Medieval

Blood of the Cross

K. M. Ashman

Published by FeedARead.com Publishing – Arts Council funded
Copyright © K M Ashman

First Edition

**All characters depicted within this publication other than the
obvious historical figures are fictitious and any resemblance to any
real persons living or dead is entirely coincidental**

More Books by K. M. Ashman

The India Sommers Mysteries
The Dead Virgins
The Treasures of Suleiman
The Mummies of the Reich

The Roman Trilogy
Roman I – The Fall of Britannia
Roman II – The Rise of Caratacus
Roman III – The Wrath of Boudicca

Novels
Savage Eden
The Last Citadel
Vampire

The Medieval Trilogy
Medieval I – Blood of the Cross

Follow Kevin's blog at:
WWW.Silverbackbooks.co.uk

or contact him direct at:
KMAshman@Silverbackbooks.co.uk

Cover design by R.M. Ashman

Rhys.Ashman02@gmail.com

Chapter One

The Kingdom of Brycheniog

Wales 1269

Elena Wyn tended the fire in the stone hearth, feeding in the extra logs to warm the contents of the pot. The sound of metal on metal echoed from the other room on the ground floor as her husband worked the ore to make a new plough blade for the manor. Elena paused and wiped the sweat from her brow. The combined heat from the furnace and the hearth meant the single living space was stuffy but it was better than the piercing cold that lay outside the thick stone walls.

Wales was in the grip of winter and the snow lay knee deep throughout the valley, forcing the villagers to stay indoors and ride out the storm. Ordinarily this meant only a few days isolation but the snow seemed never ending and they were relying on the dried fruit and salted meat they had put aside for times such as these. Throughout the summer, Elena kept pigs and chickens but though most of the birds were kept alive for the eggs, it made no sense to feed the pigs through the winter so every autumn they butchered the animals and salted the meat to preserve it for the colder months. In the spring, she replaced her stock with piglets bought from the manor farm, using the small amount of coins her husband earned from the occasional traveller needing a horse shod or a knife straightened.

Every family in the village made their own arrangements against such winters and though often the precautions were unnecessary, if anyone neglected to prepare and the weather caught them out, then the ensuing hunger was a cruel bed mate.

Elena stirred the potage, happy that it was thickening nicely. She turned to her five year old daughter sitting in the window alcove, peering at the white world outside through a crack in the shutters.

'Lowri, summon the men,' said Elena. 'The meal is ready to be served.'

The girl jumped from the stone ledge and ran to the door separating the two rooms. The blast of heat was instantaneous and Lowri waited until the sounds of clashing iron eased.

'Father,' she shouted when there was a pause, 'food is ready.'

Thomas Ruthin looked over and smiled at his daughter before straightening up and stretching his back. The young boy on the bellows also stopped and pulled a rag from his pocket to wipe the sweat from his brow. Garyn was her fourteen year old brother who worked alongside his father at the forge.

'Are you sure you haven't eaten it all, Lowri?' teased the boy.

'No, we haven't touched it yet,' answered Lowri with a haughty shrug.

'Well, that's a shame,' said Garyn, lowering his voice menacingly, 'because now I'm going to eat it all …and then I'm going to eat you.' He crouched and ran with arms outstretched toward his sister, chasing her into the living area.

Lowri squealed in delight and ran around the table before seeking refuge amongst the folds of her mother's skirts.

'Enough,' chided Elena, 'the pot is hot and you will burn.'

'He's going to eat me,' cried Lowri.

'No he's not,' said Elena, 'Garyn, leave your sister alone.'

Thomas walked in, closing the door behind him to shut out the smells of the furnace.

'It smells good,' he said taking his seat.

Elena wrapped a piece of cloth around the handle and hoisted the pot from the flames to the table.

'I put in another piece of pork this morning,' she said, 'as well as a basket of dried apples and some grain. This pot should last for three days.'

She placed five wooden bowls around the table and silence fell in the room as Elena filled just four, leaving the fifth empty alongside a knife they knew would remain unused.

'Prayers,' said Thomas and they linked hands. 'Heavenly father,' he said, 'we thank you for your bounty and pray you bring our son home safe. Amen'

'Amen,' answered the family.

Elena looked toward the empty place setting before glancing at her husband with a sad smile.

'Thank you,' she said.

Thomas just nodded and gave her an encouraging smile of his own.

'Can we start?' asked Lowri.

'Wait,' said her father suddenly, 'I've forgotten something.' He left his seat and disappeared into the workshop.

'What's he doing?' asked Garyn.

'I have no idea,' answered his mother.

'Can we start, pleeease,' whined Lowri.

'In a moment,' said Elena. 'We will wait for your father. The soup is still too hot for you to eat.'

Again they fell silent, the quiet broken only by the crackle of flames from the hearth and the sound of Lowri blowing her soup.

'Sorry,' said Thomas, re-entering the room. 'I forgot where I hid it.'

'Hid what?' asked Elena.

Thomas produced something from behind his back and placed it on the table before Garyn.

'Your mother tells me it is the anniversary of your birth,' said Thomas. 'This is a good day, Garyn so I have made you something as a gift.'

Elena's hands flew to her mouth as she gasped at the unexpected gesture.

'A gift?' said Garyn taking the Hessian wrapped package from his father. 'For me?'

Thomas looked at Elena who was beaming with delight.

'For you,' said Thomas, returning his attention to his son.

'What is it?' asked Garyn.

'Just open it,' moaned Lowri impatiently.

Garyn poked out his tongue at his sister before slowly opening the hessian and revealing a perfectly formed eating knife. The blade shone in the flickering candlelight and the highly polished oak handle was silky smooth to the touch. It was a replica of that used by his father.

'Every man should own his own eating knife,' said Thomas.

Garyn picked up the knife and held it up for everyone to see.

'It's beautiful,' said Elena.

'And well made,' said Garyn.

'I should think so,' guffawed Thomas, 'or my years as a blacksmith have been wasted.'

'Can we eat now?' whined Lowri.

'Of course,' said Elena and while three of the family lifted the bowls to sip at the hot broth, the fourth was already delving through the liquid with his knife, quietly excited at the acquisition of his first blade.

'It's stopped snowing,' shouted Lowri, early the following morning.

'Does that girl never rest?' mumbled Thomas into the horsehair filled deerskin that formed his pillow. 'The sun is not yet up and she already seeks adventure.'

'Her spirit fills me with joy each day,' said Elena, snuggling closer to her man beneath the sheepskin cover. 'Her laughter is a tonic no apothecary can hope to bottle.'

'I know,' smiled Thomas, 'and I would have it no other way. But is a few moments' extra sleep too much to ask in the morning?'

'You go back to sleep,' said Elena. 'I will take her to feed the chickens.'

'No, it's all right,' yawned Thomas. 'The little devil has me awake now, besides, I have a busy day before me.'

'Come,' said Elena. 'I'll get some bread and cheese. You light the fire.'

They descended the ladder from the sleeping platform in the rafters and Thomas smiled at his daughter's constant chatter, as he gently blew the fire back to life.

'Can we go out in the snow?' asked Lowri, peering through the window shutter. 'It looks so clean?'

'Later,' said Elena, 'call your brother first and join us to break your fast.'

Lowri went into the forge to wake Garyn. Her brother slept in the corner of the workshop in his own cot while she slept in an alcove of the main room. Her nose wrinkled at the smell and she was glad she did not have to sleep in here. It was so dirty. She ran across the workshop and pounced on the sleeping figure of her brother.

'Wake up, sleepy,' she said. 'It's stopped snowing and mother said we could play outside.'

'Go away,' mumbled Garyn and turned over to get more sleep.

'You have to get up,' said Lowri. 'Mother said.'

With a sigh, Garyn threw back the sheepskin and followed his sister into the living area.

'Hello, son,' said Thomas. 'Sleep well?'

Garyn nodded and sat at the table with his eyes shut.

'Here,' said Elena, handing him a wooden tankard. 'There is some milk left, drink it before it goes off. Now the snow has stopped I can go to the village and get some more.' She placed a chunk of cheese on the table along with half a loaf of flat bread.

'Eat up,' said his father, 'we have a busy day before us and you will need all your strength.'

Garyn produced his sheathed knife from below the table and Thomas had to stop himself laughing when he realised Garyn had slept the whole night with his new knife attached to a belt over his woollen night shirt.

'So what are you doing today?' asked Elena as she cut slices of cheese for Lowri.

'The brothers at the Abbey sent word they want a cart re-wheeled,' said Thomas. 'We have to go up there, strip the cart and bring the wheels back as templates. God willing, they may have some other work as well.' He turned to Garyn. 'Get yourself dressed boy, this commission will keep us going until the weather breaks.'

Ten minutes later, father and son trudged through the virgin snow toward the far side of the village, their heads covered with hooded capes against the biting wind that still whistled down the valley. Soon they approached the imposing walls of the Abbey and Thomas rapped his knuckles on the large wooden door. He repeated the action until they heard the sounds of bolts being drawn back and the door swung slowly inward with a lazy creak. A Monk stood inside, dressed in a full length black habit secured by a corded belt around the middle.

'Good morning' said the blacksmith, removing his hood. 'We have come about the commission…' His sentence lay unfinished as he recognised the man before him.

'Thomas Ruthin,' said the Monk in recognition. 'It is good to see you again.'

The two men stared at each other and Garyn detected a hint of anger on his father's face.

'Brother Martin,' he said. 'It has been a long time.'

'It has,' said the Monk and fell silent again. 'I forget my manners,' he said eventually standing to one side. 'please, come in out of the cold, you are expected.'

'Do you know him?' whispered Garyn once they were in the gloomy corridor.

'I did once,' said his father curtly.

The Monk turned toward them.

'Please follow me.'

The three men walked down a candle lit corridor. At the end they passed through another door and Garyn stopped in awe as they entered a large chamber decorated with tapestries depicting the glory of God and tales from the bible. Statues of angels lined the walls, staring down piously from above as they passed.

'I thought the Brothers lived frugal lives,' said Garyn.

'Shhh,' said his father.

'It's quite alright,' said Brother Martin. 'Your son is very astute and is partly correct. These corridors are for the eyes of the people of the village who expect such things from the order. We live a far more frugal existence than these surroundings suggest and you would find our cells austere in comparison. They passed through the hall and stopped as the Monk knocked on a door.

'Come in,' said a voice.

Brother Martin opened the door and they entered the sparsely furnished room. At the far side, another Monk sat at a small table writing methodically in the light from a single slit window.

'Father William,' said the Monk. 'This is Thomas Ruthin the Blacksmith.'

'Ah,' said the sitting Monk as he put aside the quill. 'I am Father William, the Abbot of St Benedict's. Thank you for coming.' He nodded at the first Monk who promptly left the room, closing the door behind him.

'Please, be seated,' said the Abbot. 'Would you care for some wine?'

'No, thank you,' said Thomas, 'we have come about the cart.'

'Yes, the cart,' said the Abbot. 'Well, there is indeed a cart that needs repair but I have to confess it is of secondary importance to the real reason you were summoned.'

'I don't understand,' said Thomas.

'I hear you are an honest man, Thomas and can be trusted to keep your silence.'

'I am a man of my word, Father, a trait that all men would benefit from.'

'Indeed,' said the Monk, 'and your son?'

'Our values are shared,' said Thomas. 'I will vouch for him.'

'Good,' said the Abbot. 'I do have a commission for you, Thomas. It is but a small task but pays well, twice the price of a cart wheel. In return, I require your silence as to what you are about to see and do. Can you guarantee this?'

Thomas only needed a few seconds' thought before agreeing. Commissions of any sort were rare during the winter, especially lucrative ones such as these.

'You have my word,' he said. 'What is the task?'

'Follow me,' said the Abbot and picking up a lit candle, led them through a second door. They crossed a courtyard before descending a winding stairway to a set of cells below the Abbey. As they walked along the corridor, they saw two plainly clothed servants struggling with a sobbing man.

'What goes on here?' demanded the Abbot.

The two men pushed the third against a wall and held him securely.

'Father,' said one, 'we caught this thief in the grounds. He stole a loaf from the kitchens.'

'Is this true?' asked the Abbot.

'Father, my children starve,' said the man over his shoulder. 'The shutter was open and I forgot myself. I will pay as soon as I am able, I swear.'

'Theft is never an option,' said the Abbot.

'But my children cry in pain at the ache in their bellies,' begged the man. 'Please, just a crust until I can get work at the manor. I beg you.'

'The times are hard,' said the Abbot, 'and many feel the pangs of hunger. How would it be if we just allowed all such thefts to be justified so? Crusts we can spare but theft is a crime that cannot be condoned.' He turned to the servants. 'Put him in a cell and tomorrow we will hand him over to the manor for judgement.'

'No, please,' gasped the man, 'Cadwallader will have my hands. My family will starve.'

'Then pray to God and hope Cadwallader is lenient,' said the Abbot.

'Father, please have mercy,' begged the man.

'The Lord will have mercy,' said the Abbot and nodded toward the servants.

The two men dragged the prisoner along the corridor before throwing him in a room and locking the door.

'Thank you for your diligence,' said the Abbot. 'See if there is warm soup as a reward.'

'Thank you, Father,' murmured the men and disappeared from the dark passageway.

'A sad testament to these troubled times,' said the Abbot and continued to the end of the corridor, stopping before a locked door. 'What you are about to witness, remains in this room,' he said and turned a large key.

Thomas and Garyn followed him into the cell and waited in the dark as the door was secured behind them. The Abbot took his candle and lit three more around the room. At first they struggled to see anything in the gloom but as their eyes adjusted, they could see the shape of a man lying on a cot facing the far wall. He was dressed in the type of winter cloak favoured by the Monks.

The Abbot walked across the room. He reached forward and shook the man gently by the shoulders. Immediately the man jumped in fright and scrambled to the back of the cot, pulling his hood across his face.

'Be calm,' said the Abbot. 'These men are friends.' He turned to the blacksmith. 'This man was brought here a few days ago,' he said, 'and as you will soon see, he is in need of your particular skills. I assume you have your tools?'

The blacksmith removed the bag from over his shoulder.

'I do,' said Thomas, 'but see no task.'

The Abbot turned to the prisoner.

'Please stand up,' he said.

After a few moments, the man struggled to his feet and stood before them with his head bowed, the deep hood covering his features.

'I am going to undo your cloak,' said the Abbot. 'We mean you no harm. Do you understand?'

The man nodded. The Abbot reached out to undo the ties around the man's shoulders and stood back as the cloak fell to the floor.

Thomas and Garyn stared in disbelief. The man was nothing more than skin and bone and every rib could be seen through his parchment-thin flesh. His black hair fell in a tangled mess around his shoulders and a matted beard fell to his chest. Around his neck he wore the iron collar of a slave with similar bands around his waist and ankles. His hands were restrained in cuffs and all were connected to each other by several short chains, restricting his movement to an absolute minimum. His face was heavily pitted from some sort of disease and they could see the unmistakable scars of the whip across his torso. Despite his appalling condition and the restrictive physical constraints, there was one more thing that kept father and son staring at him in astonishment. His skin was as black as the darkest night.

'Who is he?' asked Thomas eventually.

'He is a prisoner from the Holy-land,' said the Abbot. 'And has been sent to us by our brothers engaged on a pilgrimage to Jerusalem.'

'Since when has the order condoned slavery?' asked Thomas.

'We don't,' said the Abbot. 'and that is why we asked you here. Our brothers saved his life and I would free him from his chains.'

'But why send him here? Surely it would have been easier to free him in his own lands.'

'That is not your concern,' said the Abbot. 'All I need you to do is release his chains. Our tools barely mark the surface. Do you think you can do it?'

Thomas approached the man, who took a step backward in fear.

'Does he speak?' asked Thomas.

'Not that I know of,' said Father William. 'Though he seems to understand most of what I say.'

'What is your name?' asked Thomas facing the man, but he remained silent. 'I need to look at your chains,' continued Thomas. 'I won't hurt you.' He stepped closer and put his hands up to the collar, feeling the quality before examining the chains and the bands around the hands and feet. Thomas stepped back. 'The chains will be straight forward,' he said, 'but the collars are of quality steel. They will take time.'

'Take all the time you need,' said the Abbot. 'Enemy or not, no man will wear the yolk of slavery within these walls.'

'Do you think it is safe to release him?' asked Thomas.

'He is as weak as a new-born,' said the Monk. 'You are quite safe.'

'There are some other tools that I will need,' said Thomas, 'but I have enough to be getting on with for today.'

'Then I will leave you to it,' said the Abbot. 'The door will be locked from the outside but attended at all times. Just knock when you are ready.' He left the room and they listened as the key turned in the lock.

'Replace your robe,' said Thomas, turning to the prisoner and pointing at the garment.

The man bent, lifted the cloak up to his shoulders but due to the chains connecting his shackles to his waist he was unable to tie the cords. Garyn stepped forward and tied the knot for him.

'Sit,' said Thomas pointing at the cot. As the man dropped to the cot, the blacksmith pulled up a chair and sat before him.

'Look,' said Thomas eventually. 'I don't know why you are here but like the Father says, it is none of my business. I am an honest man, here to do an honest day's work. I mean you no harm and would like to think you will return that sentiment.' He fell silent, staring at the man, wondering if he had understood anything at all.

'Garyn, bring me another chair,' said Thomas eventually, 'I think in this case, actions speak louder than words.' He leaned forward and lifted one of the prisoners' feet, revealing the clasp around his ankle.

'The task will need the benefit of the small anvil,' said Thomas examining the clasps, 'but at least we can give him some mobility. Hand me the large file and the tongs.'

Garyn opened the sack and retrieved the tools.

'Hold these fast,' said Thomas, clasping a link of the chain in the jaws of the tongs and placing it on the chair.

Garyn did as he was told and as soon as the chain was secured, Thomas set about it with the sharp edge of the file, slowly cutting into the link. It took a long time and father and son exchanged places many times before Thomas called a halt.

'That should be enough,' he said, 'bring me the spike and the two hammers.' He placed one hammer on the stone floor and balanced the blunt end of the spike on the flat side of the hammer head. 'Hold the spike still,' said Thomas and lowered the cut link over the pointed end of the spike. Using the other hammer, he drove the link down onto the bar, forcing the link apart. Within moments the link opened enough to allow the next through the gap and the first leg was released.

'There you go,' said Thomas wiping the sweat from his brow, 'the first of many.'

They sat against the wall and Thomas unwrapped a cloth containing the remains of the bread and cheese from Elena. As they ate their meal, they watched as the prisoner stretched his leg and scratched at the scars where the chains had chafed for so long. Garyn stood up and walked over to stand before him.

'Careful, boy,' said Thomas.

Garyn broke his piece of cheese in half along with the bread and offered it to the prisoner. The man stared at Garyn for a few moments but didn't move.

'Take it,' said Garyn.

The man slowly pushed his chained hands through the front of the cloak and accepted the food.

Thomas watched as the two shared the meal in silence. Eventually he too stood and walked over with the flask of wine Elena had prepared.

'Drink,' he said. 'I have had enough.'

For the remainder of the day they worked on the rest of the chains and on one occasion, sent for the Abbot to ask if the prisoner could be taken to the forge but the request was denied, despite being assured the process would be much quicker.

'He stays here,' the Abbot had replied. 'We will pay you well for your time.' After that, Thomas and Garyn focussed on the task in hand and by the time night fell, all the prisoner's chains were removed.

'That's enough for one day,' said Thomas. 'Tomorrow we will bring a brazier and the small anvil. The collar will have to be softened before being worked but it won't be easy. We will have to protect the skin from the heat.'

Garyn packed away the tools and walked to the door. Behind them the man watched them leave but as the door was unlocked, they heard him speak for the first time.

'Wait,' he said and both men spun around in surprise.

'Masun,' he said. 'My name is Masun.'

Chapter Two

Brycheniog

It had taken three days to cut the metal from the prisoner and during that time, the only person he would speak to had been Garyn. It had only been simple phrases, asking for basic things like food or water but nevertheless, it was communication and the Abbot had given Garyn a coin in gratitude. When the man was freed, the blacksmith and his son returned to their home under oath of secrecy thinking it would be the last they heard of the matter.

It was a week later when everything changed. Once more the family of Thomas Ruthin had shared supper before retiring to their beds and it had taken just minutes before the only sounds in the house were the scratching of rats and the snores of the blacksmith but the night was only half done when Thomas was woken by someone banging on the door.

'What was that whispered?' Elena.

'I think someone is outside,' said Thomas

They both jumped as the noise came again.

'Grab a candle,' said Thomas, 'I'll see who it is.'

'Be careful,' said his wife.

Thomas clambered down the ladder closely followed by Elena. He grabbed a hammer from the forge and stood before the barred door.

'Who is it?' he asked through the planks.

'Thomas Ruthin, please open the door,' said a voice.

'Declare yourself, stranger,' said Thomas.

'It's Brother Martin from the order,' said the voice. 'Please could you let me in?'

Thomas lifted the bar and pulled the door inward slightly though tightened the grip on the hammer shaft. Behind him, Elena stretched over his shoulder with a lit candle to illuminate the visitor's face. The man stepped into the candlelight and Thomas recognised the Monk he had met a few days earlier. Behind him Elena's face dropped as she recognised the man's face.

'Brother Martin,' said Thomas coldly. 'What business brings you here at this unearthly hour?'

'The business of the Abbot,' said the Monk. 'Can I come in?'

'I don't think that is a good idea,' said the blacksmith.

'Let him in, Thomas,' said Elena, 'the past is the past and we should not deny hospitality to any man.'

Thomas stepped aside and Elena lit more candles as her husband re-barred the door.

'Please, sit down,' said Elena.

The Monk sat at the table and waited in silence until Thomas sat opposite him.

'Can we get you anything?' said Thomas. 'We have no wine but there is some mead left.'

'Thank you, I am fine,' said the Monk.

'Then let's get this done. How can we help you?'

'I have a favour to ask,' said the Monk. 'The man you freed from the chains gets weaker by the day and refuses food. He is fighting with the mind demons and we fear he is losing the battle.'

'How does this affect me?' asked Thomas.

'It doesn't,' said the Monk. 'It affects your son.'

Thomas glanced toward the door of the workshop where his son was sleeping soundly.

'Garyn?'

'Your son is the only person the prisoner has talked to,' said the Monk. 'There seems to have been a connection. We want him to come up to the Abbey and see if that connection remains. Perhaps he can bring Masun back from the brink.'

'He is but a boy,' interjected Elena. 'What possible aide could he offer? Surely you need an apothecary?'

'The soul is a mysterious thing,' said the Monk. 'Who knows what medicine it craves?'

'Can't you pray for this man?' asked Thomas.

'He is an infidel,' said the Monk, 'and we fear he is beyond God's reach.'

'Surely no man is beyond God's reach?'

'The infidels reject God's grace and seek solace only from the Devil,' said the Monk.

'Yet you protect him in the walls of God's house?' said Elena.

'We have our reasons.'

'How long will Garyn be there?' asked Thomas.

'For a few days,' said the Monk, 'perhaps a month, no more. You will of course be suitably recompensed.'

'How?' asked Thomas.

17

'We thought a cow would be a suitable reward for your family,' said the Monk.

Thomas nodded thoughtfully. The ownership of a milking cow was beyond most people's reach.

'It will be yours to keep,' continued the Monk, 'and has recently calved so her milk will last at least until next winter.'

'No,' said Elena quietly.

Both men turned to face her.

'Elena, you forget your place,' said Thomas.

'I said no,' said Elena. 'Garyn belongs here. His place is at home with us. I have already lost one son, I will not lose another.'

'You are not losing anyone,' said the Monk. 'He will be staying a short while only and will be treated well while in our care.'

'What makes you think I will allow you of all people to care for my son?' asked Thomas.

'I know it is a strange situation,' said the Monk, 'but I am not the master of my own fortune. I act on the instructions of the Abbot and he knows nothing about my past.'

'The workshop door opened and all three turned to see Garyn standing in the doorway.

'Garyn,' said Elena. 'You are awake.'

'I heard voices,' said Garyn. 'What is happening?'

'Nothing of importance,' said Elena. 'Go back to bed.'

'No,' said Thomas, 'let him stay. He is no longer a boy, Elena but a young man and as such should have a say in matters that affect him.' He turned to the Monk. 'Explain your charge, Brother Martin and either way we can move on.'

'Master Garyn,' said the Monk, 'we have need of you in the Abbey. We think the prisoner may not survive longer than a few days and thought that perhaps if he sees a friendly face he may rally.'

'But I only talked to him briefly,' said Garyn, 'I am as much a stranger to him as anyone?'

'Perhaps so, but at least he talked to you. We hope that will be enough.'

'Enough for what?' asked Thomas.

The Monk looked at the three before shaking his head.

'I can't say,' he said.

'Then Garyn stays where he is,' said Thomas. 'For all we know, you could be putting him in danger.'

'I assure you…' stated the Monk.

'Brother Martin, at least do us the courtesy of honesty. You have need of Garyn and we would like to help but there is something else here. Something you are not saying. Why do you come in the midst of the night? Surely this errand could have waited a few more hours?'

'We have nowhere else to turn,' said the Monk. 'Garyn is our last chance.'

'For what?' gasped Thomas in frustration. 'What task sends a Monk through the night seeking the aid of a boy in the business of holy men?'

'I am sorry,' said the Monk, 'the Abbot has sworn me to silence and demands the boy's attendance.'

'We do not answer to the Abbot,' said Elena 'we answer to Sir Robert Cadwallader, Lord of this manor and if the Abbot pursues this demand then we will beg audience. Let him judge the merit of your request.'

'No,' snapped the Monk a little too quickly

'Why not?' asked Thomas, staring at him. 'Why do you fear Cadwallader's involvement?'

'There is no need to go to the manor in this issue,' said the Monk.

'He doesn't know does he?' asked Thomas. 'The Lord of the manor does not know the Abbot holds a heathen prisoner from the Holy-land under his very nose. No wonder we were sworn to secrecy, the church is lying to a Knight of Llewellyn.'

'We are not lying,' said the Monk, 'but some things are the business of the church.'

'What sort of business?' asked the blacksmith?

'Brother Martin,' said Elena, 'surely you can see why we fret? Unless you share your concerns then how can we entrust you with the safety of our kin?'

The Monk took a deep breath before replying.

'You are right,' he said. 'I have been sworn to silence but we are running out of time. I will explain what I can but I do not know everything.'

'Then tell me what you can,' said Thomas.

'The man in the Abbey is indeed from the Holy-land,' said the Monk, 'but he was no soldier. He was already a prisoner of an Infidel caravan when they were attacked by a patrol of Knights in Palestine. The enemy were killed but this man bartered for his life.'

'With what?'

'Information.'

'What sort of information?'

'That's just it,' said the Monk. 'We don't know but whatever it was, it was deemed important enough for the Knights to transport him as fast as they could to the city of Acre.'

'To what end?'

'Again we do not know but it cost the lives of fifty men.'

'How so?' asked Thomas.

'The Knights were themselves ambushed on the way to Acre, but fought to the death to save this man. Apparently they were all slaughtered except one. He managed to get this man onto a ship headed for England but during the voyage the Knight died of an infection, though not before telling a fellow sailor part of the tale. The man he told was one of our brothers and he brought Masun straight here from the ship.'

'What knowledge is worth the lives of fifty men?' asked Thomas.

'That's just it, we still don't know but whatever it is, if Masun dies, then it will be lost forever.'

Silence fell as Thomas and Elena considered the tale.

'So what exactly do you want from Garyn?' asked Thomas eventually.

'To befriend Masun and help him regain his health,' said the Monk. 'We need time to gain the man's trust and glean what information we can from him.'

'But it may be worthless,' said Thomas.

'I don't think so,' said the Monk, 'for the dying Knight managed to say one more thing before he died.'

'And that was?'

'He said that Masun was the key to Christ himself!'

Thomas stared in shock, as did Elena.

'That's impossible,' said Thomas eventually. 'The prisoner is an infidel.'

'These were our thoughts also,' said the Monk. 'But don't forget, over fifty pious Knights believed enough to give their lives for him. So,' he continued, 'you now share what I know and can see the importance. I ask again, will you allow your son to return to the Abbey with me?'

'I'm not so sure…' started Thomas.

'I'll do it,' said Garyn.

Everyone looked at the boy.

'Garyn, you don't know…' started Elena.

'I'll do it,' said Garyn again.

'But…'

'Elena, leave it be,' said Thomas. 'The boy has spoken, let him be the judge.' He turned to face the Monk.

'Brother Martin,' he said. 'Garyn is our only son and we beseech you to take care of him as would we.'

'He is not our only son,' interrupted Elena quietly.

Thomas took a deep breath before continuing.

'I beg pardon,' he said, 'Garyn is the only son here. Our other boy, Geraint is in the service of the King though we have had no word from him for two years.'

The Monk nodded in understanding.

'I understand he was summoned at the last recruitment?' he said.

'He was,' said Thomas. 'When Henry needed archers, Geraint and ten others from the village answered the draft. A few months later we heard he was stationed in London but since then we have not heard a word. As you can see, his silence weighs heavily on my wife's mind, as indeed it does mine so the sight of another son leaving gives cause for concern.'

'I understand,' said the Monk, 'and be assured, he will be treated well.'

Thomas looked at Elena for acceptance but she just turned and walked into the forge. The Monk turned to Garyn.

'Get your things, boy,' he said. 'I want to be back at the Abbey by dawn. The fewer eyes that see us pass the better.'

Garyn ran back into the forge but slowed to a walk as he saw his mother sitting on his cot.

'Mother, are you alright?' he asked.

Elena wiped away the tears and forced a tight lipped smile.

'Of course,' she said, 'I'm just being silly.'

'I will be fine,' said Garyn, 'it will only be for a few days and when we have the cow we can sell milk to the travellers.

Elena smiled at the boy's reassurances.

'Come here,' she said and leaned forward to pull him into her arms. 'You just take care and come back soon.'

Garyn assured her he would and watched as his mother put some things into a hessian sack.

'I've put in a second pair of leggings and a tunic.' she said over her shoulder, 'as well as your nightshirt and your cloak.' Garyn fastened his belt around his waist and placed his eating knife in the scabbard. When they were done, they re-joined the men in the other room.

'Ready?' asked the Monk.

Garyn nodded

'Wait,' said Elena and added some cheese and a piece of pork to the sack. 'What about the cold nights?' she asked, 'will he need a cover for his bed?'

'Elena, that is enough,' said Thomas. 'You treat him like a babe.'

'We have heavy blankets he can use,' smiled the Monk. 'Rest assured, he will not go cold or hungry.'

Thomas unbarred the door and the Monk stepped outside. Garyn turned to his father and Thomas held out his arm as if to another man. Garyn hesitated before taking his father's hand. It was the first time he had been offered the manly gesture.

'Be the man I know you can be, son,' said Thomas.

'I will, Father,' said Garyn and turned to his mother.

'Worry not, Mother,' he said. 'I will be back before you know it.'

'I know,' she said, pulling him in for another hug. 'Be careful and when you come back, we will kill one of the chickens to feast like Kings.'

Garyn smiled at the thought of his favourite meal.

'I will dream of it every night,' he said and pulled from her arms. He stepped out of the door and walked toward the Monk standing a few paces away before turning to wave goodbye.

'Be safe,' called Elena quietly and watched as her son disappeared into the darkness.

Thomas followed them across the yard and as Garyn entered the treeline, the blacksmith called the Monk to him.

'Brother Martin,' he said quietly.

The Monk turned to face him.

'For the boy's sake and the demands of courtesy I have held my tongue,' said Thomas, 'but I warn you now, if anything happens to

22

that boy whilst in your care, I swear before God you will pay with your life.'

'It is sad that our paths have come to this, Thomas,' said the Monk. 'I thought the years would have long healed old wounds but I see they still weep hatred.'

'What do you expect,' asked Thomas, 'we have managed to rebuild our lives and have moved on. Now you reappear as welcome as a plague and expect us to hand over our son as if the past never happened.'

'The past is past, Thomas,' said the Monk. 'Leave it where it lies.'

'Just look after our son,' said Thomas, 'and when he is returned, stay away from my family.'

The Monk nodded silently.

'I understand,' he said and turned to follow Garyn into the wood.

Thomas returned to the house and joined Elena.

'What did he say?' she asked.

'Nothing of importance,' said Thomas. 'Come, we should retire for the morning beckons. Fret not for despite the circumstance, Garyn could not be in safer hands.'

Elena nodded in agreement, realising her husband was probably right.

But he wasn't right, in fact, he couldn't have been more wrong, for Garyn was about to be in more danger than either would ever realise.

A few hours later, Brother Martin knelt on one knee before the Abbot. He bowed his head and made the sign of the cross before kissing the Father's hand.

'Was your task successful?' asked the Abbot.

'It was,' said Brother Martin. 'The boy sleeps in a cell near the prisoner. He will be taken to him tomorrow.'

'Is he aware of his purpose?'

'He is.'

'And no others know of this?'

'Father, I had to break your instruction to get the family to let him leave. I know I have failed you but there was no other option. I accept any punishment God deems suitable.'

Father William paused, slightly shocked at the admission.

23

'Ah,' he said. 'This is a problem. How many others know of this situation?'

'Only the Blacksmith and his wife,' said the Monk. 'But they have been sworn to secrecy.'

The Abbot nodded.

'Good,' he said. 'Let the boy sleep tonight but have him taken to the prisoner at first light.' He lifted his crucifix toward the Monk. 'You acted in the service of God, Brother and that merits no punishment. Thank you, you may leave.'

The Monk kissed the crucifix and retreated from the room. Father William sat in silence for over an hour before reaching for a bell at his side. Within moments, a servant entered the room and knelt before him.

'You rang, Father?'

'Phyllip,' he said. 'Bring me the prisoner.'

'Which one?' asked the servant, 'the infidel?'

'No, the brigand you caught stealing the bread.'

The Servant nodded and left the room. With a sigh, the Abbot stood and crossed the room to face the life-sized image of the Crucified Christ suspended from a wall. Father William prostrated himself before the cross and silently prayed, begging forgiveness for what he was about to do.

Chapter Three

The Homs Gap

Syria

The dark skinned man crawled forward to the edge of the escarpment. The sun was almost up and it was important he was in place before the dawn. His white linen cloak protected him from the last of the night's chill and he knew it would also keep him from the worst of the sun's rays as he watched for the infidel patrols. Once in position between the rocks, he withdrew his knife and placed it before him, along with a water skin and a bag of food including dates and goat meat.

Abdul Malik was a scout and served in the armies of Sultan Baibaars, the region's prominent warlord and leader of the Mamluk Dynasty. Like all Mamluk warriors Malik had originally been bought as a slave and his earliest memory was being separated from his mother in the markets of Cairo but far from being the start of a life of drudgery and servitude, his purchase had been the start of a military life envied by many free men of the time.

Every Mamluk warrior had started their lives as slaves and they took great pride in maintaining that heritage. Over the centuries, previous rulers had trained slave armies to fight for them and as those armies had gained strength, they turned on their rulers and became an entity in their own right. As they grew in influence they continuing the tradition of recruiting only slaves and quickly came to dominate Egypt and Syria by virtue of their exceptional skills in warfare.

'This is good,' said Malik, surveying the valley before him.

Behind him, Ashia, a fellow scout settled in to his own position and followed Malik's gaze. The position gave a clear view for miles in both directions. It would be a long day but the task was one they were used to. The main strengths of a Mamluk scout were patience and discipline.

'It is a likely route,' said Ashia.

'It will either be this way or the valley of the snake,' said Malik. 'Either way we can be upon them within the hour. Our task is to forewarn the Amir as soon as they break the horizon, that way the Amir's thousands can meet them with full strength.'

The second scout nodded with understanding.

'It will be a great day,' he said.

Twenty miles away, Husam al Din, Baibaar's right hand man entered the tent of the Sultan. Other rulers would expect their men to prostrate themselves at their feet but Baibaars was different. He too had been a slave and to him all his men were equal except for the rule of command. Expressions of inferiority were reserved for the prayers to Allah, not to other men.

'Husam,' said Baibaars from behind a netted curtain. 'I was told you had arrived. What news from our scouts?'

'The crossed devils ride through the Homs Gap,' said Husam. 'They avoided our Halqas by travelling through the night and are within the influence of Chevalier. They will be in the safety of the castle within hours.'

'They proclaim military might and chivalry yet run like rats in the night,' said Baibaars.

'They cannot run forever,' said Husam.

'We do not have forever, Husam,' said Baibaars walking into the carpeted area of the tent. 'We need to seize the moment. Since Louis of France fell in Egypt the Christian resolve has weakened. If we wait for the right moment, we will always hold back.'

'There are still many Knights in the area,' said Husam, 'and though they are spread out between the Christian forts, any battle will bring their brothers running like dogs to a hare.'

'I do not fear the Crossed Devils, Husam. Have I not forced them to their knees at Arsuf and Anthilth? Did they not beg for mercy at Haifa and Safad? In Jaffa and Ashkalon the very walls shook at the thunder of our horses' hooves yet still they come, each generation intent on seizing Jerusalem in the name of their Popes.'

'Their holy men never set foot in Jerusalem yet send thousands to die in their name,' said Husam.

'They call themselves the Knights of God yet celebrate pain and death like none I have ever seen. When first the crusaders were victorious almost two centuries ago, it is said the streets of Jerusalem ran with blood, yet when the great Sah-la-din recaptured the city, he ordered the streets washed with rose water and they call us the infidels.'

'Allah will prevail,' said Husam.

'He will,' said Baibaars, 'but it is my destiny to rid this land of the Crossed Devils scourge before I am summoned to the afterlife. Even the Mongols tremble in fear at my name and before I die, I will see the last Crusader ship leave these shores.'

'A heavy burden to bear,' said Husam

'Yet one I welcome.' said Baibaars 'and the time to act is upon us. Allah has sent distraction to their eyes and doubt to their hearts. While they still shudder from the loss of a King, we will take them on where they least expect us. We will take their castles from them and force them to run back to their homes like beaten dogs.'

'Their combined armies are mighty,' said Husam.

'They are,' said Baibaars, 'but individually they are weak. Break them into pieces and the biscuit becomes crumb.'

'What would you have us do?'

'The infidel stronghold is no doubt Acre,' said Baibaars, 'but it enjoys the protection of the outlying castles and support from the sea. Other strongholds are the White castle, Chevalier and Tripoli. One by one we will take them apart until only Acre stands and when it is done, we will unleash Allah's wrath upon its walls.'

'Are we to lay siege?'

'Not yet. First we will provoke the garrisons of the forts to come out to face us. We will taunt them with our presence under their noses. Our people will graze their cattle within sight of their walls and move our caravans within the Homs gap as we please. We will move the villagers east denying the Christians the source of their taxes. We will pollute the wells and take what crops we need. Pastures will be burned and markets destroyed. Let them play at being Kings for their kingdoms will be wastelands.'

'They will not sit back and allow this to happen,' said Husam.,

'No, they won't and when they venture forth, we will strike like the desert snake but fade away as shadows, each time wearing them out. We will spread word of our might, kindling fear in their hearts and finally, we will lay siege to these so called impregnable walls. We cannot wait any longer, Husam. The time is right, the time is now.'

'Shall I summon the Amirs?'

'Do that and together we will draw up a plan of attrition such as the Christians have never seen.'

'How soon do we start?' asked Husam.

'We have already started, Husam,' said Baibaars, 'the first blow is about to be dealt.'

High in the mountains, Malik felt the hand of Ashia shaking him gently.

'What is it?' he whispered, instantly awake,

'A dust cloud,' said Ashia,

Instantly Malik was at Ashia's side, peering into the distance.

'A sand storm perhaps?'

'Too low,' said Ashia. 'It is the dust from many horses.'

'We will wait a moment more,' said Malik. 'We need to be sure.'

Ashia nodded but ten minutes later, both men rode as fast as they could back to their camp, absolutely certain about what they had seen. A column of Crossed Devils was riding toward Acre and though they were almost a hundred strong, they were no match for a full strength Halqa.

Fifty Miles to the south, a soldier lowered his lance toward a lone rider approaching the Castle of the King's Constable deep in the city of Acre.

'Hold,' shouted the guard, as the rider rode toward the castle gate. 'State your business, stranger.'

The horseman reined in his horse and pulled back his hood. His head was shaved bald and he wore a full beard hanging down to his chest. His hands were covered with metal gauntlets and beneath the open cape, the guard could see a chainmail shirt and the hilt of an impressive sword.

'I ride to speak to the Castellan,' said the rider. 'Who holds this honour?'

'The title falls to my master, Sir John of Cambridge,' said the guard. 'An honour bestowed by the King of England himself, Henry of Winchester.'

'And long may he reign,' said the man. 'Send word to your master, I seek audience for I have information for his ears only.'

'And who is it that demands such audience?' asked the man, 'for my master opens the gate for few men, especially those who know not his name.'

'I have been many years away from the walls of Acre, soldier,' said the rider, 'and the politics of the city changes quicker than mortal

28

man can follow. My name is Abdul Khoury, Knight Hospitaller. I have a message for this Sir John.'

The guard glanced at his Comrade. The Hospitallers were once the major military force in the region and though their fortunes had taken a downward turn in the last twenty years or so, they were still famous for being formidable warriors. They still had their own smaller castle within the walls of Acre but their main fortress lay two days inland, the castle of Krak des Chevalier.

'I will send word,' said the guard and spoke to another comrade through the bars of the inner gate. The second man turned and ran into the castle.

'Tell, me,' said the rider, 'why is the castle secured thus, are you at risk of attack?'

'There is word of Mamluk assassins in the city,' said the guard, 'and we lock down until they are caught. What of you traveller, from whence do you come?'

'From Krak des Chevalier,' said the Knight.

'A dangerous ride for a man alone,' said the guard.

'I never said I was alone,' said the Knight, 'My men rest within our order's headquarters near the sea wall Do you have a drink you can share, friend?'

The guard retrieved a skin of water from around his waist and gave it to the impressive Knight.

Khoury drank deeply before wiping his mouth.

'Clean water,' he said, 'a treat indeed.'

'We are blessed with several wells within the town,' said the Guard. He hesitated before continuing. 'Tell me, Sir Knight, I hear Krak des Chevalier is a majestic fortress, impenetrable to any who assault her walls.'

'Chevalier is indeed such a place,' said Khoury.

'It is said that the Knights of Saint John garrison the Castle and live a life of Chivalry and Piety.'

'Such is our calling,' said Khoury. He looked up as the messenger ran back across the courtyard.

'Open the gate,' cried the man, 'Sir John will see him.'

Within moments the spiked defence swung open allowing the rider through. The messenger took the horse's reins and led it to one side to a waiting groom.

'Sir John of Cambridge bids you welcome, Sire,' said the messenger 'and thanks you for your patience.'

'On the contrary,' said the Knight, 'my gratitude goes to your master for granting me audience.'

'You can leave your mount here, Sire,' said the messenger, 'it will be well cared for. Please, come this way.' The two men made their way across the courtyard toward a large set of double doors set into a far wall. Khoury knew it was the entrance to the great hall, a room typical of such places. Outside the doors, two more pike men stood at guard and up on the walls he could see strategically placed crossbow-men, leaning nonchalantly against the castellations. The messenger pushed open the doors and stepped inside.

'My Lord, Sir Abdul Khoury,' he announced and stepped to one side to let the visitor through.

Khoury stopped to look around. The hall was large and reached up to the roof without any intervening floors. The whitewashed walls were draped with tapestries and at the far end, a huge fireplace was built into the stonework, a necessary defence against the freezing nights. The darkness was lit by many arrow slits in the walls and supplemented by hundreds of candles on the many tables scattered within.

Around the walls, men at arms played games of dice atop chests of equipment or lay asleep amongst sacks of clothing and grain. Many stopped what they were doing to stare at the giant stranger but soon returned to their games with disinterest.

A clean shaven man with a rounded belly betraying an easy life walked forward to greet him. He was almost the same height as Khoury and wore a red surcoat bearing a golden dog's head coat of arms over a gleaming chainmail shirt.

'Sir Khoury,' said the man, 'welcome to Acre. My name is Sir John of Cambridge, master of this castle.'

'Thank you,' said Khoury, 'your hospitality is most welcome.'

'You speak excellent English,' said Sir John.

'Our homeland is Syria,' said Khoury, 'but the business of our order demands we deal with many nations. I also speak French and Latin.'

'Impressive,' said Sir John, 'please, you must make yourself at home.' He turned and summoned a page.

'Boy, take the Knight's cloak and gauntlets,' he said, 'and bring some fresh mead.'

The page did as he was told and within minutes, Khoury was sitting at the host's table, drinking mead from an ornate tankard.

'Good Mead,' said Khoury as he looked around the room again. 'You seem well garrisoned, Sir. 'Are these men under your command?'

'They may be,' said Sir John, 'why do you ask?'

'Sir John,' said Khoury, 'I will get to the point. I have ridden from Krak des Chevalier with a plea for aide. We have heard that a Mamluk army twenty thousand strong ride our way under the command of Baibaars.'

'Baibaars,' spat Sir John, 'a man of the devil himself.'

'You have had dealings with him?' asked Khoury.

'He laid siege to these very walls just a few years ago.'

'And your opinion of him is low.'

'What man doesn't curse the ground he walks on?' asked Sir John. 'Many in this castle had family or comrades in Antioch when it fell to his trickery last year. Despite his promises of leniency, he slaughtered every one upon the town's surrender. There is a debt to be paid.'

'He is known for such deeds,' said Khoury, 'yet is a great commander.'

'How can you say he is great?' asked Sir John.

'As a young man he was instrumental in the defeat of Louis of France engaged on the Crusade of Pope Innocent the IV,' said Khoury, 'and nine years ago he taught the Mongols a lesson in the Jezrel Valley, the first time any Mongol army has been defeated, repeating the deed later that year in the battle of Homs. Any man who can defeat the Mongols in one battle, let alone two, deserves such a title.'

'Impressive victories I agree,' said Sir John, 'but again based on tactics of subterfuge and brutality.'

'Both weapons of war, I would suggest,' said Khoury. 'Not ones we recognise within the code admittedly but successful nevertheless and greatness is defined by the victors, irrespective of the methods employed.'

'I hold no patience for such methods,' said Sir John, 'and the quicker an assassin's blade finds his heart the better.'

'Yet did not Richard the Lionheart employ similar tactics in this very place?' asked Khoury.

'That was over a hundred years ago,' said Sir John, 'and this castle was won in fair siege. The prisoners were executed as retribution for Sah-la-Dhin's trickery in holding up the advance to Jerusalem.'

31

'Almost three thousand souls sent to hell at the whim of one man,' said Khoury.

'Your words are tainted with criticism,' said Sir John. 'I would take care for though Lionheart has rested for a hundred years, his name is still spoken in awe within these walls.'

'I too hold Lionheart in admiration,' said Khoury, 'I only point out the similarity to illuminate the fact great leaders often share similar traits. Sah-la-Dhin was one and Richard the Lionheart another. This Baibaars of the Mamluk shares their ability and is destined for great things. That is why I am here. He heads toward Chevalier and if that falls, I fear Acre will be next and if this city succumbs, then our presence in the Holy-land will come to an end.'

Before Sir John could answer, a servant called out.

'Sire, the meal is served.'

'Sir Knight, we will continue this talk with full bellies. I trust you are hungry?'

'I am,' said Khoury.

'Then come,' said Sir John, 'join us for our meal.'

They walked over to the top table and took their seats. The servants brought platters of food from the kitchens and laid them out. Loaves of bread were joined by pastries and slices of roasted meat.

'Goat again,' said Sir John with a sigh. 'What I wouldn't give for just one slice of Venison.'

'It is said our predecessors ate their own clothes,' said Khoury, 'such was their hunger.'

'A different time with different challenges,' said Sir John.

The commotion died down in the hall and every man sat in silence as each said a prayer.

'Are they all Knights?' asked Khoury.

'Most of them,' said Sir John, 'does this surprise you?'

'It does,' said Khoury. 'There must be a hundred men here.'

'A hundred and ten,' said Sir John, stabbing a piece of goat with his knife. 'Fifty more in the other halls and five hundred men at arms stationed in the town.'

'A powerful force indeed,' said Khoury, 'where have they come from?'

'Some from France,' said Sir John, 'and the rest from England. They are first to arrive.'

'The first to arrive?' asked Khoury.

'You mean you haven't heard?

'Heard what?'

'There is a great army en-route from England, Sir Knight. England has finally mustered the numbers needed to defend Tripoli and send Baibaars back from whence he came.'

'The King is coming here?' asked Khoury in surprise.

'Not the King,' said Sir John, 'his son, Prince Edward is in Tunis and is expected to leave any time soon. These men came ashore over the last few days and await the rest of the army.' He paused before continuing. 'Longshanks is coming, Khoury and this time it is Baibaars who will experience the bitter taste of defeat.'

Chapter Four

Brycheniog

Garyn sat in the prisoner's cell, staring at the man facing him across the room. He had been there for several hours trying to make conversation with the bedraggled man but with no success. Brother Martin had been with them the whole time but finally he realised it was pointless and stood to leave.

'It is no use,' said Brother Martin, 'the man is obviously mad. This was a wasted journey, Garyn, come, I will return you to your family.'

Garyn stood and followed the Monk to the door.

'No,' said Masun unexpectedly and the Monk turned to stare at the prisoner.

'You want us to stay,' he asked.

Masun lifted his hand from beneath the cape and pointed his finger at Garyn.

'You,' he said.

The Monk looked at Garyn before turning back to face Masun.

'You just want him?' he asked.

The prisoner nodded.

'I have to stay here,' said the Monk.

'It's alright,' said Garyn, 'I don't mind.'

The Monk hesitated but finally agreed.

'So be it,' he said, 'but I will put a servant outside the door. One call from you and this man will be back in irons before the sun sets.'

'I will be fine,' said Garyn and waited until Brother Martin had left before taking his seat once more.

'So,' he said eventually, 'your name is Masun.'

The man nodded slowly.

'Where are you from, Masun?' asked Garyn.

'From beyond the great sea,' said Masun, 'a place of majestic sun and endless sands. A land where a man can be alone with his thoughts below the countless stars.'

Garyn swallowed quietly. It was the most he had heard the man say.

'It sounds wonderful,' he said. Silence fell again.

'And you, Gar-ryn,' said Masun. 'Where do you ride from?'

34

'My family lives nearby,' said Garyn.

'This cold place is your home?'

'It isn't always this cold,' said Garyn. 'In the summer, the sun gets very hot and we harvest the wheat in the Lord's fields.'

'The Lord Allah?'

'No,' said Garyn. 'It is what we call the master of the manor. He owns the lands around here and the people all work for him or pay him taxes. His word is law.'

'Does he have armies?'

'He has soldiers,' said Garyn, 'and many Knights but the larger armies are only raised by the King in times of warfare.' He paused before continuing. 'You speak good English, Masun. Why have you remained silent all this time?'

Masun glanced at the door.

'It was necessary, Gar-ryn, your people are servants of the Christian Gods, killers of the innocents.'

Garyn frowned.

'Who, the Monks?' he asked, 'surely they are men of peace.'

'Peace,' sneered Masun. 'In our lands they are murderers and thieves.'

'I don't believe it,' said Garyn.

'Believe what you will, Gar-ryn,' said Masun. 'I have seen this with my own eyes. Women ravaged by your so called priests and babies speared on their lances. Men scream at the hands of their torturers and whole villages burned to the ground. I have been brought here in chains, betrayed by one who wears the same cross.'

'I don't understand,' said Garyn.

Masun started coughing and bent over in pain. Spots of bloodied spittle splashed on the cell's floor and Garyn ran over to help him.

'Are you alright?' he asked as he helped him to sit up.

'Water,' gasped Masun.

The boy poured water into a goblet and held it to the man's lips. Masun drank before leaning back against the wall, struggling for breath.

'I am very weak, Gar-ryn,' said Masun. 'I am not long for this world and soon I will leave these devils behind me and travel to meet my God.'

'No,' said Garyn. 'I will ask the Abbot to bring the apothecary. He will let your blood and release the poison that ails you.'

'The only poison I have is that in my mind,' said Masun, 'memories of death and bloodshed that no man should ever see. I do not fear death, Gar-ryn, I welcome its embrace. I desire the peace it will bring and only regret I will never again stand beneath the stars of the desert and wonder at their marvel.' Masun's hand shot out and grabbed Garyn's wrist, pulling him in close. Garyn tried to pull away but despite his frail condition, the prisoner's grip was too tight. Masun stared into the boy's eyes for several seconds before finally releasing him. Garyn stumbled backward against the wall, wondering if he should call out. The two stared at each other before Masun broke the silence.

'I have a son your age,' he said quietly. 'I see him when I look into your eyes. I see the same innocence of youth and the impatience to be a man. He too wishes to don the colours of his people and fight in the name of his God, both young men believing the righteousness of their cause yet standing on opposite sides of the battle.'

'I don't know what you are talking about,' said Garyn.

'Then tell me I am wrong,' said the prisoner, 'do you not yearn to wear the armour of the crusader and ride to glory in the name of your God. Does not the pull of the chivalric codes fill your dreams?'

'I will never be a Knight,' said Garyn. 'I have no sponsor to show me the way of the Squire and my family are of humble nature. To become a Knight you need the wealth of a lord and a family name of note. I have neither.'

'Why is this so important to you?' asked Masun.

'To live a life of honour is the dream of all men,' said Garyn.

'And if you were to achieve such heights, would it be your lance that spears the children of my people, your torch that burns their homes?'

'I cannot see the future, Masun,' said Garyn, 'but I do know this. If God's glory sees fit to set me upon such a path, I will do everything in my power to meet the chivalric code and that does not include the slaughter of the innocents.'

'I believe you, boy,' said Masun eventually. 'My views on your God differ wildly but my heart tells me you say the truth. I feel my body weaken as we speak, Gar-ryn so there is something I must give you.'

Garyn looked around the cell. The man had nothing to give.

Masun saw his glance and smiled.

36

'It is not a chattel, I offer, Gar-ryn but a gift much greater, a gift so valuable that it has the power to bring the armies of Henry home and send my people back to their villages in peace.'

Garyn waited in silence.

'You have an honest heart, Gar-ryn,' said Masun, 'but what I am about to tell you, you must keep to yourself. Do not trust the men of cloaks in this place, I have heard their whispers and they cannot be trusted. Do you understand?'

Garyn nodded.

'Good, then know this. If you are willing, I will tell you a great truth. Accept my words and you will bear a burden greater than any man should ever bear. It has the power to break you or give a purpose greater than any Knight. If it is shared, thousands will die yet within one true man, it is the means to peace in both our lands. The choice is yours, Gar-ryn. Accept and bear the burden of truth, decline this burden and I will happily take it to my grave.'

'Why me?' asked Garyn quietly.

'Because you were the first man to show me kindness in this cold place,' said Masun, 'because you did not judge me by race or religion and because you are yet untainted by the greed of mortal man.'

'You flatter, me, sir,' said Garyn.

'Perhaps,' said Masun, 'but true words nevertheless. There is another reason, Gar-ryn,' he said, 'you remind me of my son.' Another coughing fit made him grimace in pain. 'Make your choice, Gar-ryn for I feel my time is limited.'

'I will accept the burden,' said Garyn.

'Then listen well, Infidel, for I fear I will not have the strength to repeat this again.'

Half an hour later, Garyn sat beside the prisoner's bed, absorbing the astonishing tale he had just been told. Masun's breath was getting weaker and he slipped in and out of consciousness. Garyn realised he had succeeded in getting the information the Abbot so desperately wanted yet something worried him. He did not know the man dying before him and had no concept of the life he had lived. Masun even worshipped the heathen God yet despite all this, Garyn had the feeling he was probably the most honest man he had ever met. The sound of keys rattled outside the door and as Garyn turned, Masun reached out and grasped his hand.

'Gar-ryn,' he said. 'Use the words wisely, or cast them from your mind. Either way is good but I ask only this. Do not share them with anyone except those you would die for.'

Before Garyn could answer, Masun gasped and his body writhed in spasm. The door burst open and Brother Martin came into the room, running to the Muslim's side. Father William stood in the doorway and as other Monks joined Brother Martin around the dying man to pray, the Abbot's face turned from concern to anger. Finally he turned to face Garyn.

'Why didn't you call?' he said.

'There was no point,' said Garyn. 'He was dying and sought only peace.'

'Your role was to glean the information from him before he died,' said the Abbot. 'Did he say anything to you? Did he share what information cost the lives of fifty Knights?'

Garyn paused. He was talking to a man of God in the depths of an abbey and he had never told a lie in his life. He glanced at the dying man before turning back to the Abbot.

'No, Sire,' he said. 'He never said a thing.'

Garyn stayed in the Abbey until they buried Masun the following day. He had asked the Abbot if they had buried him according to his beliefs but the Monks had no knowledge of what was expected so buried him with a simple Christian ceremony. Before he left to go back to the village, he was summoned by the Abbot to attend him in the Abbey.

Garyn followed the messenger and was led into one of the chapels. Rows of pews faced the far end and the Abbot knelt before the figure of Christ, high above the altar. Garyn waited until he had finished before coughing gently to attract his attention. The Abbot glanced over his shoulder before summoning the boy to join him.

'Kneel alongside me, Garyn,' he said.

Garyn did as he was told.

'Look up,' said Father William, 'and tell me what you see.'

'I see the Lord Jesus Christ,' said Garyn.

'And he sees you, Garyn. From his glorious place in heaven he sees each and every one of us, not only this temporary shell our soul calls home but also into our very hearts.'

The boy nodded, not sure where this was leading.

'You see,' continued the Abbot, 'there is nothing we can hide from him, no matter how hard we try. He knows when we are truthful but also knows when we tell untruths and as we know, lying is a sin.' He paused before looking directly into the boy's eyes. 'Have you ever lied, Garyn?'

Garyn's heart was beating faster than he had ever known. To answer truthfully was to admit he had lied the previous evening but anything else was to add even more sin to that he had already committed. He thought furiously, thinking about what Masun had said before he died. He said this man was not to be trusted yet the Abbot was a man of God and Garyn had been brought up to believe they were the voice of Jesus Christ. Surely such men could be trusted?

Within seconds he knew what he had to do. Though Masun had seemed a good man, Father William was a man of God and a native of Brycheniog. Masun must have been mistaken, there was no way a voice of Christ was untrustworthy. Garyn looked up at the life sized figure of Christ above him and silently prayed for forgiveness. He had to break a promise, he had to tell the truth.

'Father William,' he said, 'I...'

Before he could finish the doors burst open and one of the servants called out across the Chapel.

'Father,' he shouted, 'there is fire in the village.'

Father William and Garyn both turned to stare at the man. Fire was one of the most feared disasters in the village due to the thatched roofs on all the houses.

'Thank you,' said the Abbot. 'Round up whoever you can and offer aid. I will be along as soon as possible.'

'Of course,' said the man, 'the brothers are already on their way but I thought you should know, the blacksmith's house is ablaze.'

Garyn jumped up in horror and stared at the man.

'Get out,' shouted the Abbot and grabbed Garyn's arm.

'Garyn,' he said, 'the villagers will be doing what they can. We will leave in a few moments but first there was something you were going to say.'

'Leave me go,' shouted Garyn and pulling his arm from the Abbot's grip, ran through the chapel and out of the doors.

'Come back,' shouted the Abbot but it was too late. Within moments, Garyn was running headlong down the hill toward the village.

The sounds of shouting and the smell of smoke reached him long before he could see his home and as he increased his pace, he prayed his family would be alright. He turned off the path and took a shortcut through the trees. Finally he broke clear and stared in horror at the scene before him.

People from the village passed wooden buckets of water from hand to hand from the pond and the young men at the front ran as close as they could before throwing the liquid onto the blaze. They worked feverishly but Garyn could see it was hopeless, the house was an inferno.

He tried to get close but was beaten back by the heat. Brother Martin was already there and came across to comfort him.

'Garyn,' he said, 'I fear we are too late.'

'My family,' gasped Garyn. 'Did they escape?'

'I fear not, Garyn,' said the Monk. 'It seems the fire was started by the heat from the forge and they were overcome by the smoke before they could escape.'

'No,' cried Garyn, 'my father took great care to make sure the furnace was always dampened. There would not have been sparks.'

'There is no other possibility, Garyn. The snow still lies on the houses and the fire must have been started on the inside.'

'No,' gasped Garyn, 'it can't be true.'

'Come,' said Brother Martin, 'there is nothing you can do here.'

A shout came from around the back of the house and both men looked up in surprise and hope.

'We have the woman,' cried the voice, 'and she is alive.'

Garyn sprinted around the back and fell to his knees alongside his mother. Her face was blackened with smoke and her eyes were closed but they could see her chest moving slightly.

'Mother,' gasped Garyn, 'are you alright? Speak to me please.'

Elena opened her eyes and a gentle smile played around her lips.

'Garyn,' she whispered. 'You have come home.'

'I have,' said Garyn smoothing her hair from her eyes. 'And I will not leave you again. 'You will be better soon, the brothers will make you well, don't you worry.'

'Garyn,' said Elena, 'what of Lowri, I couldn't find her in the smoke, is she safe?'

Garyn looked toward the man who had rescued his mother but the farm labourer shook his head, confirming the worst. Garyn looked back at his mother and realised she was dying. Once again he was faced with the choice of telling the truth or lying but this time there was no struggle of conscience. There was no way he could let his mother die thinking her daughter had burned to death.

'She is fine, Mother,' he lied with tears running down his face, 'she escaped the smoke and is being looked after by the women.'

Elena smiled.

'Look after her, Garyn,' said Elena weakly, 'and one day, when she is safely married, seek out your brother for me. Tell him that I love him, Garyn as I love you and that we will once more meet again at the feet of the lord. Will you do this for me?'

'I will mother,' sobbed Garyn. 'I swear by all that is holy that before I die I will pass on your words.'

'Thank you,' she gasped and her body was wracked with coughing before she passed out for the last time. Garyn picked her up from the floor, shouting through his tears.

'No,' he screamed, looking up at the heavens. 'Why have you done this? What harm has she ever done to you.'

Many of the onlookers crossed themselves at the blasphemy but Brother Martin stepped forward to put his arm around him.

'Get away from me,' shouted Garyn. 'Where is your God now, Monk? What possible reason could he have to take the lives of my kin?'

'God works in mysterious ways, Garyn,' said Brother Martin. 'He does not answer to mortal man.'

'Well he should,' shouted Garyn through his tears, 'for I have too many questions.'

'She is gone, Garyn,' said a woman's voice, 'let us take care of her now.'

Garyn looked down at his mother in his arms. Her arms hung limply and her head tilted so far back, her long hair reached the ground. Her eyes that had once held so much sparkle now only shone in contrast to her blackened face. Garyn looked around the clearing. The men had stopped fighting the fire, for it was too far gone. One of them swept some empty buckets off a handcart and a woman laid her cape across the boards. Garyn walked over and laid his mother gently onto the cart.

Another cape was laid over her body and before it was raised over her head, Garyn leaned over and kissed Elena's forehead.

'Thank you, mother,' he said, 'thank you for being the best mother a boy could ever have. He lowered her eyelids and kissed her once more, Rest well, Elena Wyn. Until next we meet.' He stood back and watched as her body was covered before being wheeled away. Behind him, his childhood home blazed ferociously and he knew that somewhere within the flames lay the remains of his father and young sister. He glanced back one more time before striding across the yard toward the forest edge.

'Where are you going?' shouted Brother Martin but the only reply was the sound of crashing branches as the boy ran.

Chapter Five

The Castle of the King's Constable

'So,' said Sir John, when the last of the food had been cleared away. 'Tell me why you have graced these walls with your presence.'

'It is a tale of woe, I fear,' said Khoury. 'As you know, I bear the crest of the Hospitallers and ride from Chevalier.'

'An honourable code,' said Sir John, 'you have the respect of most men.'

'It is appreciated,' said Khoury, 'but respect is just a word when the lives of many are at risk.'

'Continue,' said Sir John.

'As you know these lands have been the centre of much strife since the church led the first crusade and took Jerusalem in 1099,' said Khoury. 'Countless men from both sides have spilt their blood in the name of religion and though we swept the infidel aside for many years, they never gave up and Jerusalem has been in the hands of the Muslims since Sah-la-Dhin.'

'You patronise me with your history lesson, Sire,' said Sir John.

'My apologies,' said Khoury, 'but it is important to establish what has gone before, in order to judge the threat of what is about to happen. My point is, Sah-la-Dhin was the greatest warrior these lands have ever known. He brought the fight back to us and even Lionheart failed to defeat him. When Sah-la-Dhin died, he left a legacy second to none and even though his factions fought amongst themselves, they still proved too strong against our Knights. To this day, those lands still under our control, only bend their knee due to the strength within our fortress' walls.'

'And your point is?'

'There is a new storm brewing, Sir John. Baibaars has managed to unite the Amirs of the outer tribes under his banner and he is about to gain the command of an army potentially hundreds of thousands strong. Already their encampments stretch from horizon to horizon out in the deserts and tales are told of many more in Egypt, all holding their reins until the call comes.'

'There have always been such rumours,' said Sir John.

'There have but this time they have substance. Nomadic tribes loyal to Baibaars seep into Palestine like blood from a wound. Those

43

who were once subservient to our banner no longer pay the cost of our protection and seek greener pastures elsewhere. Our castles are now no more than isolated islands in a sea of hatred. Yes, we are yet too strong to fear any assault but this is only the start. By stealth, Baibaars has succeeded in subduing a country that once cost a sea of Christian blood to acquire. Only we remain between him and outright victory.'

'I have heard nothing of this,' said Sir John.

'Like you said, the man has the cunning of a fox,' said Khoury, 'yet is about to gain the ferocity of a lion.'

'Our castles are impregnable, Khoury,' said Sir John, 'and Edward is already under sail. When he arrives, it matters not the size of Baibaars' army for no force can withstand an English Monarch's wrath.'

'Perhaps so,' said Khoury, 'but I fear we may not have the time. Already Baibaars has amassed a force to the east of Chevalier and they set their eyes on controlling the Homs Pass. If they succeed, Edward or any other leader will struggle to defend these lands. What we need to do is confront Baibaars as soon as possible and send him back to the East. If we are victorious it may spread doubt amongst his allies but now I know Edward is on Crusade, perhaps all we need to do is delay Baibaars' campaign until he arrives.'

'So what are you suggesting?' asked Sir John.

'We need men at arms,' said Khoury, 'a mounted army capable of taking on Baibaars in the Homs gap. If you could lend your strength, combined with our garrisons from Chevalier and Marquab we would be strong enough to drive him back.'

'What about the Knights Templar?' asked Sir John. 'Surely their swords would add strength.'

'The garrison from the White Tower are on patrol as we speak,' said Khoury, 'but number no more than a hundred men. The Tower is little more than an outpost for the Templars and is lightly manned.'

Sir John stood up and walked around the now empty hall, the rest of the men having moved into the castle courtyard for trials of arms.

'I don't know,' he said. 'With the greatest respect, Khoury, you are but one man and the request is a heavy one.'

'I have authorisation from our order's grand master himself,' said Khoury, 'Hugh de Revel.'

'Let me see.'

44

Khoury retrieved a rolled parchment from beneath his tunic and handed it over.

'This document is dated over twenty months ago and is just a general authorisation to seek aid from allied forces,' said Sir John.

'It is,' said Khoury, 'but until this time it has not been needed. Now we have need of such aid and present you with his authority.'

'And who will pay for such aid?' asked Sir John.

'Our order will pay all expenses,' said Khoury, 'but we would assume our mutual interest in this matter would preclude any claims of profit. The security of the Holy-land is in all our interests.'

Sir John walked around the room for a few moments more while re-reading the parchment.

'Is he aware of the threat?' he asked.

'We have sent a message but his location is unknown. We believe he is on pilgrimage to Rome.'

'I am sorry,' Khoury, he said. 'This authorisation is dated and the seal is obviously broken. Many things have happened between then and now. For all I know, he may not support this campaign.'

'He will,' said Khoury, 'there is no other option. If Baibaars is triumphant, the order will lose all footholds in the region and will be forced to move overseas.'

'I sympathise, Khoury but I regret I must decline your request.'

Khoury stared at the Knight before standing up and retrieving the parchment.

'I am disappointed, Sir,' said Khoury, 'and fear we will both regret this day. However, I will not beg. Please have my horse prepared.'

Sir John signalled to a nearby Squire who ran from the hall to make the arrangements.

'In different circumstances I would ride myself,' said Sir John, 'but Edward is en-route and expects to find his army waiting. How would it be if he found part of it out fighting a battle not under his command?'

'It could be months before he arrives,' said Khoury, 'and by then it will be too late.'

'The matter is not mine to assume,' said Sir John. 'My men stay here until ordered otherwise by the King or Longshanks himself.'

'So be it,' said Khoury and strode across the hall to leave. As he reached the door, a group of giggling women entered without warning and he accidentally knocked one to the floor.

'My apologies, my lady,' he said crouching down to help, 'I am surely an imbecile with the manners of a mule.'

'No apologies needed, Sir Knight,' said the woman as he helped her to her feet, 'the clumsiness was mine alone.'

As she stood, Khoury caught his breath at her extraordinary beauty. Her long hair was as red as fiery embers and her eyes were the deepest emerald. For a few seconds they gazed at each other, both stuck for words. Khoury stood a full head taller than the woman and despite the beard, she could see he was an extraordinarily handsome man with features weathered by the rigours of desert life. Finally Sir John interrupted the silence.

'Sir Khoury,' he said, 'please meet my wife, Jennifer of Orange. She hails from Ireland and has recently joined us here in Acre. Jennifer, this is Sir Abdul Khoury of Syria, Knight Hospitaller.'

'My Lady,' said Khoury, lifting her hand to his mouth. 'Please forgive my ignorance, I have been a long time away from the business of any court.'

'Again, nothing to forgive, Sir,' said Jennifer. 'Everyone must make allowances in this...' she paused, seeking the politically correct words, 'shall we say, demanding environment?'

'We must,' said Khoury, 'and the environment is indeed demanding. Can I take it you do not find it to your favour?'

'On the contrary,' interrupted Sir John, 'the ladies reside in excellent rooms and enjoy the very best of entertainment and food.'

'Of course,' said Jennifer, still looking at Khoury, 'but there is only so much entertainment a person can stomach before it becomes a chore and though the walks within the city walls are enlightening, they fall short of the greenery of England's pastures.'

'Nonsense,' said Sir John before Khoury could respond. 'You have everything you need here and besides, I expect us to be back in England within two years. Now, if you don't mind, our guest is leaving. Please retire to your rooms, I will have the kitchens send up a meal.'

'It seems our meeting is over, Sir Knight,' said Jennifer and curtsied once more.

'An all too fleeting moment,' said Khoury, 'yet one I will treasure. Fare well, My Lady.' He kissed her hand again and after a glance at Sir John, left the hall to cross the courtyard. Behind him he heard the door slam shut and Sir John's raised voice as he admonished his wife. At first, Khoury thought about going back but realised it was none of his business.

'Squire, my horse,' he shouted and two minutes later he galloped through the gate as he headed back out into the city.

Back in the great hall, Jennifer's lady in waiting had been dismissed leaving Sir John and his wife alone.

'How dare you criticise my standing in front of my guests,' he snarled. 'Need I remind you your father is indebted to me and should I cast you back from whence you came, his debts become payable.'

'If my father knew how you treat me he would gladly hand over everything he owns,' said Jennifer.

'Then tell him,' challenged Sir John. 'I can have the deeds of transfer of his lands drawn up within days should you so wish.'

'You know I will not,' she said. 'This marriage may be one of convenience but my loyalty to my family is unbreakable. God willing, his petitions will prove fruitful and when his finances are once more stable, then and only then will he hear of my plight.'

'You are lucky the fire of your mood transfers into your bed-space, My Lady,' said Sir John, 'for I tire of your disobedience.'

'Lust is not love,' said Jennifer.

'Love I can live without,' said Sir John. 'Now get from my sight and dismiss your servants. Restrict yourself to your bed chamber for I feel I will have need of your fire before this night is out.'

'You will get nothing from me,' snarled Jennifer.

'I have a lash that begs to differ,' said Sir John, 'be-gone.'

Jennifer of Orange stared at the man with hatred in her eyes but did not move.

'*Get out,*' screamed Sir John, 'or I will have you flogged where you stand.'

Jennifer flinched and turned to walk away. As she left, tears ran silently down her face for though her temper was often fierce, her real emotions were for her only.

Fifty miles away a mounted unit rode through the valley, eager to get back within their fortress walls. Their task had been one of escort and the French nobleman had been delivered as promised to Tripoli in safety. Now the riders sought only the sanctuary of their castle and the release of burden that prayer would bring. The lead rider wore chain mail armour covered with a white habit. He carried the rank of Under-marshal and above his head flew the standard feared by

47

the infidels for over a hundred years, the red cross on a white background, the symbol of the Knights Templar.

The column consisted of just over a hundred riders, twenty Knights wearing the white habits of purity over their chain mail armour, twenty Sergeants in brown tunics, the paid cavalry who supported the Templars and the rest made up of Squires and servants, each leading the spare horses and pack mules that such patrols demanded. In addition there was one more rider that stood out from the rest, a man who also wore chain mail but was clad in a habit of green. He was the chaplain, one of the spiritual leaders always present within any Templar unit and besides taking care of the Knights' divine needs, many spoke several languages.

The canter slowed to a halt as the Under-Marshal held up his hand.

Brother Mathew, the Turcopolier in charge of the patrol rode forward and reined in his horse alongside his comrade.

'What holds our advance, Brother?' he asked.

'Look,' said the Under-Marshal.

In the distance a lone rider wearing the garb of the desert sat motionless astride his horse, blocking their way forward.

'What is he doing?' asked the Turcopolier.

'Just standing there,' said Brother Steffan.

'The ground lends itself to a trap,' said the commander. 'I will alert our men. You take the chaplain and see what he wants but beware of treachery.'

The Under-marshal waited until the chaplain joined him before walking his horse slowly forward. When they were within calling range, the chaplain spoke out in the language of the locals.

'Hail, stranger,' he said. 'Are you in need of our aid?'

The man's horse fidgeted beneath him but the man did not speak. The chaplain glanced at Brother Steffan.

'Try again,' said the Knight.

The Chaplain tried a different dialect but again there was no answer. The Under-marshal looked around the walls of the narrow canyon.

'I don't like this,' he said. 'Something is wrong.'

Before the chaplain could answer, the man called out in English.

'You soil my mother's language with your dirty tongue, Holy man,' he snarled, 'it hurts my ears.'

'Curb your tone, stranger,' said Brother Steffan, 'and clear the path.'

'The path belongs to Allah,' said the man, 'and only he can decide who rides this way.'

'These lands have been claimed in the name of Christendom and we act under the banner of the one true God. Now move or be moved.'

'I see no Christian God,' sneered the man, 'just a band of intruders under a dirty flag. Allah is God of all men and he alone will decide those who pass.'

'This is your last chance,' said Brother Steffan. 'Step aside in peace or feel our wrath.'

'Your wrath will be as petals in the wind compared to Allah's retribution,' said the man. 'This land is bequeathed to our people by Allah and we claim it in his name. You will no longer dirty the holy soil with your infidel feet. Today, you ride no further.'

'Enough idiocy,' said Brother Steffan, 'you have been warned.'

'As have you,' said the man drawing his curved sword. 'Make your peace with God, Infidel for today this holy ground will be stained by Christian blood. Without another word he spurred his horse to a gallop and rode headlong toward the two Knights, his sword raised high above his head. The Chaplain's horse reared up as he tried to turn but Brother Steffan knew they had no time to get back to the column.

'Get back to the men,' he shouted, 'call them to arms.' Before the Chaplain could answer, Brother Steffan spurred his own horse and galloped to meet the oncoming rider. Though he had no lance, he knew the standard above his head was tipped with an ornamental spike and as he rode he lifted the pole from its leather socket and lowered it quickly into the charge position.

Within seconds the two men met and though the wooden pole shattered on the chest armour of the enemy rider, it had enough force to knock him off his horse. Brother Steffan spun his steed around and saw the wounded man struggling to get to his feet. The Knight dismounted and drew his large double edged sword.

'Your attack was infantile, heathen,' he snarled, 'and now you will pay the price for insulting my friends and my God.'

To his surprise the man looked up at him and smiled.

'My death is glorious, infidel' he said. 'You and your friends will not enjoy such rapture.'

'I tire of your drivel,' said Brother Steffan and with an almighty swing, took the man's head from his shoulders.

Behind him the Turcopolier had seen the attack and called his patrol to arms.

'Squires, attend the brothers,' he roared and the young men rode up quickly with the pack horses. The Knights retrieved their kite shaped shields and their steel tipped lances. The Sergeants added spiked maces to their weaponry, resting them across their saddles ready for conflict.

'You there,' said the commander pointing at a Squire, 'ride out and retrieve our standard. Place it on the head of a lance.'

'Yes Sire,' said the boy and rode his pony out to meet the returning Brother Steffan. The Knight handed over the flag and continued to the column, now busy with preparations for battle. Within minutes, the patrol was fully armoured including steel helms over their chain mail coifs and greaves over their shins.

'What possessed him to act so?' asked the Turcopolier.

'I know not,' said Brother Steffan, 'but he bars our way no longer. We should ride as soon as we can. This place is too confined for my liking.'

'Agreed,' said the commander. 'Lead us out, Brother.'

The column rode toward the end of the valley, pausing only to retrieve the flag from the Squire. The boy held up the lance as they approached and the standard fluttered once more in the mountain breeze.

'Is it secured tightly, boy?' asked Brother Steffan. 'It would bode ill if it was to become loose.'

'It is tight, Sire.' said the boy. 'I swear.'

'Good.' said the Knight as he took the lance. 'Re-join your comrades.' Before the boy could move, a sickening thud made Brother Steffan's horse back up in fright and the Squire fell to his knees with a crossbow bolt sticking out from between his eyes. As the boy fell into the dust the Knight sounded the alarm.

'Treachery,' he shouted, 'archers amongst the rocks.'

Instantly the Turcopolier knew they were in trouble. Cavalry were no use against hidden archers and if they stayed they would be slaughtered. The well-rehearsed drills kicked in and he ordered the gallop that would take them free of the ambush.

'Advaaance.' he screamed, 'clear the valley or we are doomed.'

The patrol spurred their horses as arrows flew past them. Two pack mules were hit and fell snorting to the ground, dragging one of the Squires with them.

'Keep going,' shouted the commander. 'The valley ends before us.'

Within moments they cleared the constrictions of the ravine and the hail of arrows died away but far from relief, the commander reined in his horse in horror. Between him and safety stood a Mamluk army thousands strong.

'We have to go back,' said his second in command, 'and seek another route.'

The commander looked back the way they had come. Within the rocks he could see hundreds of archers standing up from their hiding places, each cradling bows and in their arms. To escape that way would be futile for they would be felled in seconds. He looked back to the army before him and knew there would be no reckoning. The dead man back in the valley had made it completely clear, they were supposed to die.

'Fellow Knights,' he called, 'fear not the heathen before you. Stiffen resolve and remember our code. We will not fall to assassins' arrows but do what we do best. Sergeants, man our flanks. Squires, select what weapons you can from amongst the pack horses and then cut their throats. I will not supply Baibaars with valuable mounts. When you are done, you will ride alongside us as equals and any that survive this day will be Knighted by the hand of the Grand Master himself. This I promise.'

A flurry of activity ensued and within minutes, they lined up across the plain facing an army of five thousand Mamluks. At the centre of the Templar lines, the white capes of twenty Knights blew gently in the wind as they waited to meet their destiny.

'Fellow brothers,' shouted the Turcopolier, 'rejoice, for this day we will stand before our Lord Jesus Christ in all his glory.'

'Amen,' said the men and each made the sign of the cross on his own body. The Turcopolier drew his sword and held it up high.

'Not unto us, oh Lord' he cried, 'not unto us, but to your name, grant glory.'

'Vive Dieu, Saint Amour,' roared his men and as the last word of the Templar's battle cry left their lips, a hundred men and boys charged the overwhelming numbers of the Mamluk Halqa.

51

Chapter Six

Brycheniog

Garyn stood at the side of the grave and watched as the village men covered the three bodies below. His mother had been cleaned and dressed for her funeral by the women and he had said his goodbyes in the church, but the bodies of his father and his sister were just charred remains, deformed beyond all recognition. The men had collected the bodies and passed them onto the women to do what they could but there was nothing left that could be recognised and the shrouds had been sewn into bags. Usually the bodies of the deceased would be laid out in the family home but as the forge was now no more than a smoking ruin, the priest had allowed them to be placed in the church, an honour usually reserved for the wealthy or noble.

The priest had conducted the service and the church had been filled to capacity with the villagers. A blacksmith was an important part of the community and the family had been known to all.

'Master Ruthin,' said a voice, 'come away now. You need to host the wake in your family's name.'

Garyn turned and saw Elspeth, a local girl and daughter of the village fletcher.

'In a moment Elspeth,' said Garyn. 'I will follow soon.'

The girl nodded and joined the rest of the mourners going back to the village.

Garyn stared down and as the last of his family disappeared under the damp heavy soil, he made the sign of the cross on his head and chest. With a sigh, he wiped away a tear and turned away, but as he walked, a movement at the forest edge caught his eye.

'Brother Martin,' he said as he recognised the cloaked figure, 'you startled me.'

The Monk nodded silently, acknowledging the recognition.

'Garyn,' he said, 'please accept our deepest condolences but rest assured, your family are in the arms of Christ.'

Garyn didn't answer but gave a thin lipped smile in gratitude.

'I did not see you in the church,' said Garyn.

'Where possible we leave such things to the priests,' said the Monk, 'and only intervene if he is ill or other circumstances require our presence.'

'Thank you for coming,' said the boy.

'Garyn, there is something I need to talk to you about,' said the Monk.

'If it is about the prisoner, I have nothing more to say,' said Garyn.

'No it's not about him,' said the Monk, 'it is about your father.'

'What of him?' asked Garyn.

'Come from here,' said the Monk, 'for this is consecrated ground and such matters should not be discussed here.' They left the grave yard and walked a little into the wood until they found a fallen tree.

'Sit a while,' said Brother Martin.

'What's this about?' asked Garyn.

'Garyn there are some things you should know,' said the Monk, 'truths that may surprise and hurt you. However, these things need to be said and the truth must come out.'

'Continue,' said Garyn.

The Monk took a deep breath.

'Garyn,' he said, 'as you know, I am a Monk and have taken the holy orders of St Benedict but many years ago I was a different man and pursued a different path.'

'What path?'

'One of misguided violence,' said the Monk. 'I served in the King's army before selling my services to the highest bidder and fought in the Holy-land as a Secular Knight.'

'You were a Knight?' asked Garyn in surprise.

'I was,' said Brother Martin, 'but cast aside any thoughts of chivalric codes for my sword was sold to the highest bidder. Always on the side of Christianity, I hasten to add but a mercenary all the same.'

'So what happened?' asked Garyn.

'I saw the light,' said Brother Martin, 'and realised the futility of such bloodshed. Every year that passed saw more men from both sides die needlessly in the name of religion. My sword arm became weary so when I had enough money to pay for my fare, I returned home to farm my father's land.'

'So how did you become a Monk?' asked Garyn.

'Therein lies the issue,' said Brother Martin. 'During my time as a mercenary I became the closest of friends with a fellow Knight and we returned together. Within months, he fell in love with a beautiful woman, in fact we both did. Our friendship became strained for the woman did not know whom to choose.' He fell silent for a few moments as his memory wandered back through the years. 'Anyway,' he continued, 'she chose him and our ways parted. To my shame, I could not forget this woman and pursued her in secrecy, eventually capturing her mind with lies and false promises. She fell from virtue and succumbed to my advances, spending several weeks under my spell. Ultimately she realised her mistake and returned to the man who truly loved her, a man who exceeded me in all things from military skills to virtue.'

'And what has this to do with me?'

'The woman was your mother, Garyn,' said Brother Martin, 'and I loved her more than life itself.'

Garyn stared in astonishment.

'My mother betrayed my father with you,' he asked.

'Betrayal is too strong a word, Garyn,' said the Monk, 'for she was a virtuous woman.'

'Not virtuous enough to stay from your bed,' snarled Garyn.

'Garyn, you have to understand, she was a very young woman and did not know her own mind. I pursued her relentlessly, proclaiming love unrivalled. She was confused and vulnerable and fell to my charms. Do not judge her, Garyn, I alone am responsible.'

'Yet she returned to him,' said Garyn.

'She did,' said the Monk, 'for he was always the better man. Even though she had strayed, he took her back unconditionally. It was the right decision for though I still loved her, I knew she would be happier with your father. However, it also meant my friendship with Thomas was destroyed. Years of close comradeship born of mutual hardship and shared peril was destroyed by my stupid actions. We fought and your father was victorious but he spared my life, demanding I stay away. My shame was complete, I had betrayed my best friend, lost the woman I loved and faced a future devoid of anything good. In desperation I turned to the church and over time they rebuilt the pieces of my shattered soul and eventually I made peace with God.'

'That's why he was so cold to you that night in the forge,' said Garyn.

'It is,' said the Monk 'and with good reason. For eighteen years I stayed my distance but fate saw fit for me to once more intrude on your father's happiness. I didn't want this to happen, Garyn but the

54

word of the Abbot is the earthly voice of Jesus Christ and I cannot turn away from his path.'

'So why are you telling me this now?' asked Garyn. 'All you have succeeded in doing is to cast stain upon my mother's reputation. You could have kept silent and I would eventually go to my grave thinking she was the virtuous woman I have always known'

'She was virtuous,' snapped Brother Martin, 'and you should never think any other way.'

'Then why do it, Brother Martin,' asked Garyn, 'why cast the clouds of doubt before her grave is even filled.'

'Because there is something else you should know, Garyn. Something of far more concern than any deeds long in the memory.'

'Then finish your tale, Monk,' said Garyn, 'for surely this day cannot get any worse.'

'Garyn,' said the Monk, 'when the women were laying out your family, I took the opportunity to visit the church alone to pay my last respects. While I was there, I saw something that has frozen my heart.'

Garyn stared in silence, waiting for him to continue.

'What?' he asked eventually.

'I don't know how to say this, Garyn but I saw mortal wounds on your father's body. Thomas Ruthin did not die in the fire, he was stabbed from behind by an assassin. Your father was murdered, Garyn, slaughtered in cold blood.'

'Are you sure?' asked Garyn when the shock had faded.

'I am sure, Garyn,' said the Monk. 'I saw many such wounds on the battlefield and often we tended our comrades ourselves. The marks of a blade are easily recognisable if you know what to look for. It seems that someone must have taken your father by surprise and stabbed him from behind. After the first blow, the rest would have been easy.'

'And my sister?' asked Garyn.

The Monk's head lowered and stared at the floor.

'What about my sister?' repeated Garyn quietly, 'how did she die?'

The Monk looked up again.

'Her throat was cut,' he said.

Garyn gasped in horror as the news sunk in.

'I don't understand,' he said eventually. 'Why would someone want to murder my family? They never harmed anyone.'

'I don't know, Garyn,' said the Monk, 'but I promise you this. I will work tirelessly to find out and when I do, we will inform Lord Cadwallader and watch the murderers hang from the gibbet.'

Garyn stood and stared back toward the cemetery.

'What ill have I caused to be punished so?' he asked quietly.

'None of this is your fault, Garyn,' said the Monk, 'and we can only thank the Lord that you were at the Abbey that night or there could be four bodies in that grave.'

'I have no thanks,' said Garyn. 'My life is done and I would rather wear that dank soil blanket than walk forward alone.'

'On the contrary,' said the Monk, 'there is one reason to thank God he spared you and that is retribution. Being spared the grave means you can help me find the men responsible. Make this your reason for living, Garyn and when God's justice is seen to have been done, then and only then question your destiny.'

'Why would you do this?' asked Garyn. 'You broke them apart all those years ago and now, after the briefest of meetings you set yourself upon a path of justice in their names.'

'During our early years we were as brothers, Garyn, each looking out for the other in times of peril. We fought together and bled together, each pledging his life to the other, a true oath of brotherhood yet when his happiness was on the line, I stepped in and tried to wrest it from him. There is no greater treachery, Garyn, I owe your father a great debt and though there was nothing in life he would have accepted as settlement, perhaps in death , the sword of justice will partly repay the great wrong I inflicted upon him.'

'So my father was a Knight?' said Garyn. 'He never told me.'

'Being a Knight is not the glorious life young boys dream of, Garyn. Your father and I saw more horrors than any man should see. There is no glory in death only pain and suffering. After a while a man becomes immune to the horror and he loses his soul to the slaughter. We saw Knights who never spoke, yet killed any before them with raging anger, devoid of reason and immune to all but the deepest of wounds. They had descended into a living hell, the kind where no life meant anything, even their own. Their nights were filled with horrors, worsened only by the reality of their days. We did not want to become like these men, Garyn so left when we could.'

'You deserted?'

'No, we were mercenaries and saw out every contract we entered. When a chance came, we declined further riches and rode home. We had enough money to live a comfortable life and with his share, your father bought this land.'

Garyn looked up in surprise.

'I thought our land was rented from the Manor?' he said.

'No,' said the Monk. Your father once served Cadwallader's father and found favour with him. He agreed to sell this land at a fair price and it is one of the few holdings in these parts not owned by the Cadwalladers.'

'The surprises keep coming,' said Garyn. 'Not only am I the son of a Knight but a landowner as well.'

'You are,' said Brother Martin, 'and you owe it to your father to be diligent in the management of your legacy. It was hard earned and not to be lost as a fool.'

'This is too much to take in,' said Garyn standing up. 'I must get to the wake and carry out my duties.'

'Yes you must,' said the Monk. 'Pay them great tribute and when you are done, remember their lives not the manner of their deaths. There will be time enough for anger.'

'What will you do?' asked Garyn.

'I have to go back to the Abbey,' said the Monk, 'but will come again soon.'

'How?' asked Garyn. 'I thought your order seldom left the confines of the Abbey yet you have been here constantly since the fire.'

'I will not lie to you,' Garyn said the Monk. 'The Abbot has tasked me with finding out what you know of Masun's tale. He still believes the man talked before he died. I am to befriend you and find out what you know.'

'Even if I do know anything,' said Garyn, 'what makes you think I will tell you?'

'I do not expect anything,' said the Monk. 'You asked and I was honest in my response. Either you will tell me or you won't but I will not engage on subterfuge on behalf of the church. My quest will be to find the man who murdered your family and if you have any information you wish to share, then so be it. I ask no more than that.'

'There is much to think about, Monk,' said Garyn, 'and I do not know if I am willing to trust the man who once set upon splitting up my family.'

'A wise recourse,' said Brother Martin. 'Take your time, Garyn. When you are ready, let me know and we will talk again.'

Garyn nodded and walked toward the village in silence. He was tired of talking, yet knew he had many hours of tribute and discourse before him. It was going to be a long, long day.

Chapter Seven

Krak des Chevalier

'*Open the gates,*' roared the guard commander, 'Khoury returns.'

Below the turrets, a patrol of thirty men could be seen riding up the slopes of the hill toward the impressive castle. The white cross emblazoned upon the black flag identified the patrol as Hospitaller and they thundered through the gates at a gallop before slowing down to negotiate the carefully designed tunnels within Chevalier's giant ramparts. Above them, men at arms peered down through the murder holes built into walls and the ceiling, checking the patrol was indeed friendly. The unique design of the castle meant all visitors or indeed attackers had to ride along this enclosed passage to reach the main inner ward and as it was only a few paces wide, an attacking force would be constricted in a very tight space. Halfway along the passageway, it turned sharply back on itself, heading steeply upward and any attacker not taking the turn, would find themselves outside, trapped between the castle's inner and outer walls, sitting targets for the archers above. Those enemy who were lucky enough to get that far and make the turn, would be slowed to a walk and once again, become easy targets for those defenders on the other side of the murder holes.

At the end of the winding passageway, Khoury led his patrol out into the daylight of the courtyard and leapt from his horse, allowing it to walk away untended. A Squire ran to take control of the beast while Khoury strode through a doorway and up a stair to the Knight's hall.

Two servants jumped out of his way as he pushed the door open and threw his gauntlets onto a nearby table.

'Bring me water,' he said, 'and while you're at it, summon Sir Najaar to attend me.'

The servants ran from the room, realising they were better off avoiding their master when he was in such a bad mood. Five minutes later another Knight entered the room.

'Brother Khoury,' he said pausing at the door. 'You have made good time. I see the horses heave from exertion.'

'A necessary demand,' said Khoury. 'There are events afoot that demand urgency in our manner.'

'Was your petition granted?' asked the Knight.

'It wasn't,' said Khoury, 'but there are far more urgent matters that demand attention.'

'What matters are these?' asked Najaar.

Khoury reached beneath his tunic and threw a large piece of dirty fabric across to his comrade. Sir Najaar picked it up and unfurled a white flag with a red cross stitched across its centre.

'Templar,' he said.

'It is,' said Khoury. 'I took it from the dead hands of a Squire less than an hour ago, part of a patrol we found slaughtered near the crags. Fifty souls slaughtered like market cattle and their bodies butchered before being strewn across the desert floor. It looks like the boy was trying to save the banner and rode into the mountains but he stood no chance. They staked him out and opened his stomach to the midday heat. The vultures did the rest.'

'Lord have mercy,' whispered Najaar.

'This is the work of Baibaars,' said Khoury, 'and if he has gall enough to do this almost within sight of our strongholds then he must be supremely confident and we have to take steps to increase our defences straight away.'

'What would you have us do?' asked the Knight.

'Post guards at the bottom of the rock,' said Khoury, 'and at every approach to the Castle. I want plenty of warning of any attack. Send word to the villagers, we have need of labour and need it now. Offer good coin and empty the money chests if necessary. I want the ditch deepened across the approach and more stakes added. What is the state of the castle?'

Sir Najaar considered the fortress' formidable defences. The castle was built on a spur of a rocky mountain high above the valley floor. It was protected on three sides by a sheer escarpment while the only approach on the fourth side was protected by a staked ditch and a second stone wall topped with ramparts and castellations. The second wall had been an afterthought and was intended to slow any attackers down while suffering casualties from the defenders. Even if they passed this first obstacle, the formidable castle walls were impregnable. The Taluses were built from enormous blocks of limestone, smooth sloping walls hundreds of feet thick, impervious to any sort of ram or catapult. Eight towers incorporated into the walls provided dominant fighting positions and secure living quarters for the defending Knights.

The foundations rested on the mountain bedrock, precluding any undermining and the eighty foot high walls were un-scalable by any siege ladders. Arrow slits provided archers a view of all approaches and high above, machicolations stuck out from the top of the walls, protective slabs providing cover for defenders to drop things on any attacking army below. Overall it was considered impregnable and had never been taken in its current form.

'The fortress is in good order,' said the Knight. 'Our stores are healthy and we can last a year of siege if necessary.'

'Water?'

'The Cisterns are full.'

'What about the Brothers?'

'A hundred Knights in Garrison,' said Najaar, 'another hundred on escort duties. Most will be back within the month.'

'Send word,' said Khoury, 'they are to return with all speed. What about archers?'

'No more than a hundred,' said Najaar. 'Our greatest strength is Chevalier itself.'

'Your stewardship will not go unrewarded, Brother,' said Khoury, 'but I want you to commission a further defence. Arrange a palisade to be erected on the eastern approach. Build it at least an arrow's flight from the outer wall and furnish it with ramparts. I want it to be able to withstand anything short of a siege engine.'

'Of course,' said Sir Najaar.

'One more thing,' said Khoury. 'Dismantle the buildings on the eastern approach. The Burgus may be a valuable addition to the castle in settled times but a traders' market is no use in war. Give the villagers a day to move, after that, get rid of them by any means necessary. I want a clear view of any man climbing that hill.'

'At once, Sire,' said Najaar. 'Is there anything else?'

'No, that will do for now. I need to send a message to Margat, for they too will be at risk.'

'What about those men you found in the desert?' asked Najaar.

'I will send word to the White Castle,' said Khoury. 'The Templar Grand Master will want to retrieve the bodies and give them a Christian burial, though I fear there may not be much to bury.' He looked over at his Brother Knight. 'We have seen many threats, these past few years Brother but there are things afoot. Baibaars is up to something and though he has feinted such assaults on many occasions, I feel this time there will be no retreat. Brief the men and furnish the defences with weaponry. Our fate is in the Lord's hands but until that path is revealed to us, we will not be found wanting. Join me in seeking his blessing.'

Khoury drew his large sword and placing it point first on the floor, knelt before the weapon, using the hilt as a natural crucifix. Najaar knelt down to join him and clasped his hands together as Khoury prayed.

'Lord, we thank you for unveiling our eyes to the threat of those who would deny your flock your glory. Grant us we beseech thee, the strength to carry your will, the knowledge to defend your name and the humility to accept your glory. Amen.'

'Amen,' said Najaar and the two men stood up once more. Without another word, Sir Najaar left the room to prepare for battle while Khoury climbed the watchtower. From there he could send a heliograph signal to the White Castle who in turn could relay it to the garrison at Margat in similar manner.

As he climbed he knew it was important for all orders to unite in the face of Baibaars but even if they managed to put aside their differences, their combined strength would not be enough against a full Mamluk army. If the sources were right, all they could hope for is the early arrival of Longshanks' army, that or a miracle from the Lord God himself.

Longshanks looked around the port in Tunis. The docks bustled with men of all races, all busy with the task of restocking his fleet. King Louis had laid siege to the city but the Prince and the English force had arrived too late to take any part.

Longshanks had sailed with the intention of providing support to the city of Acre and the surrounding territories but had diverted to support King Louis the Ninth of France in his Egyptian campaign. Tunis had been deemed an important step toward that goal but not long after the siege had started, the French King had died and within months his successor Charles, called off the siege and joined with the newly arrived Edward in his mission to Acre.

Longshanks took command of the remaining Christian army and now intended to sail with all speed to Acre, knowing full well his presence could affect the very future of the Christian presence in the Holy-land.

'Captain, are we ready?' he called.

'Upon your word, Sire,' answered the sailor.

'Then take us out,' said Longshanks before adding under his breath, 'and pray to God we are in time.'

Chapter Eight

Brycheniog

Garyn walked through the snow toward the remains of the forge. An overnight flurry had covered the many footprints from a few days earlier and though the walls still stood proud, they were blackened from smoke and the roof had long gone. Garyn paused and stared at the place he had called home. The ruins were silent but as he watched, a movement caught his eye on the far side.

'Brother Martin,' said Garyn, 'you startled me yet again. The day has not yet begun.'

'On the contrary,' said the Monk, 'the day is half over.' He smiled. 'Good to see you again.'

Garyn walked across and joined the Monk in the ruins.

'My heart breaks to see it so,' said Garyn. 'A loving family and a lifetime of work have all gone in the blink of an eye.'

'Your family live in the arms of the Lord,' said the Monk, 'and destruction is but temporary.'

'It doesn't look temporary to me,' said Garyn.

'The walls are still sound,' said Brother Martin, 'and with new timberwork the thatch is but a week's work for skilled men. The forge can be an entity again, should you wish to pursue your father's path.'

'And who will pay for these repairs?' said Garyn. 'I have no money.'

'Your lands are substantial, Garyn. Sell part of them back to Cadwallader. That way your future is secured and you can honour your father's memory in the manner he would have wished.''

'Perhaps,' said Garyn. 'It is too soon to decide.'

'Where are you staying?' asked the Monk.

'The priest lets me sleep in the church,' said Garyn. 'I can stay as long as I want until I sort out this mess.'

'He is a good man,' said the Monk. 'Tell me, Garyn, are you aware of any enemies your father may have had?'

'No,' said Garyn, 'but if what you say is true and he fought in all those wars then there must be many men who hold a grudge.'

'No,' said Brother Martin. 'Warfare is brutal but grudges are not taken overseas unless a great wrong is carried out. Your father was an honourable man and only killed in the name of Christ.'

'Then I know of no other,' said Garyn. 'We kept ourselves to ourselves and any visitors were always welcomed with open hospitality.'

'Perhaps that was the problem,' said the Monk. 'It may have been they welcomed in a brigand without realising and he took advantage to steal what he could.'

'Perhaps,' said Garyn walking through the empty doorway to the forge. He looked up at the morning sky before returning his gaze to the snow covered remains of the workshop. 'It looks strange like this,' he said. 'It used to be so dark and was lit only by the flames of the furnace. This snow makes it look so...' he hesitated, 'clean.'

The Monk stayed quiet but followed Garyn through the ruins. Occasionally the boy would bend over and pick up a remnant from the fire, recalling what significance it played in his family's life.

'This is a broach from my mother's favourite dress,' he said, brushing the snow of the trinket. 'She would have liked this to be in her grave.'

'The dead need no chattels, Garyn,' said the Monk.

Garyn bent over again and retrieved some tools from amongst the debris.

'These will have value,' he said. 'I should come back when the snow has melted and see what I can find.'

The two men continued picking amongst the rubble, putting aside anything they thought could be of use.

'What about the warped things?' said the Monk. 'Will they be of any use?'

'Yes,' sighed Garyn, 'They can be melted down and will see life as a different item. Here's my father's tankard,' he continued, picking up a twisted metal cup and turning to face the Monk but Brother Martin didn't hear him, his brow was furrowed as he examined something in his hand.

'Garyn, did you do any commissions for the Abbey?' asked the Monk.

'We made a gate once and there was talk about some cart wheels but apart from that, no. Why do you ask?'

'Look.' said the Monk and held out the blade of a knife. 'Is this one of your fathers?'

'I don't think so,' said Garyn examining the blade. It was a typical eating knife with a pointed end for stabbing pieces of meat. 'It may be but if it is, it's not one I recognise.'

'Perhaps he was asked to repair it,' said Garyn, 'but hadn't yet told me.'

'Perhaps,' said Brother Martin. 'Do you mind if I take this?'

Garyn shrugged.

'It's not mine,' he said, 'take it.'

They carried on checking the building for another hour before heading their separate ways.

'Brother Martin,' said the servant as the Monk entered the Abbey kitchens, 'you are not tasked to the kitchens until tomorrow. How can I help you?'

'Alwyn,' said the Monk. 'I have a question to ask. Do you have a list of all the items in the kitchen?'

'There is one with the Abbot,' said Alwyn, 'but I have been here a long time and know exactly what should be here. Is there a problem?'

'I'm not sure,' said the Monk. 'Can you tell me what eating knives you have?'

'Which type?' asked the servant.

'Those with a cruciform near the hilt. We sometimes use them in the hall.'

'I know the ones,' said Alwyn, 'they were a gift to the Abbey from the manor and are used when we have guests to share the meal.'

'Can you show me one?'

Alwyn went to a cupboard and retrieved a box. Inside there was a pile of knives, each with an elm handle and a blade inscribed with a crucifix.

'Here they are?' he said and pulled one out.

'Are they all here?' asked the Monk.

'They are,' said Alwyn, 'there is a set of fifty, a beautiful gift from Cadwallader himself.'

'Count them,' said the Monk.

'I can assure you they are all there,' said Alwyn. 'I am diligent with such matters.'

'Please humour me,' said the Monk and watched as the servant counted the knives, not once but three times.

'I'm sorry, Brother Martin,' said the servant, 'there seems to be one missing. I don't know how this could have happened, I counted them myself only three days ago and they were all there.'

'Are there any others in existence?'

'No the set was specially commissioned.'

'So do you think this may be the missing piece?' He placed the twisted blade on the table. Alwyn examined it closely before looking up at the Monk.

'It is,' he said, 'but what happened to it.'

'It was found in the remains of a fire,' said the Monk, 'but I don't know how it got there.'

'It was here a few days ago,' said the servant, 'I swear it.'

'Do not fret,' said the Monk. 'Do you recall exactly when it was counted?'

'It was the night before the blacksmith's fire,' said the servant. 'I remember because it was the night that rogue tried to steal a loaf and was thrown into a cell.'

'Ah yes,' said the Monk, 'I remember. I expect he regrets the deed now, Cadwallader is not known for leniency in such cases.'

'Oh,' said the servant in surprise, 'he won't be facing justice, Brother, the Abbot set him free. In fact, he brought him in here himself and told me to give the man food for his family. I thought it was strange but obviously the Abbot thought mercy was more advantageous than punishment. Truly he is a pious man.'

'Did you stay here the whole time they were here?' asked the Monk.

'No,' said Alwyn. 'The Abbot sent me to get a blanket. He said it was a gift for the family. I was gone no more than a few minutes. Do you think that rogue stole the knife?'

'Perhaps,' said the Monk. 'Thank you, Alwyn, your help is greatly appreciated.' Without waiting for a response, Brother Martin left the kitchen and returned to his cell. It was almost time for mid-morning prayers and he had a lot on his mind.

Garyn returned to the Church and spent the next few hours chopping firewood for the Priest. As he worked the events of the past few days whirred around his mind like a storm wind, picking up the information before discarding it once more when it did not make any sense. Finally a voice dragged him back to reality.

'I think that may be enough,' it said.

Garyn looked up and saw a pretty girl standing near the churchyard wall. She was wrapped up against the winter's cold and despite the head scarf, he smiled as he recognised the attractive face.

'Elspeth Fletcher,' he said. 'Good day to you.'

'And to you,' said Elspeth with a sunny smile. 'I think you may have enough kindling for two winters.'

Garyn looked at the enormous pile he had accumulated.

'I lost track,' he murmured.

'Obviously,' laughed Elspeth before adding, 'do you have many chores today?'

'Nothing that can't wait,' said Garyn, 'though I should tidy this lot up.'

'Well,' said Elspeth, 'I have to go up to the manor for my father. Perhaps you would like to join me on the walk?'

'I would like that very much,' said Garyn.' Give me a few minutes.' He busied himself stacking the wood in the porch of the church and sweeping up the splinters before returning the axe to the tool box.

'Right,' he said, 'I am ready.'

'Then come,' said Elspeth, 'it looks like it is going to be a sunny day.'

Garyn joined the girl and they walked along the footpath until they reached the traders road leading past the manor house a few miles away.

'How are you feeling?' asked Elspeth.

'I'm not sure,' said Garyn, 'confused, I suppose.'

'Why is that?'

'I still cannot understand why someone would kill my family,' he answered, 'that and the discovery that my father was once a Knight who fought in the Holy-land.'

'Really?' said Elspeth, coming to a halt. 'Are you sure?'

'One of the Monks told me,' said Garyn, 'so I suppose it must be true.'

'But why didn't your father tell you?' asked Elspeth.

'I know not' said Garyn and they carried on walking in silence.

'I wonder if your father knows,' he said eventually. 'He and my father shared ale on many nights and was his closest friend. Do you think he told him?'

'If he did, my father never shared the knowledge with us,' said Elspeth. 'I could ask him if you like?'

'No, what is done is done and I wouldn't want to make your father feel awkward.' They carried on walking but as they crossed the stepping stones of a shallow ford, Elspeth slipped and Garyn reached out to grab her hand.

68

'Here, let me help,' he said.

They crossed the river with no further mishap before turning from the track and making their way across the fields.

'That was nice,' said Elspeth.

'What was?'

'Back there,' she said, 'when you held my hand. You could do it again if you like.' She glanced up at Garyn and he could see she was blushing furiously.

Garyn was taken aback. He tried to respond but struggled to find the words.

'I...I...Um, I suppose...'

'I am sorry, Garyn,' she said, 'I forget myself and have embarrassed you. Please forget I said anything.'

'No,' said Garyn, 'I mean, yes, I would like to do it again, if it pleases you.'

'It does,' said Elspeth with a smile and held out her hand. Garyn took it gingerly and they walked for several hundred paces in silence, each enjoying the quiet intimacy of close contact for the first time.

'This is nice,' said Garyn eventually.

'It is,' said Elspeth. 'Garyn, would you be offended if I was to say I find your company very pleasing?'

'Not at all,' said Garyn.

'And do you like me too?'

'I do,' said Garyn, 'and always have. You are the prettiest girl in the village by far.'

'Really,' said Elspeth, 'you have never said so.'

'There were far too few days outside of the forge to seek your company,' said Garyn, 'and even when our paths crossed in church or at the market, you were always with your mother or father. How could I say?'

'Are you afraid of my father?' asked Elspeth.

'Not as much as your mother,' said Garyn.

Elspeth laughed and cuffed him across the shoulder.

'Garyn ap Thomas, you say the cheekiest things.'

'Well, she is a formidable woman,' said Garyn. 'A man can talk to a man but a mother can be like a she-wolf when it comes to her pups.'

'Then why don't you talk to him?' asked Elspeth.

'Who?'

'My father, silly.'

About what?

'Well, you could ask him if you could call on me and perhaps we could walk out.'

Garyn stopped and stared at the girl.

'What are you saying?' he asked.

'Garyn, you are not making this easy for me,' she giggled. 'I am saying if you were to offer courtship, then I may not turn you away.'

'But…'

Elspeth's face fell.

'Oh Garyn,' she said, 'I am so sorry. Here you are still grieving for your poor family and I am filling your head with the silliness of girls. Please forgive me.' She pulled her hand from his and hitching up her skirts, ran up the slope away from him.

Garyn took a few moments as her words sunk in but as she disappeared over the crest, he shook himself from his surprised stupor and called after her.

'Elspeth, wait,' he cried. 'It is I who should offer apology for being such a knave.' He ran after her but as he crested the hill, saw she had stopped just a few paces further on. He came to a stop beside her, staring in awe at the sight which lay before him.

In the shallow valley below, the forests had been cleared for over a mile and in the centre of the clearing, the most impressive building he had ever seen sat serenely in the winter sun. It was much bigger than the Abbey and consisted of a fortified building, castellated along the roof edge as a defence against any attack. On either end, a large chimney stack reached up into the sky, pouring smoke into the crisp air above and three rows of windows were set deep into the thick walls, each window higher than the tallest man. To one side, a courtyard was a hive of activity as grooms saw to their master's horses and in the distance, Garyn could see two rows of soldiers practising their skills with bill hooks and maces.

'Isn't it wonderful?' said Elspeth, looking at a group of finely dressed ladies walking in the sun. 'Oh how I wish I could live such a life.'

'It is a magnificent estate,' said Garyn. 'I had no idea it was so big.'

'Have you never been here before?'

'No,' said Garyn. 'We always followed the track and did our business at the gate house. There was never any need to come up here.'

'Then come,' said Elspeth. 'It is much more impressive close up and if we are lucky, we may get something hot from the Kitchens.'

'Elspeth, about what you just said…' started Garyn.

'Forget it,' said Elspeth, 'just pretend it never happened.' Before he could reply, she ran down the slope toward the manor, leaving a trail of footprints in the sparkling snow.

Garyn ran after her and as they approached the building they both slowed to a walk. The guards at the manor door looked their way but before Garyn could voice his concern, one raised his hand and waived.

'A very good morning to you, Miss Fletcher,' said the man in a strange accent.

'And to you, Pierre,' answered Elspeth. 'Is Master Reynolds present today?'

'He is,' said the guard, 'go around to the courtyard and ask for him there but be quick, His Lordship is due back and it wouldn't be good to get in his way.'

'Thank you Pierre,' said the girl and Garyn followed her around the side of the enormous building.

'Is he French?' asked Garyn.

'What do you think?' laughed Elspeth.

'I don't know,' said Garyn, 'I have never met a Frenchman before.'

'He is from Normandy,' said Elspeth, 'and is a soldier in the pay of Cadwallader. That's all I know.'

'Who is this Master Reynolds you asked after?'

'The head stockman,' said Elspeth. 'He looks after all beasts on the manor and keeps a flock of geese on the estate. He has their fallen feathers collected for us and we use them to fletch the arrows for the bowmen. Others are collected as well but goose feathers provide the best flights by far.'

They entered the courtyard and stared around at the activity.

'It's busy,' whispered Elspeth.

Garyn didn't answer, he was too busy looking at the fascinating work going on around him. Dozens of grooms brushed vigorously at their horse's coats while younger boys carried buckets of manure out of the stables to unload them onto a waiting cart. The sound of a blacksmith's anvil brought the memories back but before he could say anything, Elspeth grabbed his arm.

'There he is,' she said, 'come on.'

They walked across the yard toward two men struggling to encourage a huge pig into a different pen. When they were successful, Elspeth coughed politely.

'Master Reynolds,' she said, 'a very good day to you.'

'Mistress Fletcher,' smiled the man, 'thank you for coming. And who is this young man?'

'This is Garyn ap Thomas,' said Elspeth, 'son of Thomas Ruthin the blacksmith.'

The stockman looked at Garyn for a few moments.

'I hear tell of a fire,' he said. 'Is it the same family?'

'It is,' said Garyn.

'Then you have my condolences, Garyn, it is a very sad state of affairs.'

'It is done,' said Garyn, 'and they have been laid to rest.'

The man nodded before continuing.

'Anyway,' he said, 'it is just as well you have brought some muscle, Mistress Elspeth,' 'for there are two sacks to convey to your father and though they are feathers, it is a load too heavy for such a pretty girl.'

'Two sacks?' asked Elspeth. 'Why so many?'

'Tell your father to double his output,' answered Reynolds. 'There are things afoot that demand increased stocks of arrows with little time to prepare.'

'Warfare?' asked Garyn.

'Probably,' said Reynolds, 'but not between Llewellyn and the house of Winchester, this time Henry's son has taken the cross and intends to Crusade.'

'To where?' asked Garyn.

'To Palestine to aid the beleaguered forces at Acre and Tripoli,' said Reynolds.

'What would Longshanks see in such a quest?' asked Garyn.

'I am not privy to the reasoning of Monarchs or their sons,' answered the stockman. 'All I know is Henry begged him not to go but Longshanks amasses an army as we speak. The Landholders' debts have been called in and taxes have risen throughout the land to pay for the Crusade. It is said he hopes to sail within months.'

'What about Llewellyn?' asked Elspeth, 'what part does our own Prince play in this?'

'He stays home,' said Reynolds. 'Though Henry formally recognised Llewellyn as the true Prince of Wales in Montgomeryshire two years ago, Llewellyn still has to pay homage. Subsequently he has instructed the lords of Brycheniog and Builth to supply Longshanks with a thousand bowmen and fifty Knights. Cadwallader himself intends to take the cross and join Longshanks on Crusade.'

'Really?' gasped Garyn, 'but surely he is too old?'

'It is true he is fifty years old,' said Reynolds, 'but he is a man of great stature and has many campaigns behind him. Perhaps he sees this as a last opportunity to seek Christ's blessing before he dies. He is taking ten Knighted men with him from the estate and a hundred archers from the outer villages. Anyway,' he continued, 'enough idle gossip, I'll get the sacks and you can take them to the fletcher. I'll be back in a few moments. Reynolds walked into an outbuilding leaving Garyn and Elspeth outside.

'Another Crusade,' said Garyn, 'and so many men from this manor. I wonder if there would be room for one more?'

'Who?' asked Elspeth.

'Me,' said Garyn.

'You are no archer, much less a Knight,' she said, 'besides, I don't want you to go.'

'You are right,' sighed Garyn. 'I chose the forge while my brother chose the sword. He marched from my mother under a patriotic banner and she died not knowing whether he lives or dies. A question I ask myself most days.'

'Make way for Cadwallader,' shouted a guard and everyone in the courtyard rushed against the nearest walls to stand in honour of the manor Lord. Garyn and Elspeth did the same and moments later, a troop of ten mounted men in Chainmail armour rode through the gate.

The lead horse was enormous and wore full barding, the armour so necessary for mounts in battle and beneath the armour, a Caparison saddle blanket embroidered with the coat of arms of the Cadwallader household, hung low about the horse's legs. As they pulled up, the fully armoured Knight lifted the visor of his helmet.

'Take this one away,' he shouted as he dismounted, 'he is lame. Have another ready for me tomorrow. If we don't settle on four mounts soon I will have to travel to London and purchase the horses I need. That is a distraction I could do without.' Two Squires ran forward to take the Knight's gauntlets and unstrap his armour while a third led the limping horse away. A page brought a flagon of water and as Cadwallader drank, his gaze fell upon Garyn standing against the wall.

'You there,' said Cadwallader. 'I know not your face. Who are you?'

'My name is Garyn, Sire,' said the boy, 'Garyn ap Thomas, Son of Thomas Ruthin

'Ruthin,' said Cadwallader, 'the blacksmith?'

Garyn nodded silently.

'Come here,' said Cadwallader.

Garyn glanced at Elspeth before walking across the courtyard to stand before the Lord of the manor.

'You look like him,' said Cadwallader eventually, 'and will have his stature. Be proud of your father, Garyn, he was a great man.'

'People keep telling me this,' said Garyn, 'yet I knew him only as a father and a blacksmith. I never knew he was a Knight. He chose not to share his past with me.'

'A strange choice but one I respect,' said Cadwallader. 'Perhaps he wanted to steer you from the Knight's path to keep you from harm.'

'That wasn't his decision to make,' said Garyn. 'A man should choose his own destiny.'

'Agreed,' said Cadwallader, 'but a father should also keep his children from harm. He did what he thought was right.'

'I hear you are taking the cross,' said Garyn. 'Perhaps there is room for an extra Squire amongst your men.'

'You are no Squire, Garyn. A Squire takes many years to learn the code before having to prove himself in battle. I have no doubt you would be a man of honour but it is too late for you to follow the path of chivalry. Go home and rebuild your father's business, these matters are above you.' Cadwallader turned and walked away, leaving Garyn standing in the middle of the courtyard alone.

A Squire walked up to him and spoke quietly in his ear.

'How dare you try to claim the path of the chivalry, peasant,' he snarled. 'Get yourself back to your pig farm or whatever pauper's place you crawled from. Knighthood is for the gentry, not the lowly.'

Garyn turned to face the similarly aged boy but Elspeth ran across to grab his arm.

'Garyn, come away,' she hissed, 'this is not the place.'

Garyn looked around and saw many people staring at him, including all the Squires.

'Come on,' said Elspeth again and dragged Garyn to where Reynolds was waiting with two sacks of feathers.

'Don't even think about it, young man,' said the stockman, 'they all train in the art of warfare and each could beat you within an inch of your life without breaking sweat.'

Garyn swung the larger of the two sacks up onto his back.

'For trainee Knights, their courtesy leaves a lot to be desired,' he said and stormed out of the gate, his ears ringing with the jeering of the Squires behind him.

Chapter Nine

Krak des Chevalier

Sir Najaar knocked loudly on the door of Khoury's chambers.
'Enter,' called Khoury.

Najaar walked in and Khoury could see he was covered with the dust of the road.

'Brother Najaar,' he said, 'you are back earlier than I expected. How went the patrol?'

'Sire,' said Najaar, 'I have grave news. A Mamluk army is but a day away and heads in this direction.'

'Are you sure?' asked Khoury, standing up.

'Yes, Sire. I saw the dust from their feet with my own eyes.'

'At what Strength?' asked Khoury.

'Unknown as yet,' said Najaar, 'but already their lead units besiege the White Castle. The main force follows on and the talk in the village is that Baibaars himself leads the army.'

'If Baibaars leads then his target must be Chevalier,' said Khoury. 'We are not strong enough to take on a Mamluk army but luckily, our predecessors made these walls thick enough to withstand a nation. Pass the word, stand to the garrison. Have our herdsmen bring in the cattle and man the outers.'

'Sire, the villagers have sent petition and seek sanctuary within our walls.'

'Grant entry to all that request it,' said Khoury, 'but in the outer ward only. It looks like Longshanks has let us down and we are on our own in this matter. Prepare for siege, Sir Najaar and pray that God strengthens our arms.'

Twenty miles away, Sultan Baibaars rode at the head of his mounted army. Behind him, a seemingly endless caravan of carts followed the Mamluk warriors, carrying the supplies the army would need in their campaign against the Christians.

Hassam rode up and joined the Sultan.

'Majesty,' he said, 'our Halqas dominate the Homs gap and already the White Castle trembles before our assault. Do you wish me to hold back our swords until you get there to witness their capitulation.'

'No, Hassam,' said Baibaars, 'the White Castle is but a distraction. Let our Amirs tear it down for the one I want is Chevalier and I would make it my focus. Send in the Halqas to surround the castle and lay waste to any hope of succour in the area. Lock them in their precious fortress, Hassam, let them think their walls are impregnable for in their arrogance they forget who it is they face. No army is too big to fall to Baibaars and no castle too strong to withstand my wrath. We will give them a gift, Hassam. We will give them the gift of this night to sleep safely within their walls. Tomorrow, our offerings will be horror, pain and bloodshed.'

'Get a move on,' shouted a Knight at the crowd of villagers pouring through the gate in the newly formed wooden palisade. 'One more hour and these gates will be barred.'

The villagers shuffled forward, each burdened with what belongings they could carry. Behind them, on the horizon, thousands of mounted Mamluk soldiers rode slowly toward Chevalier intent on laying siege.

All along the palisade archers were busy placing piles of arrows in strategic places. The approach to the castle was not very wide and they knew their arrows would cause devastation before any battering rams got anywhere near.

'Leave the animal here,' shouted the Knight at an old man leading a mule through the gate. 'There is no need of beasts of burden within the castle.'

'My wife can't walk, Sire,' said the wrinkled man. 'Please let us through.'

'I will not allow your diseased animal, old man,' said the Knight, 'but will not deny you the sanctuary of the Castle. He stepped forward and lifted the woman from the mule.

'Unload your things and follow me,' he said, 'your wife will be waiting within Chevalier.' With that, the fully armoured Knight strode back toward the imposing fortress with the old woman in his arms, surrounded by two hundred terrified villagers.

Within hours, Baibaars' army surrounded the mountain upon which Chevalier sat. His warriors set about looting the village before setting it alight and building their own tented encampment out on the plain.

From his position in the gate tower, Khoury could see the smoke rising from the White Castle in the distance and he knew that further along the gap, Castle Margat was already under siege.

'Are the men ready?' he asked.

'Yes,' said Najaar.

'Then take ten Knights and support the palisade,' said Khoury. 'I do not expect it to hold out against the hoard but our archers can cause many casualties before they even reach the outer wall. Do not sacrifice our men needlessly, pull them back when they can do no more. Their services will be needed within these walls before this is over.'

'Yes, Sire,' said Najaar and left the Castellan alone with his thoughts.

Out on the plain the enemy army swelled and were like ants upon the ground.

'Bring your wrath, Baibaars,' said Khoury to himself as he watched them prepare their camps, 'for no man has yet breached these walls and they will not fall until every Knight's blood has stained the walls red. This I swear by all that is holy.'

The following morning Najaar stood atop of the archer's ramparts waiting for the assault to begin. On either side of him, fifty archers waited patiently, each with their bows already strung in anticipation and a hundred arrows at their feet. On the slopes below he could see thousands of men making their way up the hill and in amongst them he could see carts heavily laden with the catapults such sieges inevitably brought. A lone rider broke free and rode toward the palisade.

'Hold your arrows,' called Najaar to his defenders.

The man came close before reining in his horse.

'Who speaks for your Castellan?' he called.

'I do,' answered Najaar, 'what do you want, Mamluk?'

'I come with my Majesty's blessing with offer of leniency,' said the rider. 'Baibaars himself recognises the greatness of your Castle and believes it would be a shame to destroy such magnificence. He offers terms of surrender with guarantees of safety for all. Commit to his request and our armies will be gone before this same sun sets.'

'Tell Baibaars that surely a warrior King such as he must know we will not yield,' answered Najaar, 'and though his warriors are many, they will be like a wave upon a rock.'

78

'Even a rock erodes from many waves,' said the messenger. 'Look before you, Christian. This Halqa is but ten thousand strong. Baibaars has a hundred times this many, you do not have a chance.'

'We have every chance, Mamluk,' answered Najaar, 'for we are the Knights of St John De Hospitaller. Our name is feared throughout your tribes and there will be no submission.'

'There were indeed days when your name struck terror into our villages,' said the messenger, 'but not this day. Our country is united once more, Christian and rides with the spirit of Sah-la-Din at our side. Your time here is done, Christian, take your ships and leave this land to those whom Allah decrees.'

Najaar nodded to a nearby archer and an arrow ripped through the air to embed itself in the floor at the horse's feet, causing it to jump in alarm.

'You have our answer, Mamluk,' said Najaar. 'Now be gone for there is a battle to be fought.'

The messenger rode forward a few paces before answering.

'You had your chance, Christian,' he shouted, 'now pay the price.' He spun his horse and as he galloped away, slid sideways in the saddle to snatch the arrow from the ground without losing any speed. Najaar watched him go and turned to the defenders.

'To arms, Brothers,' he called, 'and face the heathen with courage and honour. Count not their numbers for God is with us and for those who do not survive this day, look down on us with pride from the Kingdom of the Lord.'

Baibaars took the arrow from Husam and waited for the explanation.

'Majesty,' said Husam, 'the Castellan's voice sent this in response.'

'It is no more than I expected, Husam,' said Baibaars. 'Their arrogance knows no bounds. Give the order to attack. Tear down their walls and bring me the head of the Castellan.'

'Yes, Majesty,' said Husam and left the tent to start the assault.

'Here they come,' roared Najaar, 'archers prime your bows and release on my command.'

Before them, hundreds of men carrying round shields and curved swords raced up the hill toward the palisade, each roaring their battle cries and beseeching their God for victory.

The defenders notched their arrows and aimed high into the sky. The slopes before them had been carefully paced out and markers placed at various distances, allowing the archers to know how high to aim their arrows.

'Steady,' shouted Najaar as the enemy approached the first marker, 'steady...Release.'

A hundred arrows shot high into the morning sky, followed seconds later by a second volley. Within moments the hail of death fell amongst the Mamluk infantry and though most raised their shields against the arrows, many fell beneath the deadly barrage.

'Keep firing,' shouted Najaar, 'show them that every step they take comes with a heavy price.' Over and over again the air filled with arrows but despite their losses, the Mamluk army continued onward until finally, the last man fell and the slopes fell silent. All over the hill the ground was littered with the corpses of over three hundred men, none of whom had got anywhere near the palisade.

Suddenly the air was ripped apart by the sounds of the defenders cheering but Najaar knew it meant nothing.

'Silence,' he roared, 'report casualties.'

'No casualties, Sire,' came the reply from one of the Sergeants.

Another Knight walked over and stood alongside Najaar, staring out over the corpse littered killing ground.

'Brother Sabra,' said Najaar. 'This is your first siege I understand.'

'It is,' said the fellow Knight, 'and the tactics of the Mamluk fascinate me. They have sacrificed so many men for so little gain.'

'Baibaars knows what he is doing,' said Najaar. 'Look to the flanks, he has observers watching how we defend the walls and will use this information to his advantage. A few hundred or so of his lower ranks are but a small price to pay for this knowledge.'

'What do you think he intends to do?' asked Sabra.

'I don't know,' said Najaar, 'but we will soon find out.'

The wall fell silent again and the morning quiet was disturbed only by the occasional groan of any wounded men still on the battlefield, suffering in the heat. Apart from appointed lookouts, the men on the Palisade took the opportunity to rest from the sun until Najaar's voice echoed around the hill once more.

'Stand to,' he called, 'here they come again.'

Every man returned to their positions and this time saw warriors with longer shields walking slowly toward them.

'Prepare arrows,' shouted Najaar, 'steady…release.'

Again the air filled with arrows but this time the effect was less devastating. Few men fell due to the shields but it soon became clear they had no intention of assaulting the wall. Instead they covered the slopes with piles of blackened hay before retiring once more.

'They build a palisade of grass,' said an archer, 'what use is that?'

Najaar turned his face into the welcome breeze before realising the significance.

'That's no ordinary grass, soldier,' he said, 'it is fire grass. Damp hay soaked in flammable oil. The breeze is with him and he prepares for the next step.'

Within moments a line of Mamluk archers appeared and lay clay pots on the ground before them.

'Archers,' said Sabra,' but surely they are out of range.'

'Their arrows are not meant for us, Brother Sabra but the fire grass. The pots before them contain embers from their fires.'

The Mamluk archers dipped their arrows into the fire pots before aiming at the bales of hay around the slope. As each bale was hit it burst into flames sending clouds of black oily smoke toward the palisade.

Najaar turned to the defenders.

'Tie a cloth around your faces,' he shouted. 'Tear your clothing if you must but form a mask against the smoke.'

Within moments the defenders were coughing violently as the smoke billowed over the wall. Their eyes stung from the acrid fumes and they crouched behind the timber, desperate for fresh air.

'Here they come again,' shouted a voice and the sound of thousands of screaming men filled the air as the second attack began. This time they reached the wooden wall and the defenders heard the sound of siege ladders thumping against the other side.

'Ladder poles,' shouted a voice and many archers exchanged their bows for long poles, notched at the end to take a ladder rung and used them to push away the ladders, sending the men upon them hurtling down to the floor. The smoke was rapidly dispersing and the defending archers once more rained their arrows amongst the Mamluks. Some attackers succeeded in getting over only to be met by the maces of the Sergeants. Eventually the sound of horns echoed around the hill and the attackers turned and fled down the hill as defending arrows cut them down like hay.

The wall fell quiet again and this time there was no cheering.

'Casualties?' shouted Najaar.

'Three dead and two wounded,' came the reply.

'Get them back to the castle,' ordered Najaar. 'Archers replenish your stocks for the main assault is about to come.' He turned to Sabra. 'A strange assault, Brother,' he said, 'Baibaars is a ruthless man yet I struggle to understand the aim of that attack. Even with the smoke, they would have been turned.'

'Sire,' said a voice, 'I think I know what they have done.'

The Knight turned and saw a man peering down to the base of the wooden walls on the enemy side.

'More fire grass,' continued the man, 'but this time it is piled high against the walls.'

Najaar looked for himself and saw he was right but as well as the fire grass, there was something more concerning. Almost all the wooden wall was soaked with black oil, the result of hundreds of clay pots smashed under cover of the assault.

'So that's it,' said Sabra. 'They intend to burn us down.'

'It was always a possibility,' said Najaar, 'and Baibaars is a clever man. Without a source of water, there is nothing we can do. When he sets the wall alight, all we can do is withdraw.'

As he spoke a line of enemy archers approached once more and within moments the defenders heard the thud of arrows hitting the wooden walls. Black smoke billowed from the fire grass once more but this time, the intense flames caught the oil soaked timbers alight and the wooden wall was soon ablaze.

'Pick up your weapons,' shouted Najaar, 'and retire to the outer walls. The Palisade is lost to us.'

The defenders climbed down the ladders and ran back across the open ground toward the outer wall. The stone wall also stretched from one cliff edge to the other and its structure meant fire would be no use to the attackers. The ditch at its base was similar to the one at the base of the main fortress and filled with pointed stakes. Any man falling in was doomed and the high parapets provided ample protection for defenders.

Najaar led the men through the archway and watched as the stout door was secured with metal bars sunk deep into the stone walls. Though it wouldn't hold against battering rams, the murder holes meant any such weapons being employed would cost them dearly in lives.

'Deploy along the walls,' ordered Najaar, 'and get some rest. The palisade will take time to burn and I expect Baibaars to savour his minor victory before continuing the assault.' He turned to one of the soldiers. 'Take word to the Castle,' he said. 'Tell them to bring food out for the men. They will eat on station.'

'Yes Sire,' said the man and ran to the castle behind them.

Najaar climbed the winding staircase of one of the small towers and exited onto the ramparts. His men were already there, each sat with their backs against the wall passing a goatskin water bag between them.

'You did well, men,' said Najaar, 'but know that the worst is yet to come.'

'We lost the outer palisade,' said one.

'It was but a temporary defence designed to hold him up,' said Najaar, 'and today his army is weaker by several hundred souls. It has not been a wasted day.'

The expected follow up assault never materialised that day, nor the day after, but any thoughts of a reprieve were cut short on the third day, when the look-outs reported activity at the remains of the palisade.

'Something's happening,' one called and every man on the ramparts stood to gaze across the open ground.

At first the brow of the slope meant the actions of the Mamluks were hidden from their eyes but eventually they saw teams of horses dragging something up onto the plateau.

'What are they?' asked a page, peering over the battlements.

'Siege engines,' said a Knight, 'and if I am not mistaken, they have built Mangonels.'

'I count ten,' said the page. 'Is that bad?'

The Knight glanced over at a comrade who returned the worried look in silence.

'Think of the most destructive catapult you have seen, boy,' said the Knight, 'and then multiply its force by ten. A Mangonel is capable of sending rocks the size of a man through the walls of most castle defences. Ten of them will drop this wall within hours.'

'Since when has Baibaars had Mangonels?' snapped Sir Khoury half an hour later.

83

'He must have picked up the knowledge during his campaign,' said Najaar. 'Perhaps he has captured engineers who make them for him.'

'Wherever the source, this is not good,' said Khoury. 'Are they already set up?'

'The bases are in place and the workmen construct them as we speak,' said Najaar. 'The component parts were already made and need only be fitted. I estimate they will be complete before the day is out.'

'How many?'

'At least ten,' said Najaar.

'Even the stone of the outer wall will struggle against ten Mangonels,' said Khoury. 'We must do something to lessen their impact and we must do it tonight.'

'Understood,' said Najaar and they spent the next few hours making their plans.

The sky was at its darkest when Khoury made his move. Twenty men slipped silently out of the gate and along the edge of the escarpment toward the fully assembled Mangonels. As they neared they dropped to their knees before crawling as close as they could to the campfires of the unsuspecting Mamluk guards.

During battle the main role of the archers was to supply cover to the men at arms with their bows but during the battle itself they had a secondary role. When the use of arrows was impossible due to the close quarter battle, many were often called upon to despatch the enemy wounded with their knives and all archers were skilled with the smaller blade. It was this skill that was needed this night and finally the first two archers crawled forward to begin the silent assault.

They approached the looming shape of the first Mangonel keeping low to the ground as they neared the guards' fire. Two of the Mamluk were asleep, wrapped in their thawbs while the two others talked quietly, keeping themselves warm by the flames.

The two archers made their way around the back of the siege engine and inch by inch, closed in on their enemy. Finally they were in range and with a nod of agreement, both silently ran the last few paces to reach the guards. At the last moment the Mamluks heard the approach and turned in confusion but it was too late, the blades sliced deep through their throats and their cries of alarm were silenced by hands across their mouths.

The archers lowered their victims gently to the floor and stared into the darkness for any sign they had been seen but the night remained silent. Quickly they slit the throats of the two sleeping guards before signalling those behind them it was safe to continue. The remaining men crawled past to carry out their part in the sabotage and as they passed, they handed over leather water skins full of flammable oil similar to that used by the Mamluks earlier that day.

Slowly the Mangonel guards were overcome and one by one the war machines were smeared with the oil. The Sergeant in charge of the assault started to hope they would complete their task unnoticed but it wasn't to be and the night silence was torn apart as a guard raised the alarm. Down on the slopes the enemy camp burst into life as the Mamluks raced to arms. The Hospitaller Sergeant gave up any pretence at subterfuge and shouted toward his own command.

'We are discovered,' he shouted, 'give the signal, the rest of you, set the fires.'

A flaming arrow cut through the darkness high above and at each of the seven Mangonels already captured, the archers dipped prepared brands into the Mamluk fires before setting light to the oil sodden timbers of the catapults. The oil took a few moments to catch but when it did, the flames licked quickly up the ropes.

'Make haste,' roared the Sergeant to his men, 'make sure they are well alight.' The machines were now lit by the flames of their own fires but the Sergeant knew they could be easily extinguished. Below them, hundreds of men had started to run up the hill and the few defending archers re-strung their bows in anticipation.

Within moments twenty arrows flew through the air but the darkness and the spread out nature of the counter attack meant few found their mark.

'There's the signal,' shouted Khoury back at the outer wall, 'open the gates.'

The wooden doors swung inward and the drawbridge crashed down to span the spike filled ditch. Within seconds, a hundred mounted Knights led by Khoury himself thundered across to support the archers on the front line.

'Make way,' shouted Khoury and the archers stepped aside to allow the Knights through. Within moments the horses smashed into the disorganised Mamluks on the slopes and the Hospitallers slashed their swords through unprotected flesh and bone, taking advantage of the confusion and darkness.

Khoury reigned in his horse and looked around the mayhem. The surprise was total but though the Knights' domination caused havoc, he knew it would be only minutes before the slopes were swarming with Mamluk reinforcements.

'Enough,' he roared, 'back to the outers.' The Knights turned their horses and galloped back up the hill past the now blazing siege engines. The archers were already racing back to safety, their job done as behind them, the shouts of thousands of Mamluk warriors filled the night sky.

Minutes later all the attackers raced across the ditch to safety.

'Raise the drawbridge,' shouted Khoury,' every man to the ramparts. Squires secure the horses, Sergeants in arms, prepare to defend the walls.'

Men ran everywhere to their stations, fully expecting a full assault in retribution but apart from a flurry of arrows, the attack never came. Najaar and Khoury stared across the open ground toward the blazing siege engines.

'Seven Mangonels destroyed,' said Najaar, removing his helmet, 'a task well done, Brother.'

'Three yet remain,' said Khoury and we will surely hear their voice before this thing is done.'

'We have done what we can,' said Najaar, 'the rest is in the hands of God.'

'How did they manage this?' demanded Baibaars, 'where were the guards?'

'Sire, there were four guards on each machine,' said the commander. 'They were taken by surprise.'

'Four only?' shouted Baibaars, 'the importance of these machines warranted four hundred. Who is responsible for this?'

The commander nodded to a man at the entrance and moments later, two guards dragged in a tethered warrior.

'This is the man.' said the commander.' Shall I have him beaten?'

'You will have him disembowelled,' spat Baibaars, 'along with the rest of his unit and you, commander, you will be staked out in the sun. This man failed in his duty but you failed my trust completely. Guards, take them away, I have no use for imbeciles.'

The guards fell on the two men and dragged them away to their fate, as Baibaars turned to Hassam.

'What damage has been caused?' he asked.

'We have lost seven Mangonels,' said Hassam, 'and another is damaged. That can be repaired but the others will take weeks.'

'Weeks we do not have,' said Baibaars. 'Set the remainder upon their task at first light and do not stop until the outer wall is breached.'

'Yes, Majesty,' said Hassam and left the tent. As he climbed the slope to the Plateau, the first screams of the condemned men echoed through the night. It was to be the first of many.

Chapter Ten

The Castle of the King's Constable

Jennifer of Orange sat before a mirror in her room. Her handmaiden, Lucy, sat alongside her cradling a bowl of cold water as Jennifer bathed her split lip with a piece of clean linen.

'My Lady,' said Lucy, 'it looks so painful, why do you put up with it?'

'I have no choice,' sighed Jennifer, turning her head to better see her blackened eye, 'if I run, then my father will suffer.'

'But you cannot go on like this,' said Lucy. 'He will surely kill you.'

Jennifer sighed again and examined the bruising on her face.

'You are probably right,' she said. 'What life is this to be no more than a piece of meat to a man I loathe?'

'Then end it, My Lady,' said Lucy. 'Flee for England as quickly as possible and tell your father of this man's treatment. Even if he hasn't resolved his debts, he can petition the King for leniency. Anything but this, I implore you.'

Jennifer turned to face her.

'You are wise beyond your years, Lucy,' she said, 'but how can I find a berth aboard any ship in Acre. Sir John would know about it within hours and I would be dragged through the city in chains. He would take great pleasure in setting me to the stocks and I would die of shame.'

'Then leave from another port,' said Lucy. 'There are many fishing villages along the coast. Flee from Acre in the night and seek passage to Cyprus. From there, you can make your way to Italy and then back to England.'

'And how do you see two lone women undertaking such a treacherous trip, Lucy? We would last but hours on our own.'

'There are many Mercenaries within Acre who have no allegiance to Sir John,' said Lucy. 'If you can find the money, we need escort as far as Cyprus only. There we can throw ourselves under protection of the church.'

'Your plan may have merit,' said Jennifer. 'I have some funds of my own and my jewellery alone could pay for at least two protectors for a month but how do we find such men?'

'Leave that to me, My Lady,' said Lucy, 'I will make discreet enquiries.' She started to brush Jennifer's hair as they talked about their plan, completely unaware that their conversation had been overheard by a servant outside of the door.

The following morning, Jennifer woke in alarm as her bed chamber door flung open and two soldiers marched in, along with a priest.

'What's happening?' she asked, 'what are you doing in here? Get out at once.'

'They are here at my command,' said Sir John following them in. 'Get dressed, wife, you are going on a trip.'

'To where?' demanded Jennifer, 'I have agreed to no such arrangements.'

'No, but I have,' said Sir John. 'You are going to Tripoli for a few months. With the Father's help,' he nodded toward the priest, 'I have arranged chambers there for you in a secured compound. Unfortunately you will not be able to come and go as you please, as it is a convent and closed to the world but at least you will be safe.'

'Safe from what?' asked Jennifer.

'From yourself,' said Sir John, 'get dressed, you leave within the hour.'

'But, what about my maid?' she asked.

'She won't be joining you,' he said. 'In fact, she won't be joining you ever again.' He turned and walked out of the room, slamming the door behind him.

'Wait,' shouted Jennifer, 'what do you mean? What have you done with her?' She ran toward the door but the two soldiers stepped across to bar her way.

'Let me past,' she screamed but they did not move.

'Better do as he says, My Lady,' said the priest, 'or you will be travelling as you are.'

An hour later, Lady Jennifer of Orange sat alone in the back of a covered cart. An armed guard of eight mercenaries rode alongside and she peered out of the cover as the cart rumbled through the gates leaving the castle behind them. On the walls above she could see Sir John staring coldly down but any feelings toward him, good or bad were immediately swept aside as they turned a corner and the site of three bodies hanging from a gibbet swung into view. The first two men were obviously Mamluk and had signs around their necks proclaiming the word, 'Assassin' but the third made her gasp in shock and she had to stifle a scream of horror.

Swinging gently in the wind was the naked and beaten body of Lucy and around her neck she also had a sign. *'Traitor.'*

A few days later, Sir John stood on top of the castle walls once again, though this time he wasn't sending a treacherous wife into captivity, but watching a relief fleet jostle for position in Acre's harbour. Prince Edward, son of the King of England, Henry Winchester had arrived at last and with him, he had brought an army of a thousand men. Rumour had it that he also had at least two hundred Knights and Sir John knew that these alone would send messages of fear to the Mamluk hoard. He turned to one of the servant's.

'Is everything ready?' he asked.

'It is, Sire,' said the man. 'We have prepared a feast for the Knights in the main hall while the rest of the soldiers will be fed in their quarters. Prince Edward will not find us wanting.'

'Good,' said Sir John, 'see that he doesn't. With his sponsorship, I may yet find a route to the court of Henry when we return to England. Set out my equipment, I will greet him in full colours.'

'Yes, Sire,' said the servant and hurried away to prepare the polished armour. It had been a long time since Sir John had struck a blow against any enemy capable of fighting back, unless of course, you counted his wife.

Longshanks stayed aboard the ship as the fleet unloaded. The cargo ships had already arrived and supplies were being carried on carts up to the castle. One of his Knights approached.

'Sire, the ships with the horses wait their turn to dock. Do you want to wait?'

'No, we have been too long without meaningful exercise,' said Longshanks, 'assemble the men, we will march through the city. Have the horses brought up when they arrive.'

'Yes Sire.' said the Knight and left to make the arrangements.

An hour later, Edward Longshanks marched at the head of his Knights toward the castle. His heart swelled at the thought of following in Lionheart's footsteps and though privately he dreamed of capturing Jerusalem, he knew that his army of only a thousand, even including two hundred Knights, were there mainly to aid Acre and without the support of the neighbouring countries, Jerusalem would remain but a dream.

Jennifer of Orange walked beside her cart, taking the opportunity to exercise her legs. They had been travelling for three days and the incessant rocking of the cart made her feel sick.

Four of the mounted Mercenaries rode alongside but the other four were somewhere over the horizon, checking the way forward was clear. Jennifer stumbled on, desperate to reach wherever it was she was being sent. Her initial anger had been replaced with a desperation for civilisation, no matter what the restrictions. The cart drew to a halt and the driver stood on his seat to peer further into the distance.

'What's the matter?' asked one of the soldiers, 'why have you stopped?'

'Something is wrong,' said the driver and pointed to the horizon.

Everyone followed his gaze and saw a lone rider coming slowly toward them, his body slumped across his saddle.

'It's Momani,' said the soldier, referring to one of the horsemen who had ridden forward, 'and he is wounded.'

Two of the men spurred their horses but had not gone a hundred strides before they reined them in once more.

'In the name of God,' said one, 'this cannot be.' Before them the whole horizon seemed to come alive as untold numbers of Mamluk horsemen crested the hill. For a few moments, both guards just stared in astonishment, they had never seen such an army.

'Come on,' shouted the soldier to his comrade, 'we have to get out of here.'

'What about Momani?' shouted the other rider.

'Leave him, he is already dead.'

Both soldiers turned and galloped back the way they had come. As they passed the wagon, they pulled up alongside the other two horsemen.

'Turn your steed, Brother,' shouted one, 'and escape this place. A whole Mamluk Halqa rides this way, the others are already dead.'

'What about her?' asked one of the riders.

'Leave her,' came the answer, 'we were paid to protect her from brigands, not the entire Islamic state.'

'Wait,' shouted Jennifer, 'what's happening? 'You can't leave me here?'

'He is right, My Lady,' said one of the horsemen, 'the cart will slow us up. This way we may survive.'

'Take me with you,' she shouted, 'I can ride behind you on your horse.'

'Sorry Lady,' said the man, 'your fate is sealed. Make your peace with God.' With that he spurred his horse to follow his three comrades already galloping across the sands, leaving the woman alone with the driver of the cart.

Jennifer turned in panic and saw the lines of Mamluk riders coming closer, hundreds of horses interspersed with as many camels. Behind them, she could see hoards of warriors on foot, each wrapped against the desert heat, their weapons gleaming in the blazing sun. The driver jumped from the cart and ran forward to meet them, pleading for his life and holding out his arms extolling the virtues of Allah the Just.

The lead riders rode by him without acknowledging his presence, galloping after the distant mercenaries but as the next wave neared, a group of ten broke from the main body of the Halqa and approached the cart. As they neared, one of the riders drew his sword and decapitated the driver without breaking stride.

Jennifer's hand flew to her mouth to stifle the scream that threatened to erupt and watched in horror as fountains of blood spurted from the dead man's neck, leaving streaks of red staining the scorching white sand. Expecting to die, she quickly composed herself and made the sign of the cross before tilting her head back to look up to the Lord.

'Holy father,' she whispered, 'welcome me into your glory I beseech thee.'

The lead riders reached her but the expected blow never came. Instead the man who had killed the driver, leaned down and wiped his blade on her dress. The rest of the riders laughed at the gesture and circled their camels around her, talking in a language she didn't understand.

Finally another man rode up and lowered the fabric from around his mouth.

'Who are you?' he asked.

'I am Jennifer of Orange,' she replied, 'wife of the Castellan of Acre.'

'A prize indeed,' said the man and spoke to the others in his own language.

'What are you saying?' demanded Jennifer drawing a small knife from amongst her skirts. 'Keep your filthy hands off me because I swear I will cut my own throat before succumbing to your disgusting needs.'

'Put your little knife away, Lady,' said the man. 'We are Mamluk and have honour to exceed any of your so called Knights. You will come to no harm from us, you have my word but you will become our prisoner and when the time is right, will be ransomed back to the Christians. Can you ride?'

'I can,' said Jennifer.

The warrior whistled and a boy riding a camel came over, leading another camel behind him.

'I can't ride that,' said Jennifer, 'and besides, it stinks.'

'As do you, Lady,' said the warrior. Walk or ride, the option is yours. Without another word the group headed back to the passing throng leaving the boy, the woman and two camels behind them.

Jennifer turned to the boy and realised she had no choice.

'Come on then,' she said, 'let's get this over with.'

Chapter Eleven

Brycheniog

For the next few days, Garyn stayed around the Church, helping the Priest repair a storm damaged roof. There was no sign of Elspeth and Garyn thought he had ruined any chances of wooing her he may have had. He visited the ruins of his family home on a daily basis, often staying several hours before wandering back to the church again, devoid of any idea what he was going to do. Finally he realised he was going nowhere fast and resolved to do something with his life. He laid a sprig of winter Holly on his family's grave before walking to the village and that evening, found himself knocking on the door of Elspeth Fletcher.

'Master Garyn,' said Jayne Fletcher, opening the door.' It's good to see you, come in.'

He entered the house and found himself in a long room with an open hearth. To one end of the room, bundles of arrows lay tied together, waiting to be delivered to the manor and many more lay un-fletched on the table.

'Garyn,' said, Elspeth standing up in surprise. 'What are you doing here?'

'Um, I have come to see your father,' said Garyn, 'and would beg audience.'

The man at the table looked up at the boy before standing up. He brushed the feathers from his jerkin and walked around the table to stand before Garyn.

'Garyn ap Thomas,' he said, 'welcome to my home. I am sorry about your family, your father was a good friend.'

'Thank you Sir,' said Garyn.

'What can I do for you?' asked the Fletcher.

'Sir, first of all I have brought you a gift,' said Garyn, handing over his birthday knife. 'I know it isn't much but it is all I have.'

'Thank you, Garyn,' said the Fletcher, placing the sheathed knife on the table, 'but what have I done to deserve such a thing?'

'Nothing Sir,' said Garyn, 'at least not yet.' He took a deep breath and looked around before continuing. 'Sir, I seek permission to call on your daughter and to go out walking.'

The room fell silent and Elspeth blushed furiously, staring at the floor. Her mother smiled broadly and stared at her husband in anticipation.

'Really,' said the fletcher. 'Well, I think you had better take a seat. Woman, bring ale. There are serious matters to discuss here.'

Elspeth's mother brought two tankards as her daughter cleared away the unfinished arrows from the table. Elspeth's eyes caught those of Garyn but he turned away quickly, afraid he might lose his nerve. When the table was cleared, the two men sat opposite each other and drank the ale in silence.

'Elspeth, come away,' said her mother, 'we will take a walk. This is men's business.' Mother and daughter left the house and walked down to the village. The Fletcher took another long drink from his tankard before breaking the silence.

'So, Master Garyn,' he said. 'What makes you so interested in my daughter?'

'Well, Sir,' stuttered Garyn, 'she is clever and makes me laugh. When we talk, I am enthralled at her words and I find her company pleasing.'

'And…?'

'And what, Sir?' asked Garyn.

'Your answer is well practised, Garyn yet tells me nothing. Tell me how you feel about her and why I should allow this to happen.'

Garyn hesitated.

'I find her very fair of face, Sir.'

'My daughter is a very pretty girl, Garyn. I would imagine all young men of your age find her attractive. Why should I choose you?'

'Other boys may see her beauty,' said Garyn, 'but I see far more. Her being glows about her and her face fills my every thought. Even now, though my days are yet dark, her presence sends rays of light to my deepest soul. I find myself longing to see her smile and hear her laughter each and every day. I hurt when I do not see her, sir and have come to realise, my world is darker without her.'

'Poetic words,' said the Fletcher, 'but words do not fill hungry mouths. What can you offer her that others cannot?'

'I know my father and you were once friends and thought you may be amenable to the idea.'

'Let's get something straight, Garyn,' said the fletcher, 'yes we were good friends but that has no bearing on who I allow to court my daughter. The decision will be made on merit alone. So I ask again, what future can you offer her?'

'Well, as you know, Sir, the forge is but a ruin. However, I learned the trade at my father's anvil and intend to rebuild my family's home as good as it once was. A blacksmith can earn a good living, Sir and I would not be found wanting as a husband.'

'A husband,' said the fletcher in surprise. 'I think you get ahead of yourself young sir.'

'My apologies,' said Garyn, 'but I have to be honest and say that I see our future together.'

'And does she share this view.'

'I don't know,' said Garyn quietly, lowering his gaze to the table.

'Well, that is a conversation for another day,' said the Fletcher. 'A Blacksmith is indeed an honourable trade, Garyn but the task you set yourself is a stern one. How do you intend to accomplish this alone?'

'My father had some land,' said Garyn, 'so I will sell some pasture to the manor or the church. With the money I will hire labour, restart the business and establish a place in the community.'

The fletcher nodded.

'An admirable intention,' he said and sat back in his chair to consider his decision. Finally he sat forward and withdrew the gifted knife from its sheath.

'This is a fine knife, Garyn,' he said. 'Did you make it?'

'No Sir, the work is of my father's hand.'

'I thought so,' said the Fletcher, 'he was a very skilled man. Do you share this skill?'

'I think so Sir, I have been taught well.'

'You have fine intentions, Garyn but as yet there is no evidence that you are able to meet them so my decision is this. Yes you may call on my daughter but there are conditions. First of all, you will act toward her with the utmost honour and will not seek carnal knowledge outside of wedlock.'

'I would never do such a thing, Sir,' said Garyn.

'Remember, Garyn, I was once your age and such promises are hard to keep. Anyway, the second condition is this. You will rebuild your family home as intended and in this I will offer help. However, you will not seek marriage until you can bring me a knife such as this, made by your own hand, from your own forge. That way, I know your trade is true and her future is secured. During this time, Elspeth will not be bound to you by any promise and she can walk away at any time. Are we agreed?'

Garyn nodded quietly, willing to accept any conditions imposed.

'I have plenty of time, Garyn but I have only one daughter. Do not let her down and do not break her heart. Understood?'

'Yes Sir,' said Garyn.

'Good,' said the fletcher, 'now, when was the last time you ate?'

'I had oats at the church yesterday, Sir.'

'Then take off your cloak, Garyn, for today you will dine with us.'

Garyn held back a smile. It had all been far easier than he had thought.

The next few weeks were magical for Garyn and he spent at least an hour with Elspeth every day. He even managed to sell a pasture to the manor farm and held a promissory note for enough money to hire labour as soon as the weather broke. Occasionally the Fletchers allowed him to eat with them and such evenings were amongst the happiest he had ever spent. On one such evening he coughed politely and asked for attention.

'I hope you don't mind,' he said, 'but I have a poem and beg permission to read it to Elspeth, here in front of her family.'

'You are literate?' said Elspeth's father in surprise.

'I am, Sir. I learned at my mother's knee .'

'Then proceed, Garyn,' he said and sat back in silence, impressed at the young man's ability to carry out the traditional custom.

'It's not very long,' said Garyn, 'and not very good.'

'Get on with it,' said the father with a forced smile.

'It's called, Elspeth Fletcher,' said Garyn and took a deep breath before starting

'Elspeth Fletcher, fair of face.
Easer of nightmares, creator of laughter.
Hair of softest down with sparkling streams captured in your eyes
Patient be for soon the wind changes and happiness beckons.

Already you hold my heart and soon yours will be mine
For evermore.'

He looked up nervously.

'That's it,' he mumbled.

'That was lovely, Garyn,' said Elspeth's mother.

'Hmm,' not bad said Elspeth's father. 'The next will be better I expect.'

'Thank you, Garyn,' said Elspeth as he handed her the parchment. 'I will keep it close to me always.'

The following morning Garyn woke to find an overnight storm had washed the snow from the ground and he made his way up to the forge to start clearing the mess. For an hour he dragged burnt timbers from the rubble, piling them against a nearby wall but had hardly made any difference when he heard a voice behind him.

'Garyn ap Thomas?'

Garyn turned and saw a hooded Monk behind him

'Brother Martin?' he asked.

'No,' said the Monk removing his hood, 'Brother Martin is unavailable. My name is Brother Steven and I am here on the Abbot's business.'

'What does he want?' asked Garyn.

'He asks you meet with him this morning to discuss a matter of greatest urgency.

'I have nothing to say to him,' said Garyn.

'Perhaps not but he has words you may want to hear.'

'Nothing he says has any interest to me,' said Garyn. 'Tell him my answer remains the same and I want nothing more than to proceed with my life.'

'He has word of your brother,' said the Monk and watched as Garyn froze to the spot, his mouth open in astonishment.

'What word?' asked Garyn eventually, 'is he alive? Where is he?'

'All will be revealed at the Abbey,' said the Monk. 'Come, there is no time to lose.' He turned and headed back up the trail, closely followed by Garyn.

Half an hour later he was once more in the Abbot's cell, though this time alone as he waited for Father William to arrive. Eventually the door opened and the Abbot walked in, pausing to genuflect before the cross before taking his seat behind the simple wooden table.

'Hello Garyn,' he said. 'Thank you for coming.'

'The Monk said you know where my brother is,' blurted Garyn. 'Please tell me what you know.'

'All in good time, Garyn,' said Father William, 'please be seated.'

Garyn sat on the offered chair and stared at the Abbot.

'Garyn,' said Father William. 'As you may know, the word of Christ crosses many boundaries and places such as this exist across the known world. Pilgrims travel between them on a daily basis and many of those chosen to serve God spend their lives walking the paths of the humble in a mission to spread the gospels.'

Garyn nodded silently.

'Subsequently, our network is vast and we have Brothers all over the world from here to Jerusalem itself so when we need certain information, it is only a matter of time before that knowledge is unveiled before us.'

'And you have used this network to find my brother?' asked Garyn hopefully.

'I have,' said the Abbot. 'He is alive and well and still serves in the army of the King.'

Garyn sat back and breathed a sigh of relief.

'Where is he?' he asked. 'I need to go and see him.'

'That won't be so easy,' said the Abbot. 'He was sent on an expeditionary force overseas in preparation for the forthcoming crusade by Longshanks and currently serves in Palestine.'

Garyn's face dropped.

'Furthermore,' said the Monk, 'when Longshanks arrives in the Holy-land, your brother will be posted to the lead units on any assault against the heathen. Unfortunately, Crusades are brutal and most such men fail to come back.'

'How do you know all this?' asked Garyn.

'His location was easy to find,' said the Monk. 'The nature of his posting was a different matter. At the moment he is just one more archer in Longshank's army but when my letter arrives at Acre in a few weeks, he will be posted to the more dangerous roles within the garrison.'

'You sent a letter requesting this?' asked Garyn, his brow creasing with concern, 'but why?'

'In order that you are more amenable to an agreement,' said the abbot. 'You see, Garyn, I still believe that heathen prisoner told you something the night he died. You may protest otherwise but I know different. I want that information, Garyn and unfortunately you have forced my arm. The only way to get you to share what you know is by dangling something worth more to you than your own life, the life of your brother. So, the arrangement is simple. You give me what I require and I will send a follow up letter, not only removing him from harm's way but begging his release from the army. I have certain influences, Garyn and assure you my request will be carried out.'

Garyn stared in disbelief before standing up and walking around the room, his mind racing from the information. If the Abbot was telling the truth then this could be a way of getting his brother home but if he was lying, then all that would happen is that he would hand over the information for nothing.

'Take some time, Garyn,' said the Abbot, 'but not too much. My letter will take a week or so to arrive at Acre but any follow up could be months later. A lot can happen in that time.'

'What if you are lying?' snapped Garyn, 'what if there is no letter and you don't know where he is?' All this could just be a ruse.'

'It could,' said the Abbot, 'but can you take that risk? Could you live with yourself knowing your brother's life was in your hands and you let it slip through?'

'You know I couldn't,' said Garyn, 'but I will not relinquish the information on an empty promise.'

'Ah, so the heathen did share information with you?'

Garyn hesitated, realising he had slipped up.

'He did,' he said finally, 'but not everything. 'He told of a relic, hidden in a secret place. Something so holy it could start or end wars in its name.'

'What relic?' snapped the Abbot'

'He wouldn't tell me,' said Garyn, 'he said the lives of too many men would end if the knowledge became available.'

'What about the location?'

'He gave me directions and some other clues,' said Garyn, 'but that is all, I swear.'

'Tell me the directions,' said the Abbot.

Garyn shook his head.

'I have said enough,' he said. 'What about my brother?'

'Tell me the rest and I will have the letter sent this very day,' said the Abbot.

'No,' said Garyn. 'I want proof he is alive first.'

'And how do you propose I do that?'

'I want to see him,' said Garyn. 'Have him brought back and I will tell you everything I know.'

'It will take too much time,' said Father William, 'and the situation in the Holy-land deteriorates by the day. By the time we get him back and you share the information, it may be too late to seek the relic.' It was the Abbot's turn to fall silent as he pondered his actions.

'There is another way,' he said eventually, 'one where we will both benefit.'

'And that is?' asked Garyn.

'You can find it for me,' said the Monk. 'Go to the Holy-land and seek this relic in my name. When you have found it, travel to Acre and present it to someone there who will act on my behalf. When he is in receipt of the relic, he will arrange the release of your brother.'

'How can I go to the Holy-land?' asked Garyn. 'Such things are beyond normal men.'

'On the contrary,' said the Monk. 'Pilgrims make the journey every day with no more than the clothes they stand in and a belief in God. You on the other hand are a wealthy man and can pay for such passage.'

'I have no wealth,' said Garyn.

'You have the money from the sale of your father's land.'

'That money is to rebuild the forge,' said Garyn, 'It is an investment in my future.'

'A future without your brother, it seems,' said the Abbot.

'There is much to think about,' said Garyn. 'I will leave now and consider your words.'

'Do that,' said the Abbot, 'but the decision must be made soon for the next ships leave for the continent within the month. You will need to be on one of those ships.'

'I will return tomorrow with my decision,' but I have one more question. 'Up until now, your messenger has always been Father Martin. Is he here?'

'Father Martin is no longer with us,' said the Abbot. 'He left the Abbey weeks ago.'

After a sleepless night, Garyn finally walked back up to the Abbey with his decision. Again he waited until the Father finished prayers but finally they stood before each other in one of the chapels.

'I have thought of your offer,' said Garyn, 'and made a decision. I will do as you ask and travel to Palestine to find this relic. Assuming I am successful, I will then meet with your representative. That much is agreed.'

'Go on,' said the Abbot.

'However,' continued Garyn, 'there will be no exchange in return for an unfulfilled promise. I will hand over what you seek only when I see my brother released. When he is safely on a ship, Then and only then will I will hand the relic over.'

After consideration, the Abbot nodded.

'It seems we have an arrangement,' he said, 'but know this well. I have many contacts throughout the Kingdom and overseas. Any sign of treachery on your part will not bode well for your brother, or indeed you. Do you understand?'

'I understand,' said Garyn, 'but am only interested in the return of Geraint. The relic is but a means to an end.'

'Then be gone,' said the Abbot, 'for I would imagine you have a lot to arrange.'

Garyn left the Abbey and walked down the hill. He had no idea where he would arrange passage to the Holy-land but knew the place to find out.

Cadwallader sat in the main hall of his manor house, talking quietly to his fellow Knights. A servant entered and asked to speak to him.

'Sire, there is a Garyn ap Thomas at the door, he begs audience.'

'Let him in,' said Cadwallader. Garyn was shown in to stand humbly before the lord of the Manor.

'Master Garyn,' he said, 'twice within a month. What errand brings you to my door once more?'

'Sire, I have a boon to ask,' said Garyn. 'I seek passage to the Holy-land and would request I share your journey.'

'Garyn, we have already discussed this,' said Cadwallader.' My Knights and Squires already prepare and we sail within weeks. You are no archer and my pike men have already sailed. I cannot carry pilgrims and will not demean your father's name by enrolling you as servant. Go home and tend to your lands.'

'Sire,' said Garyn. 'I will go to Palestine with or without your help. I would rather ride under your banner but will travel alone if necessary. Is there anything I can do to change your mind?'

The Knight stared at him in admiration.

'You have a determination that is admirable, young man,' he said, 'and there may be a way. Foot soldiers I do not need and Knighthood is beyond you. Yet there is always room for cavalry in any unit. I assume you can ride so what I suggest is this. Go home and hone your skills as a rider. Be back here in three weeks and we will test your horsemanship as well as the lance. I don't expect you to be an accomplished cavalryman but there will be a long ride through Europe and you will need to earn your keep. Do this and I will find you a place amongst the horsemen but I am not promising anything.'

'Thank you, Sire,' said Garyn, 'it is enough.'

'Sire,' called a voice from a corner, 'I suspect the boy does not even own a horse. How can you allow him spurs?'

Garyn recognised the Squire who had insulted him weeks earlier and though he felt his anger rise, he held his tongue.

'Is this true, Garyn?' asked Cadwallader. 'Do you have a horse?'

'Not yet, Sire,' said Garyn. 'But I know where to get one.'

'Then you will have your chance,' said Cadwallader. 'I will see you in three weeks.'

As he left the Manor, Garyn diverted toward the courtyard where they had obtained the feathers. As he entered he spoke to a groom, asking about the whereabouts of the stockman, Reynolds. The groom pointed toward the stable and Garyn entered to find the man sweeping out a stall.

'Master Reynolds,' said Garyn.

'Hello again,' said the stockman, before peering over Garyn's shoulder. 'Is Miss Elspeth not with you today?'

'No Sir, I am alone.'

'To what end?' asked the man.

'Sir, I am looking to buy a horse,' said Garyn, 'and would seek your recommendation as to where I can get one.'

103

'Well,' said the man scratching his chin thoughtfully, 'I suppose you could go to any of the farms, they have plenty of work horses. You may pick up a bargain.'

'I don't need a work horse, Sir, I need a Courser or even perhaps a Destrier.'

The man stared at Garyn in surprise.

'Why would you want a charger?' he asked. 'Lord Cadwallader has already made it clear there is no route to Knighthood open to you.'

'I know that,' said Garyn, 'and have turned my sights away from that path but he has offered me the chance to ride as light cavalry if I can pass a test.'

'When is this test?' asked Reynolds.

'Three weeks,' said Garyn.

'Impossible,' said Reynolds. 'Have you even ridden a horse before?'

'I have on occasion,' said Garyn, 'when we had to deliver our heavy commissions on a cart.'

'A cart horse and a Charger are completely different animals,' he said. 'It cannot be done.'

'I have to try, Sir,' said Garyn, 'for the sake of my family.'

Again the stockman stared in silence.

'Do you have any money?' he asked eventually, 'for horses of that nature do not come cheap.'

'I have this,' said Garyn and handed over the promissory note he had earned from the sale of the land.'

'It is a handsome amount,' said the man, 'but falls short of any beast here. You may find something suitable in the other villages.'

'I do not have time,' said Garyn. 'Do you not have anything within that price range?'

'There is one,' sighed the stockman, 'and I have already been tasked with selling him. He is a strong steed but suffers with an injury and it would be a wager to get him fit in time.'

'I'll take it,' said Garyn.

'But you haven't even seen him,' said Reynolds.

'I don't care, it is my only chance. Where is it?'

The stockman took the note and led Garyn to the far end of the stables.

'Before we go on, Master Garyn,' he said, 'let me give you your first lesson in horsemanship. This horse has quality breeding and is not a beast of burden. If you are to bond as you must, then do not

104

refer to the animal as it. The beast will become your comrade and if you are unlucky enough to ever ride him into battle, he will be the closest thing to a friend you will have. Understood?'

'Understood,' said Garyn.

'Good,' said the stockman and opened the stall door.

'Garyn, this is Silverlight, your new Courser.'

Garyn stared at the huge horse, taking in the strength and beauty, recognising the animal as the horse rejected by Cadwallader weeks earlier.

'He is wonderful,' he said smoothing the animal's back.

'He is,' said the stockman, 'and was selected as one of Cadwallader's mounts for the coming crusade but fell lame at the last moment. He is on the mend and I can't promise he will be ready within three weeks but he is the best I can do.'

'He is perfect,' said Garyn. 'Can I take him away today?'

'No,' said the stockman, 'I will prepare him for you. I know what works with him and he has the best chance of recovery here.'

'But how will I learn?'

'You can take a loan of a smaller animal to learn the basics,' said Reynolds. 'I will attempt to make him ready but will need him right up to the last minute.'

'Thank you,' said Garyn.

'I think you set yourself on a fool's errand, young sir but admire your spirit. Now, we will select a steady animal for you to ride away, one that will be patient with your clumsiness.'

Garyn followed him out across the courtyard. Within the hour he was riding slowly away on a much smaller horse. Across his lap, he carried a wooden training lance, a gift from Reynolds.

'He is going to get himself killed,' said a groom with a laugh, 'he has no idea of horsemanship.'

'Perhaps not,' said the stockman, 'but you can't take away from his determination. The boy has spirit.

Chapter Twelve

Krak des Chevalier

The first missile from the Mangonels flew straight over the outer defences and landed harmlessly on the ground between the outers and the castle itself. The defenders looked on quietly, knowing full well it was only a matter of time before the Mangonels operators adjusted the settings and brought their machines in range. Mangonels were essentially catapults but rather than rely on tensioned rope to provide the power they used the force of gravity instead. Giant boxes full of rock were hoisted up high within the framework of the catapult and when they were allowed to drop, the attached arm revolved around a pivot expending extreme force to fire its missile upward. The addition of a sling at the end increased the power even more and a Mangonel could fling heavy loads hundreds of paces before smashing against any fortress walls. It was the most powerful siege engine of the time and the one most feared by any castle defenders.

By reducing the weight in the boxes the range was lowered and three shots later, the first boulder smashed against the outer wall. Immediately the upper blocks disintegrated at the impact and two men fell to their deaths amongst the rubble. A cry of fear rang out amongst the defenders as the first impact was quickly followed by two more.

'Hold firm,' shouted the Sergeant at arms as some made their way to the towers. Move to either side for they will target the breach. 'Keep your heads down until ordered otherwise. When they attack, they will be funnelled through a killing zone and be easy pickings for our arrows.'

Over and over again the hail of boulders came and piece by piece, they knocked down the wall until the breach was no more than a pile of rubble almost twenty paces wide. Across the Plateau, Baibaars stood alongside Hassam and watched as the wall fell before him.

'Majesty,' said Hassam, 'the breach is complete. Shall I have our forces advance?'

'No, Hassam,' said Baibaars, 'we will be patient. Have the Mangonels change their aim and work the breech wider. We will not send any more men to unnecessary death. Instead, have them replenish the siege engines. Put every man to the task and ensure the hail of rocks goes unabated throughout the night. Change the crews regularly and give the Christians no respite. We will press the assault tomorrow, Hassam but we will do so over the rubble of their puny defence.'

Inside the castle, Najaar and Khoury watched the assault unfold from the top of the gate tower.

'It seems the Sultan thinks on his feet,' said Najaar, 'and his tactics changes like the wind. In times past he would assault any breech with unfettered aggression but this time, his patience will deliver benefits.'

Khoury looked at the remains of the outer wall. Occasionally the Mangonels would change the nature of their missiles and send clay pots containing burning oil to smash amongst the ruins, lighting up the targets for the Mangonel operators.

'Have you withdrawn the men?' asked Khoury.

'I have,' said Najaar, 'and they now man the arrow slits of the castle. At least the Mangonels will be useless against Chevalier itself, the walls are far too thick to fall.'

'You are right,' said Khoury, 'but it seems this Baibaars has more tricks up his sleeve than our archers have arrows. Who knows what he will come up with next?'

For the rest of the night, the sound of rock smashing against rock reached the castle and by the time dawn came, the outer wall was no more than a line of rubble across the Plateau. Once again Khoury looked down at the eastern approach and watched as the Mamluk army moved their camp up onto the level ground where the Palisade once stood. There was no way out of the castle, now, the real siege had begun.

'Shall we move the Mangonels forward?' asked Hassam.

'Yes,' said Baibaars but do not target the walls, send the missiles into the inner courtyards. Arm the slings with clay pots and fill them with burning oil and human waste. The walls may be strong but human spirit is easily broken. And bring me my engineers, there is no time to waste. There is rain in the air and that will only hinder our progress.'

For days the expected attack never came and even the Mangonels fell silent as a rain storm swept in from the west causing the timbers to swell and the ropes to stretch. Life was difficult in the castle as the two thousand strong garrison waited with frayed nerves, unsure what to expect next. The villagers between the outer defences and the inner ward huddled in makeshift tents and awaited their fate.

For ten days the Mamluks held back their forces and even Khoury wondered what their next move would be but unbeknownst to him, Baibaars' engineers had found the one weakness in Chevalier's formidable defences, the South west corner. Subsequently, early on the eleventh morning, the defending Hospitallers' world fell in on them.

A deafening crash echoed around the castle and clouds of dust billowed into the air. Sergeants called the castle to arms and soldiers ran everywhere, trying to find out what had happened. Sir Khoury ran down from his quarters brandishing his sword and met Najaar leading a group of Knights toward the outer walls.

'What's happening?' shouted Khoury.

'The Western tower has collapsed Sire,' shouted the Knight.

'Tunnellers,' spat Khoury, 'Baibaars must have undermined the tower, It's the only place the walls are not embedded into the rock.'

'The damage is done, Sire,' said Najaar, 'we have to get swords down there or the outer ward will be overrun.'

'Then summon the Knights,' shouted Khoury, 'and deploy to the breach, this is no skirmish, Najaar, we fight for Chevalier itself.' The sound of hundreds of warriors charging to the assault reached the defenders' ears along with the screaming of the panicking villagers as they realised the Mamluks would be through the breach in minutes. As one they ran toward the inner gate, desperate to seek the safety of the inner castle and away from the Mamluk army. High on the outer wall, archers sent their lethal arrows toward the massed hoards and though many enemy fell, it had little impact on their number.

'Make way,' roared Khoury, forcing his way through the terrified villagers, 'stand aside.' The Hospitaller Knight forced his way through, leading almost two hundred Knights toward the breach. As they ran, the lead warriors of Baibaars started to pour over the collapsed wall into the inner ward.

'For God and glory.' screamed Khoury and swung his mighty sword toward the first of the enemy. Immediately he was set upon by dozens of warriors, each screaming the name of Allah, but the Knights were also accompanied by hundreds of men at arms and they fell upon the enemy in an equally religious fervour. All around him, fellow Knights accompanied smashed into the warriors. Swords cut men in half and maces smashed skulls while up above, the archers picked their targets carefully. The Garrison's foot soldiers used their pikes to force back the flanks, but still the Mamluks poured through the gap.

As the battle raged, the frightened villagers ran to the inner gate causing mayhem at the drawbridge.

'Keep them moving,' screamed a sergeant, 'force them to the back of the courtyard, we have to clear the gate.'

Khoury fought like a madman, as did his fellow Knights, carving their way through waves of marauding Mamluks. The Hospitallers were heavily armoured so any damage from a warrior lucky enough to land a blow from their smaller curved swords was minimal. Over and over again they forced their way through the oncoming warriors, trying to reach the opening in the wall, knowing full well that if they could reach the breach then the defence would be easier. If not, the waves of Mamluks would just get stronger and eventually the outer ward would be overwhelmed.

'It's no good,' shouted Najaar over the sound of battle, 'they are coming faster than we can kill them. We have to withdraw.'

Khoury looked back toward the main gate.

'There are villagers yet in the outer ward,' he shouted. 'I will not sacrifice them to these heathen. A few more moments brothers, that's all I ask.'

They renewed the counter attack but the shock of their charge had dissipated and the enemy were becoming organised. Behind those who had taken the breach, fresh warriors were forming up, though this time in organised ranks and wielding larger shields. Within moments several hundred had formed solid lines, ten deep that stretched from the outer to the inner wall and though defenders' arrows rained down from above, the raised shields of the rear ranks ensured few warriors fell from the missiles. A horn sounded again and the few Mamluk assault troops still fighting withdrew behind their comrades' lines and the fresh threat stared at the Hospitallers across the body littered outer ward.

Khoury looked around his scattered force, each man breathing heavily from the exertion of battle. Some leaned on their swords to catch their breath while others stood proud, staring the enemy squarely in the face, goading them to further assault. Every one of the Knights was covered in blood and Khoury could see at least a dozen lying motionless on the battlefield either dead or seriously wounded.

'Regroup,' he called, taking advantage of the lull in fighting, 'Sergeants, collect our fallen and take them to the chapel. The rest of you, form up in line abreast, prepare to withdraw. The battle is lost, Brothers but the fight goes on. We will reform within the fortress. Mooove!'

The Knights ran to their stations and within moments, two forces faced each other across the open space of the outer ward. The distance between the walls was narrow and at this point, no more than thirty men could stand side by side and still wield weapons. The Hospitaller ranks were no more than eight deep while the Mamluks stretched back to the breach with more pouring through by the second.

'Sire, the villagers are secure,' shouted a voice and Khoury breathed a sigh of relief. Though his men were far better combatants, the sheer number of the enemy meant there was no way they could prevail.

'Withdraw,' he shouted and the Knights walked backward toward the doors of the inner castle. With a roar the Mamluk's charged and the Knights ran to the entrance of the vaulted corridor that led to the inner defences. The overwhelming force of enemy numbers forced their way up the slope of the covered walkway, fighting the Knights every step of the way but above them, hidden defenders fired arrows through the murder holes and their casualties mounted. Finally the pressure eased and the Mamluks withdrew back down the slope to exit back into the outer ward.

'Quickly,' shouted Khoury, 'press the advantage, we have to close that gate.'

With renewed energy the Knights raced down the narrow corridor forcing the Mamluks back until the front lines of the enemy were once more outside. Sergeants dragged bodies out of the way and the huge doors were swung shut before being barred from the inside. Instantly the sound of battle fell away and Knights dropped to their knees, some in exhaustion while others knelt to pray.

'How many lost?' asked Khoury.

'I'm not sure,' said Najaar removing his helm, 'but I estimate twenty Knights and twice that, men at arms.'

'A heavy price,' said Khoury and looked up the enclosed corridor that was the only entrance to the inner castle. Bodies lay everywhere and rivulets of blood ran between the dead and the wounded.

The sound of running men echoed down the quiet corridor and within moments, the castle Squires appeared, each brandishing knives. They fell on the enemy wounded, slitting their throats and sending them to their Gods. The Knights watched on in silence, immune to the brutality. It was an action of war and if they had fallen, they would have expected the same.

Khoury struggled to his feet.

'Brothers,' he said. 'We have work to do. Have the wounded cared for then see to your own wounds. Najaar, instruct the Sergeants to barricade these gates with stone. I want this access denied them. The rest of you, get some rest.' He strode up the ramp toward the inner ward and heard the rest of the Knights standing to follow him. He had led these men for five years and knew every one of them by name but despite leading them in battle on many occasions this was the first time he feared for their lives. Chevalier had been built to be impregnable but those who designed her buttresses, had never factored on Baibaars. The man was a military genius.

Baibaars looked up at the inner fortress. It had been several days since his forces had captured the outer ward and a deathly quiet hung over the battlefield. He had removed the bodies of his own fallen and had sent word to the Castellan, granting an hour's truce for them to retrieve their dead. Khoury himself had led a heavily armed guard slowly from the giant doors and stood in silence as a group of Squires collected the defenders' dead. When the battlefield was clear, the Knights retreated into the inner castle, with Khoury bringing up the rear. Before he entered the gate his name rang out across the blood-stained ward.

'Sir Khoury.'

Khoury turned and stared at a man in front of the Mamluk guards.

'Who is it?' asked Khoury quietly

'It is Baibaars himself,' gasped Najaar over his shoulder. He is rarely seen on a battlefield.

'What do you want?' Baibaars shouted Khoury.

'To talk only,' said Baibaars. 'Meet me man to man and talk as equals.'

'Sire, it may be a trap.' said Najaar. 'If you go out there we will not be able to support you. He is in range of our archers, I can have him cut down where he stands.'

111

'No,' said Khoury quietly. 'The fact he stands already within range of our arrows shames us with thoughts of such an action. The man seeks parley, I will see what he has to say.'

'Sire, you are walking into the arms of a devil.'

'Not a devil,' said Khoury, 'but a misguided believer in a different God.'

'They are surely the same thing,' said Najaar.

'Perhaps,' said Khoury. 'But I will trust him.'

'He can have you killed in a heartbeat.'

'All men die, Brother Najaar but there is no better reason than for a man to fall when seeking peace for his people.' He walked forward before unstrapping his sword belt and letting it fall to the blood stained grass.

'I will hear you, Baibaars,' he called, 'and entrust your honour with my life.'

Baibaars unstrapped his own belt and stepped forward, leaving his own sword behind. Moments later they met in the centre of the silent field that days earlier had been a maelstrom of pain and death.

'Sir Knight,' said Baibaars, using Khoury's formal title, 'your name is known to my people as a fearsome warrior.'

'And yours echoes across borders, Sultan Baibaars,' answered Khoury. 'For years I have killed men who fight in your name and now you stand before me, unarmed. An opportunity many men would not pass up.'

'You are not any man, Khoury,' said Baibaars, 'besides, you would find me a hard man to kill.'

'What do you want, Baibaars?'

'I want you to surrender the castle,' said Baibaars. 'You have fought well, Khoury but we both know it is a futile endeavour. The castle will fall to me today, tomorrow or next month but fall it will, even if I have to dismantle it block by block.'

'And every block will cost a Mamluk life,' said Khoury.

'But why?' asked the Sultan. 'Your men will die, my men will die but at the end of the killing, the castle will still be mine. You cannot win, Khoury, spare your men their lives.'

'I disagree,' said Khoury. 'As we speak a great army approaches and will drive you back to Egypt. All we have to do is be patient.'

'If you speak of your English army, then you will have a long wait, Khoury. The French King died at Tunis and Longshanks' fleet floundered in a storm and he repairs the damage in Cyprus. The relief upon which you pin your hopes of reinforcement is yet months away.'

'You lie,' said Khoury, 'I would have heard.'

'I am many things, Khoury but I am no liar. My words are true but it does not fall upon me to convince you. That is a matter for your own conscience. The times are changing, Sir Knight and the tide turns once more in my nation's favour, Soon the Christian influence in our ancestor's lands will be no more and you will be driven from this place like sheep before the wolf. I will not insult you with falsehoods, Khoury, the importance of this place as access to Jerusalem is second only to Acre. This is a magnificent fortress and I would have it undamaged so I offer you this. Surrender the castle to me and I will recognise your valour. Your men can leave fully armed and under their colours. You will be granted safe passage to any destination along with any civilians who wish to join you.'

'A noble gesture,' said Khoury eventually, 'but you have been known to go back on your word before. How do I know I can trust you?'

'If you refer to Antioch, it was not I but one of my generals who broke the bond. Your people are too quick to lay both blame and glory at my feet.'

'Your generals are heralds of your word,' said Khoury, 'and act in your name.'

'They do,' said Baibaars, 'but sometimes young men are eager for glory and their actions undermine those of better standing. I am not proud of Antioch, Khoury but rest assured that the man responsible for sullying my name took over a week to die.'

'I am but a warrior of Christ, Baibaars,' said Khoury, 'and will have to seek his guidance in this, as well as that of my men.'

'I understand,' said Baibaars, 'but know this. The offer is for all inside the castle. There will be no differentiation between civilian or Knight. Either you all leave and live, or you all stay and die, the blood of the villagers will be on your hands. I will give you two days, Khoury, then there will be no more talk. The castle will be brought down around your heads and any survivors will be dragged out for the vultures.'

'Perhaps we will,' said Khoury, 'but I promise you this, it will be over the bodies of a thousand Mamluk.' He turned to walk back to the castle but Baibaars' voice rang out once more.

'Christian Knight,' he called.

Khoury stopped but did not turn around. His body stiffened for the impact of an arrow but the pain that came was from words, not blades.

'You say you are a man of Christ,' said Baibaars, 'so ask yourself this. What would he do, Christian? What would your Jesus do?'

Khoury waited as the words sank in but did not respond. Instead he marched back to the Castle walls and through his waiting men. Without speaking he continued up the covered vaults toward the inner ward, his mind in turmoil as he battled the demons within his own head. A heathen king had just administered a wound bigger than Khoury had received in any battle, the cut of self-doubt. As a Knight his honour demanded he defend the castle to the last, even if he lost his own life in the process but as a Christian, he had vowed to defend the lives of the lowly and if he lost the battle, as he knew they eventually would, then the blood of all the villagers would be on his hands.

Whichever path he chose, Khoury knew one of the two ideals he held most precious would be ripped from his very soul, faith and honour.

Chapter Thirteen

Brycheniog

Garyn took the horse to the hills beyond the village and spent the next few days in the saddle sharpening his riding skills. He was no stranger to riding but as a potential lancer, he knew he had to be so much better. For several days he stayed away from the village, riding for miles during the day and sleeping in an abandoned woodsman's hut by night. Gradually his confidence rose and after two weeks, he rode back to the village, comfortable in the saddle. He tied the beast to a tree and knocked on the Fletcher's door.

'Garyn,' gasped Elspeth, coming to the door. 'Where have you been? We thought you lay hurt in a ditch somewhere.'

'I have had business to attend, Elspeth. I am sorry I have neglected you but there are things afoot that need to be taken care of.'

'What things?' asked Elspeth, noticing the horse for the first time. 'Is that yours?'

'No, it is a loan from the Manor,' said Garyn. 'Elspeth, I need to talk to you. Will you walk with me?'

The girl closed the door and walked alongside him toward the village.

'What is it, Garyn, what's wrong?'

'Elspeth, there is no easy way to say this,' he said, 'but something has happened that means I have to go away for a while.'

'What are you talking about?' asked Elspeth?'

'There is a lot that I would not burden you with,' said Garyn, 'but I will say this, my brother is in peril and I have to go and help him.'

'To London?'

'No, to the Holy-land.'

Elspeth stopped and stared at him.

'You are taking the cross,' she said simply, referring to the oath of a crusader.

'No,' said Garyn, 'I am not. I go as a paid man and when my brother is safe, I will return I swear.'

'But we have made plans,' said Elspeth quietly. 'Shared our dreams and saw a future together.'

'I know.' said Garyn earnestly, 'and those dreams will still come true but I cannot abandon my brother, Elspeth, he is all I have left.'

'You have me,' she said.

'I know,' said Garyn, 'but Geraint is my flesh and blood. I have lost the rest of my family, Elspeth, I cannot lose him as well.'

'Nobody comes back from crusades, Garyn,' said Elspeth.

'My father did.'

'He was a Knight, paid men are expendable. You will share the fate of your brother and I will never see you again.'

'I will return, Elspeth, I promise.'

'No,' she said quietly, walking backward away from him, 'you won't. I can feel it in my heart.'

'Elspeth,' said Garyn, 'please don't do this. I have to help my brother and when I am done, I will waste not a moment before returning to your side. We can still build that home and raise a family, all I ask is a year. Grant me that and I will never stray from your side again.'

'I…I don't know, Garyn,' said Elspeth, 'I have to go.' She turned and ran back to her house as fast as she could, desperate he wouldn't hear her sobs.

'Elspeth,' cried Garyn and ran after her but as he approached, a voice rang out stopping him in his tracks. It was her father.

'Garyn ap Thomas,' shouted Fletcher. 'Hold right there, young man and turn to face me. I would have explanation.'

Garyn stopped and turned to face Fletcher. The man's face was one of controlled rage.

'Sire,' started Garyn, 'I haven't hurt her I swear.'

The fletcher threw his bundle to the ground.

'Really,' he said, 'my daughter runs with more tears than I have ever seen her cry and you say you haven't hurt her. Why do I find that difficult to believe?'

'Sire,' said Garyn, struggling to find the words, 'I haven't laid a hand on her I swear, it's just that I have to go away and she sees it as a betrayal.'

'Where are you going?' asked Fletcher.

'On Crusade,' said Garyn, 'but as a paid man, Sir not a Knight of the cross.'

'What on earth possesses you to do such a thing?' shouted the fletcher, 'you are signing your own death warrant.'

'Sire, I have no choice,' said Garyn staring at the floor. 'It is a matter of honour.' He explained about his brother but withheld the details about the relic and the abbot.

'And where is your brother?' asked Fletcher.

'I think he is in a place called Acre,' said Garyn. 'I won't know until I get there. Wherever he is, I have to go and help him.'

'You are no swordsman, Garyn you are a blacksmith. Crusaders spend years perfecting their skills before setting out. You may as well throw yourself off the Cerrig edge and be done with it.'

'Even if you are correct,' said Garyn, 'I have to try. I love your daughter, Sir but I also love my brother and he is all I have left of my family. I will honour my pledge to both her and you but beg a gift of a year to save my brother.'

The Fletcher calmed down and stared at the boy.

'What passage have you obtained?' he asked quietly.

'As a paid horseman of Cadwalladers command,' answered Garyn.'

'You know mercenaries are often first into battle before the Knights?'

'It is a price I have to pay,' said Garyn.

'Do you have any skills?'

'I can ride but that's about it.'

'And he has accepted you?'

'If I pass a test,' said Garyn.

'What test?'

'I don't know but it will involve a horse.'

'Come with me,' said Fletcher and walked to his house. They went inside but there was no sign of Elspeth.

'Sit down,' said Fletcher and Garyn waited as the man brought a flask of ale.

'Garyn,' he said eventually when they both had a tankard before them, 'I am not happy you have hurt my daughter. She has set her heart on settling down with a family of her own and I know she thinks a lot of you. To her, your promises were empty and she is hurting, that is to be expected. However, I see the honour in your path. I am not happy you are going, Garyn and I think this will end in more heartache for Elspeth, however I also recognise that a man's fate is often chosen for him.' He paused and drank from his ale as Garyn waited for him to go on.

'Anyway,' continued Fletcher, 'I cannot speak for my daughter, she is her own woman. I however, will help you. You say this test is in a week and I suspect it will take the form of lance work. Any horsemen are required to be masters of the lance and if you are inept, I fear you will be denied passage. Your father wasn't the only one with secret's Garyn, I too once rode under the King's colours.'

Garyn's eyes widened in surprise.

'That's why you were friends with my father,' he said quietly.

'It is,' said Fletcher. 'I never rode alongside him for I was no Knight, however, I saw battle on several occasions and even won a tournament once. Our friendship was a belated one and born from mutual respect.' He paused and drank again. 'I will help you as best I can, Garyn,' he continued. 'A week is nothing but if I can teach you to at least stay upright, you may have a chance. The rest you will have to learn during the journey. Meet me in the back meadow tomorrow with your horse and we will see what we can do.'

'Thank you, Sir,' said Garyn and stood up.

'One more thing, Garyn,' said Fletcher, 'my daughter is hurting and that is not good. I will have a word and ask her to come and see you but if she deems it is ended between you, then you will honour her wish.'

'When do you think she will see me?' asked Garyn.

'Perhaps tomorrow, perhaps never,' said Fletcher. 'The choice is hers. Is that clear?'

'Yes Sir,' said Garyn.

'Now go,' said the man, 'until we meet tomorrow.'

The following day, Fletcher kept his promise and spent the morning with Garyn, teaching him the finer points of riding and lance work. They set up buckets on poles and Garyn made pass after pass, trying to hit the buckets with the cumbersome weapon but it took three days until he hit the first one. After that he got better until he was successful with two out of every three passes. Finally the night before the test came and Garyn led his pony back toward Elspeth's house, accompanied by her father.

'She still hasn't come,' said Garyn.

'I will not force her, Garyn,' said Fletcher, 'she knows her own mind.'

'I know but if I am successful tomorrow, then I will march with Cadwallader within days. I may never see her again.'

118

'Your choice, boy.' said Fletcher. 'Now, tie the horse and come inside. I have something for you.'

Garyn once more sat at the table and waited as Fletcher climbed the ladder to the sleeping loft before returning with a Hessian wrapped package. He laid it on the table and looked at Garyn.

'Open it,' he said.

Garyn undid the leather straps and unveiled a beautiful longsword in an ornate scabbard. The hilt was of polished oak capped with a pommel of gold.

'It is wonderful,' said Garyn pulling the weapon from the scabbard. 'Is it yours?'

'No Garyn,' said Fletcher, 'it belongs to your father, at least it did. He asked me to keep it for him a long time ago as he was afraid you and your brother may find it and ask too many questions. Take it, it is yours.'

Garyn stared at the sword again.

'I have never handled such a weapon,' he said. 'What will I do with it?'

'Use it every night, Garyn,' said Fletcher. 'Every time you stop, get a feel for it. Ask the others to practise with you for there may come a time you need it. You will never be an expert but it just may save your life. Now, it is time for you to go, I have done what I can. Good luck, Garyn and may God go with you.'

Garyn thanked him and left the house, all the time looking for Elspeth but there was no sign. Finally he rode back to the ruins of the forge, resigned to the fact she never wanted to see him again. His heart hurt but part of the pain was the fire that burned to get his brother back. All he had to do is get through the following day.

The next day Garyn rode his horse to the manor. The field before the imposing building was alive with people and animals as servants loaded carts with supplies. A company of armed men were milling about, saying their goodbyes to loved ones while a row of chargers were being held by brightly coloured Squires, waiting for the Knights to arrive from the Manor.

Flags of several houses were stuck in the ground and the air was full of excitement as they waited for the Lord of the manor to lead them to war. Garyn rode through the throng, looking for the stockman. Instead he found the Squire who had warned him off weeks earlier.

'What do you want here, peasant?' cried the Squire. 'I think the latrines have already been emptied.'

'I am here for the test,' said Garyn.

'What test?' asked the Squire, 'there are no tests today.'

'Cadwallader himself promised me,' said Garyn. 'If I pass the test, then I can ride with you.'

'Well as you can see,' said the Squire, 'our day of leaving has been brought forward. He has other things on his mind so I suggest you leave.'

'I am going nowhere,' said Garyn, 'unless Cadwallader tells me himself.'

The Squire scowled and turned to his comrade.

'Hold this,' he said and handed over the reins of the magnificent horse.

'Listen boy,' said the Squire, 'either you leave now or I will pull you from this mule and beat you in front of all these people.'

'I am going nowhere,' said Garyn.

'Then you will suffer the consequences,' said the Squire and reached up to grab Garyn.

Within moments both young men were fighting on the floor and were surrounded by cheering people. The Squire was obviously the better fighter but Garyn had the arm strength of a blacksmith and held his own.

'Hold,' shouted a voice and the circle opened up to reveal Cadwallader striding toward them. 'What goes on here?'

'I am here for the test,' said Garyn, 'but am denied by this gaudily clad jester.'

The Squire lurched at him again but was held back by his comrades.

'What test?' asked Cadwallader.

'You granted me an opportunity to prove myself,' said Garyn, 'as a lancer of your cavalry.'

'Oh yes,' said Cadwallader, 'so I did.' He looked around at the sea of expectant faces. 'I am a man of my word,' he said, 'so you will be given your chance. Come with me, you too, Master Dafydd and bring a lance.' The Squire shook himself loose and followed Cadwallader out onto the open field, picking up a lance from a soldier as he passed.

'Someone bring me a target,' shouted Cadwallader and as a servant ran over, the Lord of the manor turned to Garyn. 'Mount your horse,' he said, 'and take the Lance from Squire Dafydd.' Garyn did as he was told and the Squire turned to walk away.

'Stop there, Squire Dafydd,' said Cadwallader. 'You too have a role to play.' The two boys stared at him as he gave his instructions.

'War is a serious business,' he said, 'and there is no place for braggarts or troublemakers.' He looked at Garyn and Dafydd in turn.

'You, Master Garyn, must learn that warfare is not an art to be learned on a whim, while you Squire Dafydd are too quick to cause trouble. I need men on this Crusade, not boys, men who can trust each other and, if necessary die for each other.'

They all fell silent for a moment as the words sunk in.

'So,' he said eventually, 'what we will do is this. Garyn, you will ride to the end of the field. Squire Dafydd will stand here and hold the target.' The servant handed Dafydd a round painted board the size of a man's head. 'That is your mark Garyn and you will have but one run. Miss the mark completely and you stay here. Pierce it and you will ride with us as a trainee, however, pierce any part of Squire Dafydd and you will suffer the same fate as him. Whatever wound he receives at your hand, you will receive from mine, even unto death.' He turned to the Squire. 'You sir, should know better. You are schooled in patience and chivalry yet still you are the cause of upset amongst your peers. During the trial you will hold the target upon your head. If you move, you will no longer be a Squire in my household but a kitchen boy, serving the farm hands while your comrades crusade alongside me. Now, this is the chance for both of you to redeem yourselves. Do you understand?'

'But…' started the Squire

'I said do you understand?' shouted Cadwallader.

'Yes Sire,' said both.

'Then let's get this done,' said Cadwallader. 'Garyn, ride out.'

Garyn rode his horse to the far end of the field and turned around to see Dafydd standing in the middle of the field holding the target at his side. The crowd ran forward for a better view, forming a lane down which Garyn would make his approach. He swallowed nervously, he had expected a stern test but this was beyond anything he had imagined. During his training with Fletcher he had only been successful on two out of every three runs and the bucket they had used was twice the size of the target now held by Dafydd. This was going to be twice as hard and this time, two lives were at stake, the Squire's and his own.

'Ready,' called Cadwallader, lifting his arm in the air.

Garyn lifted the lance in acknowledgement while Dafydd lifted the target onto his own unprotected head.

'Begin,' roared Cadwallader and brought his hand down sharply.

Garyn swallowed nervously before taking a deep breath.

'One steady ride, boy,' he said to the horse, 'that's all I ask.' Without further ado, he kicked his heels into the horse's side and galloped toward the Squire.

Dafydd faced the horse as it thundered down the field toward him. His fellow Squires were watching in awe and though the thought of his head being split apart at the end of a lance was terrifying, the rejection of his comrades and dismissal from the his privileged path to Knighthood frightened him even more. He took a deep breath, tightened the grip on the target and closed his eyes.

A few seconds later the target was smashed from his head and a cheer rose from the crowd, closely followed by a cry of concern. Dafydd opened his eyes and turned to see Garyn sprawled in the dust after being thrown from his horse at full gallop. He ran over and knelt beside Garyn and tapped him lightly on the side of his face.

'Are you alright?' he asked.

Garyn opened his eyes and stared at the blurred image above him.

'I think so,' he said, 'what happened?'

'You lowered the lance after the impact,' said Dafydd, 'and the weight speared the floor causing you to be thrown off. A poor use of skill but one that is common to new riders.'

Dafydd offered his hand and pulled Garyn to his feet as Cadwallader approached. Garyn's face was covered with blood and the Knight pulled aside the boy's hair to check the injury.

'Your skull is intact,' he said, 'so no damage done.'

Garyn stared at him but said nothing.

'A target well hit,' said Cadwallader, 'now, if you two don't mind, we have wasted too much time.'

'But what of me?' asked Garyn.

Cadwallader turned to the Squire.

'Well?' he said

Dafydd nodded.

'He has a lot to learn,' said Dafydd, 'but he will do.'

122

'Good,' said Cadwallader, 'then get yourselves cleaned up. I have a crusade to join.' He walked away to continue the preparations as the crowd dispersed.

'Make way,' called a voice and Garyn turned to see Reynolds leading the magnificent charger through the crowd.

'I believe this belongs to you, young sir,' he said.

Garyn looked up at the magnificent beast in awe. The horse's eyes were bright and the ears twitched in interest at the sounds around him. The stock man had also supplied a simple horse blanket as well as a basic saddle and reins.

'Is he well?' asked, Garyn, smoothing his hand down the animal's muscular neck.

'As well as he can be,' said Reynolds. 'Take it easy but by the time you get to Palestine, he will be as strong as ever. Treat him well, Garyn and he will become your greatest friend.'

'Thank you,' said Garyn and waited until the crowd had gone back to their business. He spoke quietly to the horse, letting the animal get used to his smells before leading him over toward the activity before the Manor.

Finally the group was ready to go and the armed men stood at the front of a small column of carts filled with supplies. Garyn had mounted Silverlight and waited for the command to ride. Cadwallader rode down the column and stopped beside him.

'An excellent display, Master Ruthin,' he said before glancing down at the parcel laid across the boy's lap. And what is this?'

'My father's sword, Sire.'

'Can you use it?'

'Not yet but I will learn.'

'You will have to,' said Cadwallader, 'and quickly for I cannot carry baggage.'

'Like you said, Sire, I am no Knight and never will be. I will learn or die.'

'Still, it is a shame you have no instructor.'

'He does now,' said a voice and both men turned to see a hooded man ride from within the courtyard.

'Who are you?' asked Cadwallader.

The man removed his hood.

'Brother Martin,' said Garyn. 'I thought you had long departed this place.'

'I did,' said Brother Martin, 'but returned to pay a debt. I wronged your father and cannot repay him but I can pay you in his name.'

'How?'

'By accompanying you to the Holy-land,' said Brother Martin. 'On the way I will teach you the skills of war and the way of the brotherhood.'

'I cannot carry baggage, Monk,' said Cadwallader.

'I can pay my way,' said Brother Martin and reached inside his cape before tossing over a purse of coins. 'This is for my passage and when I am there, I will fend for myself.'

Cadwallader felt the weight of the purse.

'Gold?' he asked

'Silver,' said the Monk. 'I am a man of very few needs.'

Cadwallader nodded.

'So be it,' he said. 'Master Ruthin, it seems you have got yourself a Squire.' Cadwallader rode off leaving Garyn to stare at the Monk.

'You don't have to do this,' said Garyn.

'I know,' said Brother Martin, 'but I want to, for my own sanity.

Garyn nodded and they both looked up as the column started to move.

'This is it then,' said Garyn, 'the path is opened before us.'

Before Brother Martin could answer, a voice rang out across the field.

'Garyn,' it echoed, 'wait.'

Garyn spun Silverlight around and saw Elspeth running down the slope toward him. Behind her, he could see her father standing at the forest edge. Garyn spurred the horse and galloped toward her before jumping off and sweeping the girl into his arms.

'Elspeth Fletcher,' he said eventually, staring into her eyes, 'I thought you were lost to me.'

'I am so sorry, Garyn,' she said, 'I did not know my own mind. I thought you were abandoning me but now I see your task is a noble one and if I were in your shoes I would surely take the same path.'

'It is but a temporary state of affairs,' he said, 'and I promise you I will return within the year.'

'I will wait for you, Garyn,' she said, 'I swear. Not one year but two. Take care, Garyn and bring your brother home.'

Garyn leaned forward and kissed her for the first time and though her father looked down from the hill above, he lowered his eyes at the inappropriate gesture.

'Be safe my love,' said Elspeth stepping back. 'I will pray for you every night.'

Garyn watched her run back to her father and blew her a final kiss before mounting his horse and riding to join the column. As the pace slowed to cross a bridge he found himself alongside Squire Dafydd as they each waited their turn.

'So,' said Garyn, 'are we alright?'

'I think so,' said Dafydd. 'Like I said, you have a lot to learn but your skill with the lance was impressive. Not many novices could have hit that target off my head and I will admit to having my eyes closed at the point of impact.'

'That's interesting,' said Garyn, 'so were mine.'

Leaving the Squire open mouthed he spurred Silverlight forward and joined Brother Martin at the front of the column. His Crusade had begun.

Chapter Fourteen

The Port of Messina

Italy

Garyn and Dafydd walked through the port, fascinated by the buzz of activity around the moored fleet. They had been travelling for almost a month, first by ship across the channel to Calais and then by horseback, down through France to Marseilles on the Mediterranean coast. On the way their party had joined with other crusading groups until over a thousand men at arms reached Marseilles. The combined lords had paid a handsome price for a fleet of Merchantmen to carry them to the Holy-land. Forecastles had been added to the ships as defensive positions and they had sailed without incident to land in Messina days earlier. Cadwallader took the opportunity to resupply the ships and ordered his men to spend time ashore, before the fleet embarked on the final leg to Acre.

'Another few days,' said Dafydd, 'and we will set foot in the Holy-land.'

'Your eagerness is impressive,' said Garyn.

'I am indeed eager,' said Dafydd, 'it is the dream of all Knights to serve the lord against the infidel so why wouldn't I be?'

'You are no Knight,' said Garyn, 'at least, not yet.'

'No, I have three years left in service,' said Dafydd, 'but out here, opportunity can fall at the feet of a man and a Squire can be elevated to Knighthood earlier than expected.'

'What sort of opportunity can cut short service?'

'An act of bravery worthy of a Knight,' said Garyn. 'All I have to do is carry out such a feat and I could well be endowed with the honour before my time.'

'Why are you in such a hurry?'

'It is my calling,' said Dafydd. 'My father's line were all Knights and my ancestors fought at Hastings. I was apprenticed to the house of Cadwallader at the age of ten and served the Lordship's table as page before taking the mantle of Squire. It is the true path of every Knight but I am impatient and want to carry my family's coat of arms into battle.'

'Do you not fear death?'

'I fear only the manner of the falling,' said Dafydd. 'To die in battle is a noble end and a chivalrous death ensures quick passage to our Lord's glory.'

'But what about the pain?'

'If pain is the price demanded then that is what I will pay.'

'Have you ever seen a dead man?'

'Who hasn't? These are hard times, Garyn. Starvation and disease take many at home and brigands are hung regularly at the crossroads outside his Lordship's estate.'

'I hear battle is a different thing altogether,' said Garyn. 'Combatants slip in the entrails of the fallen, wounded men crying in agony and seas of filth turning the air rancid.'

'These are the tales of cowards,' said Dafydd, 'besides, those who allow themselves to fall in such circumstance do not deserve to be called Knights. No, I will not fall, Garyn. My fate is to be victorious and win recognition on the field of battle, like my forefathers before me. When I return home, I will rise to the court of Llewellyn himself as a trusted man. What about you, Garyn, what glory do you seek on this crusade?'

'Just the life of my brother,' said Garyn quietly.

'Even if you find him, he will surely be in service to a master so what makes you think he can return home with you?'

'I will worry about that later,' said Garyn. 'First I just need to know he is alive.'

The two young men carried on walking around the port watching the stores being loaded onto the waiting ships. The task was almost done and they knew they would be sailing with the tide.

'Acre is but a few days away,' said Dafydd, 'destiny beckons.'

Before Garyn could answer, a young woman caught his eye from a side alley, beckoning them over.

'What does she want?' he said, pointing at the girl.

'I don't know,' said Dafydd, 'but I intend to find out.'

The two boys walked over.

'Pretty Lady,' said Dafydd with a slight nod of the head. 'I am Squire Dafydd Ap Jon. This is my friend, Garyn Ap Thomas. How can we be of service?'

The girl looked around nervously but didn't answer.

'Do you speak English?' asked Garyn.

'Engleesh bad,' she said, 'but I try.'

'What can we do for you?'

'You are pretty boys,' she said. 'I find your faces very pleasing to me.'

'Thank you,' said Dafydd. 'You are also very pretty.'

'You are very kind,' said the girl. 'I am called Zara. I live very close by. You would come home with me, yes?'

'Why?' asked Garyn. 'Is there a problem?'

'No problem. I have very nice house and very nice bed. You come with me and have nice afternoons with me. Very cheap.'

'She is a whore,' said Garyn quietly.

'No not whore,' said the girl. 'Very good girl but hungry. Please, you come with me. One coin only.'

'Come on Dafydd,' said Garyn, 'let's get out of here.'

'Why?' said Dafydd. 'Whore or not she is very pretty and we are not likely to see many women in the Holy-land, at least, not many willing to share their beds. Perhaps she has a friend for you too.'

'Yes, many friends,' said the girl. 'I bring friend, yes?'

'No,' said Garyn. 'I am promised to another. You go, Dafydd, I will wait here.'

'How far is your house?' asked Dafydd.

'Here,' said Zara, pointing toward a whitewashed building at the end of the alley. 'We go now, yes?'

Dafydd grinned at Garyn.

'Go back to camp,' he said. 'I have several coins on me so may be a while.'

Garyn shook his head and laughed.

'Don't let Cadwallader find out,' he said, 'he'll have you shovelling horse shit from here to the Holy-land.'

Dafydd laughed and threw his cloak to Garyn.

'Here,' he said. 'Take this. She may be pretty but I don't trust her one bit. I'll see you later.'

Garyn started making his way back to the ship but as he walked away he felt something in the inner pocket of Dafydd's cloak and realised his friend had forgotten to take his purse. Laughing to himself he turned to catch them up but as he entered the alley, he paused and stared in confusion at the scene before him. At the end of the alley, two men were climbing through a window and into the house of the whore.

Garyn ducked behind a broken crate, not sure what to do. It seemed obvious to him that the men were in league with the whore and intended to rob Dafydd of anything of value. He thought about running for help but knew there was no time. Since leaving Wales Dafydd had become a close friend and Garyn knew he couldn't leave him to his fate so without any more hesitation, ran up the alley and climbed through the window.

Inside the room was dark, the only light coming from the open shutters. From somewhere up ahead he could hear the muffled sounds of the girl and his friend and for a moment he thought he had been mistaken as the unmistakable sounds of their union whispered through the darkness but within moments their intimacy was interrupted by the crash of a door being kicked open and the sound of shouting

Garyn knew he had to get there quickly. He ran through the darkness, searching for the source of the noise. Dafydd's voice roared above the rest as the sounds of a fight echoed through the house. Garyn burst through a door and saw his naked friend swinging a stool in the faces of two knife wielding attackers. Without thinking he launched himself onto the back of one sending him sprawling to the floor. Dafydd took advantage of the situation and smashed his stool into the distracted second man. Within seconds they had overpowered the attackers but without warning the screaming girl launched herself onto Garyn's back, her hands reaching around to claw at his eyes. Dafydd spotted the danger and swung his fist to smash the girl in the face, breaking her jaw in the process.

'Come on,' he shouted, 'let's get out of here.'

Garyn paused alongside the screaming girl as she held her shattered jaw, the blood pouring through her fingers.

'What about her?' he shouted, 'we can't just leave her like this.'

Dafydd grabbed Garyn by his jerkin and dragged him toward the door.

'Forget her,' he said, 'if you hadn't arrived I would probably have a knife in my back by now.'

With one last backward glance, Garyn ran down the corridor closely followed by Dafydd carrying his clothes. Once in the open, the Squire got dressed quickly as Garyn kept looking up the alleyway toward the house.

'Here they come,' he shouted as the two men ran out of the house and down the alleyway toward them. 'Come on.'

They raced along the dock back toward the fleet but as they ran, the shouts of the pursuers echoed around the dockyard and the attackers' comrades joined in the chase.

'Faster,' shouted Garyn as the group gained ground on them but though they were young, the locals closed them down. Frantically they ducked into the houses, hoping to lose them in the maze of alleyways but within moments they were lost and found themselves in a dead end.

'Shit,' cursed Dafydd and they turned to face the attackers.

Both boys drew their knives and prepared to face the mob, knowing full well they could not prevail against such numbers.

'There's no way we can beat them all,' gasped Garyn.

'Maybe not,' answered Dafydd, 'but we can take as many as possible with us.'

Garyn nodded grimly and both braced as the gang ran toward them. To Garyn's surprise, Dafydd didn't hold back but raced toward the attackers, causing them to falter in their rush. At the same time he heard a roar from behind the attackers and an unseen figure fell upon them, wielding a sword with a fury unrivalled. Garyn joined in the attack with his knife and within minutes, five men lay at their feet while another three ran from the alleyway in fear of their lives.

Garyn paused and looked at the scene around him. Dafydd was down on one knee, catching his breath while the man who had come to their aide walked amongst the wounded, checking they posed no further threat to them.

'Brother Martin,' he said. 'What are you doing here?'

'Just as well for you I was,' said the Monk. 'Are you wounded?'

Garyn looked down at his blood soaked body but felt no evidence of any wound.

'I don't think so.'

'Good, then let's get out of here before they return with their comrades. These docks are a hive of whores and brigands.'

'I noticed,' said Garyn. 'Dafydd, come on, we have to go.'

An hour later they were back on board one of the ships, thankful for the security afforded by the ship's guards. The Captain of the ship walked over and looked down at the blood soaked boys.

'What happened to you?' he asked.

'We were attacked by brigands.' said Garyn.

'Nothing to do with women I suppose?' said the Captain sarcastically. 'Don't bother answering that, I don't need to know. Anyway, we sail within the hour and before we do, I want you clean.

Filth breeds disease and I will not have disease on my ship. Get those clothes washed.'

'How do we do that on board a ship?' asked Garyn.

'Easy,' said the Captain and grabbing the boy by the scruff, threw him overboard into the water, much to the delight of the watching sailors.

Dafydd burst out laughing but moments later found himself falling through the air to plunge into the dock water alongside Garyn. He came up coughing and spluttering, his shoulder length hair strewn across his face.

'I can't swim,' he screamed.

'Then drown,' roared the Captain and again the watching men laughed as the two boys clung to the rope ladders draped down the side of the ship.

'Stay there until your clothes are clean,' shouted the Captain, 'or next time I'll pull up the ladders.'

Garyn looked up at the dockside crowd enjoying their plight. In amongst them was the Monk.

'Brother Martin,' shouted Garyn, 'do something.'

The Monk reached inside his cloak and threw something in the water beside the boys.

'What's that?' asked Garyn.

'A wash rag,' said the Monk. 'Potash soap is beyond my means but at least that sack cloth will clean your skin.'

Again the crowd laughed and watched as the boys started to wash the blood from their clothes with one hand while clinging tightly to the rope ladder with the other.

'Welcome to the Crusades, Master Garyn,' called the Monk, 'and enjoy your bath for there will be very few chances to bathe where we are going.'

Chapter Fifteen

Krak des Chevalier

Khoury sat inside his quarters in the southern tower. For two days the Mangonels had hurled their rocks against the inner walls but though many of the upper castellations had been destroyed, the main walls were largely intact. Despite this, Khoury knew it was only a matter of time. Even now the enemy could be sending their tunnels under the castle, undermining the walls at their weakest points. He had deployed listeners around the walls, Squires who lay with their ears against the floors of the lower rooms, listening for any sound of tunnelling. If successful, he would start tunnels of his own to confront the enemy in a subterranean battle but as yet the earth had remained silent.

His mind was in turmoil. If he surrendered the castle his honour would be stripped but if he held and the castle fell, then all the villagers within the walls would die horrible deaths because of his decisions. The order of St John was dedicated to protecting the lives of pilgrims on the road to Jerusalem but innocent villagers were no less vulnerable and deserved their protection. Approaching footsteps in the corridor outside made him look up and he awaited the knock on the door.

'Sire, it is Sir Najaar,' said the Squire on door duty.

'Let him come.' said Khoury and stood as his comrade entered his room.

'Sir Najaar, you look tired,' said Khoury.

'No more so than the rest of the men,' said Najaar. 'The bombardment is relentless and we have to keep an ever sharp watch for siege engines.'

'Are the men getting enough rest?'

'As much as they need,' said Najaar.

'Good, ensure they do for I feel this will end in confrontation sooner than we think.'

'The walls are stout, Sire and we have stores enough for many months. I am told there are no soft spots under the inner wall so any attempt at tunnelling will prove fruitless. We are impregnable.'

'No castle is impregnable,' said Khoury, 'for walls are only as strong as the hearts of those who defend.'

'Then my stance remains the same,' said Najaar, 'we are impregnable.'

Khoury smiled at his fellow Knight's resolve.

'So,' continued Khoury, 'what brings you up here at such a late hour?'

'Sire, I have this,' said Najaar and handed over a tiny rolled parchment secured with twine.

'A message?' said Khoury.

'One of our homing pigeons landed just before it got dark,' said Najaar. 'I would have brought it earlier but the bird was elusive and reluctant to roost. We had to bring it down with an arrow.'

Khoury cut away the twine and unravelled the wafer thin parchment.

'Najaar, my eyes are not what they used to be he said. Please read it out.'

Najaar squinted his eyes to read the tiny text.

'Sir Khoury. We are unable to lend aid to your cause. You are to negotiate favourable terms with Baibaars and regroup at Acre. The honour of your men is noted.'

Najaar looked up at Khoury with shock in his eyes

'Surely this cannot be true,' he said.

'Who is the signatory,' asked Khoury.

'Hugh de Revel.' said Najaar quietly

'The Grand Master himself,' said Khoury. 'This is indeed a direction unexpected.'

'It must be a forgery,' said Najaar. 'No Knight would surrender a castle so easily.'

'Has it been easy?' asked Khoury. 'We have many dead and face an unwinnable siege.'

'It may be difficult,' said Najaar, 'but I refuse to believe it is unwinnable. Relief could be just days away and we should at least withstand until our supplies are meagre.'

'What relief would this be?' asked Khoury. 'The grand master has stated there is none deployed.'

'I hear Longshanks of England is on Crusade. Perhaps he will support our resistance.'

'Longshanks will have his eyes on other targets,' said Khoury. 'No, the chance of relief is minimal and I will make my decision based on the facts available. With regards to the message being a forgery, do we know if the pigeon was one of ours?'

'The pigeon master assures me it was one of a basket sent to Acre a month ago,' said Najaar. 'This does not mean however that they have not fallen into enemy hands.'

'I agree said Khoury but it is also possible the message is authentic. Leave me to my musings, Brother, I have much to think about.'

Najaar lowered his head in deference before leaving the room.

The following morning saw those Knights not on duty at the walls deep in prayer within the bowels of the castle. When the priest concluded the service, they each made their way to the great hall to break their fast. The mood was quiet as two of their comrades had been killed during the night by a huge rock sent over the walls by the Mangonels. When the meagre meal of oats and dried dates was done, Khoury stood to address the men.

'Brothers,' he said, 'fellow Knights. By now you will have heard of the message I received last night from our Grand Master. In it he instructs our surrender to Baibaars and to seek the best terms we can.' A murmur rippled around the room. 'Like you I had my doubts,' he continued, 'but everything seems in order. The signature matches that of Hugh de Revel and the pigeon master has confirmed the bird is indeed ours. There is reason to doubt the message is true.'

'It could be a Mamluk trick,' said a voice from the back of the room.

'It could,' said Khoury, 'but we have no way of finding out. The choice is simple. Stay and eventually succumb to the Mamluks, costing the lives of all within these walls or take the opportunity to save the lives of the innocent.'

'We cannot surrender,' said another voice. 'Our honour will be as mud beneath the infidel feet.'

'Ordinarily I would agree,' said Khoury, 'but this is an order from the Grand Master himself. Those who know me well know I do not fear the enemy or the thought of a long siege. However, the times are changing and the Holy-land is under assault on many fronts. Our strength may be needed elsewhere to do what it is we do best, protect the innocent. To die needlessly here for the sake of our pride is an insult to our order and to God himself. We have the chance to not only save the villagers but to continue our cause wherever it may be needed.' Khoury paused and looked around the expectant faces.

'To this end,' he continued, 'I have this morning sent my Squire out to meet Baibaars with a petition of surrender.'

'No,' shouted several men rising from their seats.

'Disgraceful,' shouted others, 'they will think us cowards.' The room descended into a chorus of shouts from both supporters and critics of the decision.

Khoury called for quiet without success but suddenly the sound of an upturned table crashing to the floor stunned the room into silence. Everyone looked toward Brother Najaar who stepped up onto the food tables and strode above them, using his sword to point at some of the naysayers.

'Silence your babble,' he shouted, 'and show some respect to our leader.' He walked across to one of the vocal Knights. 'You, Brother Serril, answer me one question. What is more important to you, the walls of this castle or the life of an innocent?'

'That's not a fair question,' started the man.

'It is an easy question,' shouted Najaar, 'but I respect you too much to demand an answer.' He carried on walking and pointed at another Knight.

'Which is held dearest to you, Brother Joseph, your vows of obedience and servitude or your pride?'

The man lowered his head as Najaar continued along the table, finally stopping before the most vocal of the doubters. He raised his sword and drove it into the oak table before him, leaving it swaying as if in a gentle breeze.

'And you, Brother Shimal,' he said,' bravest of us all. Nobody doubts your faith yet I ask you this. Which do you hold dearest, your honour or a child's life.'

This time he waited for an answer and stared at his comrade.

'You know the answer,' said the Knight quietly.

'As do you,' said Najaar and looked up to face the room. 'Our leader has led us into many battles and fought shoulder to shoulder in the deepest of adversities. He alone decides the direction we take and even though we may disagree with him, his word is our bond. He has made a decision and no, I do not agree with it but I will carry out his will unto death.'

He pointed at the hilt of the sword now motionless before him. 'This is a weapon of death,' he said, 'but is forged in the shape of a

135

cross. Some here would do well to remember that. The protection of innocents is the holiest of our paths and today we have the chance to save hundreds. Yes it may be a trick and we could lose our lives but the life of one child is worth the sum of everyone in here. Remember your vows, Brother Knights and do not forget we are but shepherds in God's holy plan.' He paused and looked around the room before continuing.

'Now, enough meaningless talk and pay heed to our leader. The talk so far has been only of honour, let it now be of humanity but let me say this and heed me well. Should any man talk of cowardice in this room, no matter how brief the slight, then that man will meet me in a trial of arms this very morn, even unto death.' He withdrew his sword from the oak table and jumped down to the floor before turning to face Khoury once more.

Khoury bowed his head slightly in acknowledgment before continuing to address the Knights.

'As I said, I sent petition to Baibaars and he has responded thus. He promises full safe passage from Chevalier to all within. We can remain armed and ride under our colours.'

'Are there any conditions?' asked Najaar.

'Only that we go straight to Acre,' said Khoury. 'We will be shadowed by a full Halqa and if we deviate from the road, they will fall upon us with no mercy.'

'And you believe him?' asked Brother Joseph.

'I have to,' said Khoury, 'there is no other option.'

'And when is this to happen?' asked Najaar?

'At dawn tomorrow,' said Khoury. 'You will have noticed the Mangonels have already ceased their barrage and the rest of the day will see no threat of assault. Use the time well to pack what you need but give preference to the needs of the villagers. Remember, they have no home and are frightened. I recognise your fears and yes, there is a risk of treachery but we are well versed in the ways of war and should the Sultan break his bond, then we will make them pay the price of falsehood and take tenfold our number to the grave with us.'

The gathering broke up and the men went about their business. There was much to do and less than a day to do it. Finally only Khoury and Najaar were left in the hall.

'You have my gratitude,' said Khoury.

'I just hope you are right,' said Najaar and followed the others out into the courtyard.

'So do I, Brother,' said Khoury to himself when Najaar had gone, 'so do I.'

The following morning saw all the Knights of St John lined up behind the gates of the castle, almost two hundred fully armoured men riding their equally impressive war horses. To one side stood the frightened villagers, each clutching at the meagre belongings they had managed to bring from their homes prior to the assault. Despite the numbers, the courtyard was strangely quiet as they waited for their leader to join them.

Within moments a Squire appeared from around the corner closely followed by the order's flag bearer and Sir Khoury, resplendent in his armour. They paused at the centre of the waiting Knights.

'Brothers,' said Khoury, 'fellow Knights….servants of God. Today I ask a great deal. I ask you to trust me in my judgement and place your fate in the hands of the Lord. The other side of those gates waits a great army outnumbering us a thousand to one. Baibaars himself has granted safe passage and I believe him. However, should he resort to the trickery of the Infidels, then we will give a good account of ourselves and fall in the knowledge that we serve the one true God.' He turned to Najaar. 'Brother, you will lead us out under the banner. Take fifty men and form the vanguard. The villagers will follow flanked by fifty either side, the rest will bring up the rear. Should treachery be the order of the day, we are to form a perimeter and defend the villagers to the last man. Is that clear?'

The Knight nodded his understanding.

'Right, send word to the gates. Sir Najaar, lead us out and may God go with us.'

The sound of the horses hooves echoed down the covered corridor as the column made their way to the gates leading out onto the plateau. As they approached, a team of sergeants pulled away the locking bars and swung them open revealing the dusty world outside. The column made their way out and nervous hands rested on the pommels of their swords as the strength of the enemy was revealed before them. All across the plateau thousands of Mamluk warriors stood silently as the Knights left the castle. Each was dressed in the white thawbs of their people and everyone dressed the same, underlying the common theme of their slave ancestry.

The Column continued slowly, matching the pace of the slowest villagers. To one side, Khoury saw Baibaars sat upon a white charger, watching them closely as they passed. Khoury turned his horse and rode slowly toward the Sultan, stopping a few paces short.

'You have your castle, Baibaars.' he said. 'I hope now you prove to be a man of your word and give my people safe passage.'

'My word is good, Christian,' said Baibaars. 'Tell them to ride in safety unto Acre. But know this, one heartbeat after the last have entered those city gates they once more become my mortal enemy and should I see them on the field of battle, I will cut them down with as little thought as a scorpion kills its prey.'

'Understood,' said Khoury, 'though you may find that this prey fights back.'

Baibaars nodded in acknowledgement.

'And your word, Sir Knight,' he said, 'how honourable do you hold that?'

'Dearer than my life,' said Khoury.

'Then travel in safety, for my Halqas will ensure you are not endangered on your journey.'

'Until we meet again,' said Khoury.

'Until that day,' answered Baibaars.

Without another word, Khoury turned his horse to re-join the column.

Husam al din approached Baibaars.

'Sire, do you want me to give the order to cut them down?'

'Not this time,' said Baibaars. 'I will allow them their lives for there will be a time for killing soon enough but there is one more thing I would take from this man.'

'Which is?'

'His pride,' said Baibaars. 'Once they are down on the plains, send a rider and give the Christian a message.'

'What message?' asked Husam.

Baibaars pointed to something on the floor to one side.

'One that will wound him more than any blade,' he said.

An hour later, Khoury rode alongside Najaar at the head of the column. The tension had eased and they started to believe they would actually make it.

'Sire,' called a voice, 'a rider approaches.'

Several of the Knights turned and drew their swords but Khoury stood them down,

'Put away your swords, Brothers. He is a messenger only.'

The rider approached and bowed slightly with respect though never took his eyes from the Knight.

'Sir Khoury,' he said, 'my master, the illustrious Sultan Baibaars berates himself for forgetting your gift.'

'What gift?' snarled Najaar, 'what trickery is this?'

'No trickery,' said the Mamluk, 'a simple gift to demonstrate the graciousness of our people in allowing you your lives after your humiliating defeat.'

'This was no defeat,' said Najaar, 'it was a negotiated surrender instigated by us. Magnanimity is ours.'

'Perhaps this will tell otherwise,' said the messenger and threw a linen bag at Khoury's feet. 'Travel well, Sir Knights for we will meet again on the field of battle.'

Khoury waited until the rider was well on his way back to the plateau before dismounting and looking inside the bag. What he saw made his blood run cold as he realised the implications.

'What is it?' asked Najaar.

Khoury took one corner of the bag and upended it, tipping the contents onto the desert floor. At first Najaar didn't recognise the bundle of feathers and blood and he looked at Khoury in confusion.

'I don't understand?' he said.

'Pigeons,' said Khoury, 'the rest of the homing birds that were supposed to be in Acre. Hugh de Revel sent no message of surrender, Najaar, it was all a falsehood. The bird courier must have been captured and Baibaars used them against me. He is right, Brother, we have just suffered a humiliating defeat. I just gave up the most powerful castle in the Holy-land as a result of a simple forgery.'

Ten days later, the city of Acre appeared on the horizon and the column paused for a rest before the last leg of their journey.

'Sire, the Halqas have gone,' said Najaar, 'but a smaller unit remains on a distant hill. I assume they wait to see we reach the city.'

Khoury didn't answer but sipped from his water skin, deep in thought.

'It has been a long journey brother,' he said eventually, 'in more ways than one.'

'It is done, brother,' said Najaar, 'put it from your mind. Within the day we will sit amongst fellows under the same crest and thank the lord for our deliverance.'

'Not, I Brother,' sighed Khoury. 'From here you travel alone.'

Najaar turned in his saddle to look at his comrade.

'What nonsense is this? We ride together unto the arms of our order.'

'I can't Najaar, I have made an unbreakable oath and intend to keep it'

'What oath?'

'I promised Baibaars that when the column was safe, I would deliver myself into his custody as hostage. The Mamluk patrol waits for me.'

'What?' gasped Najaar, 'you never said anything about this before.'

'I knew there would be protest,' said Khoury, 'so kept my council.'

'Brother, you cannot go back,' said Najaar, 'we will not allow it.'

'The decision is not yours to make,' said Khoury. 'Hugh de Revel said to pursue the best terms I could and my custody was Baibaars' demand. There was no other choice.'

'But the letter was fake. There is no honour in keeping a bond made on falsehoods.'

'The letter was fake but the terms of surrender were made between Knights. Baibaars has delivered his part of the deal by providing safe passage. I will not go back on my word and run like a brigand. No, the die is cast and I will return with Baibaars' men. If the Lord is merciful, perhaps our paths will cross again but until that day, this must be goodbye.' He held out his arm and after a moment's pause, Najaar grabbed it in respect and friendship.

'The unit is yours to lead now Najaar,' said Khoury. 'Lead them to safety in the Lord's name and do not seek retribution for Baibaars' trickery. This land changes with every dawn and I fear the path of our order is misted before our eyes. Lead them to a future where they continue to serve the poor and if that lays on far off shores, then so be it.'

'I hold the reins of leadership only until the day you return, Brother,' said Najaar.

'Then until that day,' said Khoury before turning his horse and galloping back along the column.

'Where's he going?' asked a fellow Knight as he passed.

'To fulfil an oath,' said Najaar, 'and to do what all men should aspire to. Redeem his honour.'

Chapter Sixteen

Acre

Dafydd looked over at the city with fascination. The fleet had arrived at last and after a journey of almost three months by land and sea, the Holy-land lay before him. The entrance to the harbour was protected by a single tower rising from the sea and a huge chain stretched at water level between the tower and a stone building on the far shore.

'That's the Tower of flies,' said a man alongside him. 'The chain protects the harbour from sudden seaborne assault and is only lowered to the sea floor to allow friendly ships passage.'

'A strange name for such an imposing structure,' said Dafydd.

'A name is a name,' said the sailor with a shrug and went about his duties.

As the fleet waited Knight and Knave alike looked at their destination with awe and wonder. This was where Lionheart ousted Sah-la-Dhin's occupying forces less than a hundred years earlier and had subsequently gone on to slaughter almost three thousand Muslim prisoners before campaigning toward Jerusalem.

The perimeter of the ancient city was walled, a necessary defence against the repeated attacks from various adversaries across the centuries yet one side was open to the sea. This was the important factor that ensured the city was always difficult to besiege due to the constant availability of resupply from neighbouring Christian countries. At the far edge of the city eight towers looked inland, giant sentinels always on the lookout for the infidel.

'Do you know the names of the towers, boy?' asked a voice and Dafydd turned to see the Captain behind him.

'No Sir.'

'They all have names,' said the Captain, 'and you will know them well within days. That one there is called The Tower of the Countess of Blois and guards the only landward gate into the city. Step through those gates and you should sleep with one eye open.'

'Who was she?' asked Garyn looking at the tower.

'Some Frenchwoman who died over fourty years ago,' said the captain. A granddaughter of King Louis VII of France I believe.'

'And that one?'

'That one is known as the Accursed tower and pray you never have to sample her gifts. Any who enters those walls are seldom seen again.'

'Why?'

'It is a place given over to the confinement of prisoners and hostages. Pain and torture fill her walls and tales of atrocities poison the breath of any who have been lucky to escape.'

Dafydd balked at the thought of being confined in any space in the sweltering heat and was about to ask more questions when the chain started to disappear below the sea and the signal came to dock.

'Man the oars,' roared the Captain, walking away, 'take us in, easy now.'

Within moments the anchor had been stowed and banks of oarsmen eased the ship toward the dock. Garyn joined Dafydd on the bow and watched as the vessel nestled snugly against the stone quay.

'Secure the ropes,' shouted the Captain, 'and drop the rails. Prepare the ramps.'

Ten minutes later Garyn walked down the gangplank and onto the dock. At long last he was in Acre, the gateway to the Holy-land.

The town was alive with activity and it seemed to Garyn there was hardly any space that wasn't filled with someone either making their way to the business of the day or standing still and staring at the new arrivals. The column had been met by representatives of Sir John of Cambridge and while the Knights and Squires were led toward the far castle, the common soldiers were led through the heart of the town and into a row of dilapidated stone buildings. Finally they stopped before a door obviously damaged by a recent fire.

'This is it,' said the soldier, 'your quarters for the duration of your stay.'

'Are we not to stay at the castle?' asked Garyn.

'The castle?' answered the man with genuine surprise, 'I think not, young sir. That place is not for the likes of you or me. Only nobility sleep there, along with Knights of the realm. Even as we speak, Longshanks is being entertained by Sir John. Your master will be welcomed there as will all the other lords on Crusade but your bed lies within these walls. Be thankful for the shelter for those who once made their homes here now sleep beneath the stars.'

'They have been turned out?' asked Garyn.

'They have,' said the guide, 'but worry not, they were the lowest of the low and deserve no better.'

'But...' started Garyn.

'Garyn,' said Brother Martin, 'let it be. You are in a different world now and you would do well to talk less and listen more. You find us a bed space and see if you can find stabling for the horses when they arrive. I will join you shortly.'

'Where are you going?'

'I have business to attend,' said the Monk, 'but will return before dark.'

Garyn watched him go before the guide called him forward.

'Here you go, young sir, a castle of your very own.' He showed Garyn an open doorway and followed the boy in. The room was ten paces long and the same in width. In the corner a stone stairway led up to an open flat roof, bordered on all sides by small walls.

'This is good,' said Garyn. 'At least there is plenty of space.'

'I would grab the best space you can quickly,' said the guide, 'the ships are arriving every hour and before long the rooms will run out. I need to fit another ten in here before the day is out so stake your claim while you have the chance.'

'Another ten,' asked Garyn.

'At least,' said the man. 'Make the most of it as it's either this or you sleep on the sand by the dock.'

Without another word he left the building and disappeared into the city. Garyn looked around before dropping his pack in an alcove toward the back. He climbed the stairway and sat out on the roof watching the bustling streets below. Though it looked fascinating, he knew that if he was to find his brother, he wouldn't be here long. His journey lay on the other side of the city walls, out in the lands of the Mamluk.

Up at the Castle, Sir John of Cambridge welcomed Cadwallader outside the great hall.

'Cadwallader,' he said grasping the Knight's arm, 'good to see you again old friend.'

'Sir John,' said Cadwallader. 'I am surprised to see you still here. I thought you would be long since buried.'

Sir John laughed at the joke.

'Me dead? Oh no my friend, my flesh ages it is true but my soul is as young as those two Squires that once crept into the servant girl's quarters.'

'Good days,' said Cadwallader with a smile recalling the incident many years earlier. 'So, are you going to invite me in or shall I stay out here like a beggar?'

'Though I worry for my ale stock, you are of course my guest,' smiled Sir John. 'Please, step inside.'

The two men entered the hall and were immediately attended by two pages.

'Bring ale,' said Sir John and one of the boys disappeared down the corridor. 'So,' said Sir John sitting back. 'You made it.'

'We did,' answered Cadwallader. 'A pretty uneventful trip in all. The overland march was tough but the sea journey was fair. I lost only two men.'

'Fortune indeed,' said Sir John. 'I am told that Longshanks lost hundreds on a similar journey though truth be told, many fell to disease at Tunis.'

'Is the Prince here?'

'He was,' said Sir John, 'but has led a force out into the field. Baibaars is a thorn in our side and Longshanks rides to make a statement. His column is almost two thousand strong and includes outriders from both the Hospitallers and Templars.'

'A somewhat strange allegiance I would suggest,' said Cadwallader.

'Perhaps so but needs must. You arrive at a pivotal time, Robert. The future of the Holy-land hangs in the balance. Baibaars is proving to be a worthy adversary and the tribesmen rally to his call. As we speak he dominates all the lands south of here all the way around to Egypt and as far north as Antioch. Eastward also belongs to him and he controls the Homs gap.'

'Surely the gap is controlled by Krak des Chevalier?'

'It was until about a year ago when the Castellan was tricked into surrendering the castle by Baibaars. Since then we fight a reactive war, responding to the actions of Baibaars instead of taking the fight to him. That's why the arrival of Longshanks is so important. At least he rides out with a strong message of defiance.'

'I didn't realise it was so bad,' said Cadwallader.

'Well you do now. Antioch is lost to us, Tripoli is under siege and as for Jerusalem, well, any thought of a Christian Knight walking those sacred streets again are nothing more than dreams of boys. No, I fear our time in the Holy-land is limited, Robert and we build stick dams against a flooded river.'

'I can't say your words are comforting, Sir John,' said Cadwallader as the ale arrived. 'I have travelled far to help secure these lands alongside Longshanks.'

Sir John picked up his tankard and held it up in salute.

'Then let's drink to that,' he said, 'and hope your expedition is not in vain.'

They knocked the tankards together before drinking deeply of the ale, two fellow Knights with completely different views of their place within the Christian east.

'So how is your beautiful wife, the Lady Jennifer?' asked Cadwallader.

Sir John placed his tankard on the table and looked down in silence.

'Alas, she is dead, my friend,' he said eventually. 'Killed by a Mamluk patrol not a year since.'

Cadwallader shook his head in sadness.

'My friend, I had no idea,' he said. 'I am so sorry for your loss.'

'It is a tragedy indeed,' said Sir John, 'but we have to be strong. God's work demands it. Let the subject be changed my friend, tell me about the green fields of home.'

The conversation went on long into the evening with much ale flowing. Other Knights joined them in the hall, each happy to have arrived at last and they sat around the tables deep in conversation about the campaign before them. Cadwallader and Sir John got slowly drunk and recalled shared tales of boyhood pranks where they had grown up together as Squires to the same Lord. Finally Sir John remembered something and changed the subject.

'Robert,' he said, 'I almost forgot. A month or so ago I had a message delivered from Wales. An old acquaintance sent word of a young man who sets out on a mission to find his brother. Apparently he rides under your command. Do you know of him?'

'I do,' said Cadwallader, 'his name is Garyn ap Thomas, son of Thomas Ruthin.'

Sir John's eyes narrowed slightly.

'Thomas Ruthin? His name is known to me.'

'It should,' laughed Cadwallader, 'he unseated you in a joust tournament in London many years ago.'

Sir John nodded slowly as he remembered but did not share Cadwallader's smile.

'I remember,' he said. 'A journeyman of ill repute as I recall.'

'But unequalled skill, as his victory over you proved.'

'So this boy,' continued Sir John, 'Ruthin's son. Is he a paid man?'

'Only as far as the journey is concerned,' said Cadwallader. 'He is now his own man and free to serve any master.'

'Like father like son,' said Sir John.

'I suppose so but the son is no Knight. He is a lancer at best and short of experience. Why do you ask, do you want to enlist him?'

'No,' said Sir John, 'but the letter begged favour and held a grudge against him. I would hear from his own mouth why an esteemed Abbot demands the imprisonment of his brother until a certain pledge is filled.'

'Sounds intriguing,' said Cadwallader.' I will have him sent to you.'

'Is he not here?'

'Like I said, he is no Knight so shares the billets of the men at arms. I will have him brought at first light. Until then, my tankard is dusty through little use. Is this the way you treat an old friend?'

Sir John sighed.

'Your thirst has not been missed, Sir Knight. Perhaps we should put the ale barrels in the heart of Jerusalem and watch as you take the city single handed.'

'Perhaps you should,' laughed Cadwallader, 'perhaps you should.'

Brother Martin walked through the streets of Acre, heading toward the Hospitaller quarter. The order had held a base there for many years and their headquarters was even larger than the Castle of the King's Constable and almost as fortified as the Templar Castle in the northern edge of the city. He walked confidently, the memory of the streets coming back to him from the years he had spent as a hired Knight. His stride was purposeful as although the city was filled with soldiers, there was still an underbelly of desperation The lower classes who lived hand to mouth, who would not think twice about cutting the throat of any man thought a weak target. Hidden eyes watched him go,

147

aware he had the gait of a man able to take care of himself. Mistakenly they took him for a Knight of the order and let him pass, knowing that any attack on a Hospitaller would incur a terrible retribution. As he approached the Hospitaller castle he turned left and disappeared down a side street, seeking the alleyway he had frequented so many times before. Finally he stopped before a small door set back amongst the dirty white-washed walls of tightly packed buildings.

He knocked hard on the wood several times until it eased inward and a wrinkled woman peered around the door.

'What do you want?' she asked peering into the Monk's hood. 'We've done nothing wrong.'

'I know,' said Brother Martin gently, 'I am not from the order. I am a pilgrim and seek an old friend. He used to live here.'

'What name was he?'

'Ahmed Mubarak, he was a guide for my unit many years ago and I come in hope he still lives.'

The woman paused as she considered the Monk's words. Finally she looked up and down the alleyway before stepping to one side and letting him in.

'Go through to the back,' she said, 'and up the stairs. You will find him outside.'

The Monk did as directed and found himself out on a flat roof typical of the houses in Acre. To one side was a makeshift shelter and beneath it an old man lay on a straw mattress covered with a goatskin. Beside him, a pretty young woman was sitting on a stool keeping the flies away with a feathered fan.

'Ahmed Mubarak,' said Brother Martin, 'is that you?'

The man turned his head slightly but did not look up.

'Speak again, stranger,' he said weakly, 'for the voice is familiar to me.'

'And so it should,' said Brother Martin. 'We spent many nights under the desert stars as you taught me the ways of your people.'

A faint smile played around the Arab's mouth.

'And if my memory doesn't play tricks on me,' he said, 'many days riding weary horses into battle. My friend Martin, can it be you have returned to this accursed place once more?'

'I have,' said the Monk, 'and have come directly to find the greatest friend I have ever had.

'You honour me, Sir,' said Ahmed, but still did not rise from the bed. 'I trust this is not a visit without purpose?'

'Just as astute as ever,' said Brother Martin, 'I need a guide and hoped I could tempt you to join with me once more, two old men on one last quest.'

'A last quest,' said Ahmed. 'What I wouldn't give for such an opportunity but alas, I will have to turn you down.'

'I can pay you, Ahmed,' said Martin walking around to the foot of the bed, 'I have enough coin to ...' The words fell away as he saw the man up close for the first time in many years. Immediately he could see his trip had been in vain as he focussed on the two clumsily sewn wounds where the man's eyes had once been. Eventually Ahmed broke the heavy silence.

'I assume your sudden silence means you have noticed the reason I must turn you down,' he said.

'By all that is Holy,' said Brother Martin, 'what happened to you?'

'It is a gift from one of Baibaars' generals,' said Ahmed. 'I was caught scouting for a Templar patrol and tortured by the Mamluks. They staked me out and pinned back my eyelids in the midday sun. I would have died within hours but the patrol counter attacked and released me from my bonds but not before my eyes had boiled dry in their sockets.'

'I don't know what to say,' said Martin sitting on the side of the bed.

'It would have been better if they had killed me there and then,' said Ahmed. 'A blind man has only begging as a trade and my family starve most days. I am a burden to them and lack the courage to fall on my own blade. Perhaps you could do it for me?'

'Never,' said the Monk, 'and strike that thought from your mind. I am here now and will do what I can to help your plight.'

'You owe me nothing Martin. Any debt was always paid in full and it was a sad day when you left. Is Thomas Ruthin with you?'

'No, he died many months ago by an assassin's blade, though his son travels at my side. That is why I have come, he has a quest to fulfil but needs a trusted guide. I thought you were the man but obviously that is not now possible.'

'Alas, I wish it were,' said Ahmed. He turned his head to face the girl.

'Misha, take a coin and bring ale from the market for our friend.'

'There are no coins left, master,' said the girl. 'They have been used on fodder for the goat.'

'Water is fine,' said Brother Martin quickly, steering the conversation away from embarrassment on behalf of his friend. 'Ale disagrees with me these days.'

'Then bring water,' said Ahmed, 'and make sure it is clean. Draw fresh from the well.'

'Yes master,' said the girl and ran quickly down the stairs.

'I thought she was your daughter,' said Brother Martin.

'No,' said Ahmed with a sigh. 'She fills a very unique role in our life, a servant of a beggar. How low is that?'

'A strange situation indeed,' said Brother Martin. 'How did this come to pass?'

'I saved her from certain death years ago and she promised service in gratitude. Alas, her life is now as wretched as mine.'

'What stops her from running away?'

'She is from an honourable tribe and has sworn to serve me until the day I die.'

'What family do you have?' asked Martin.

'Only my wife, Maysam. My sons died at Antioch. Maysam cooks at the Templar Castle but the money barely covers food. Often I sit outside with the begging bowl but the population struggles as much as me. Anyway, enough of my woe, friend, Allah has seen to bestow this fate upon me and I must accept his will. What about you? Tell me of this great quest so I can join you in my dreams.'

Brother Martin paused, wondering whether to share what he knew. This man had been his most trusted friend for many years and he saw no need to mistrust him now.

'I don't know the details,' he said, 'but I do know this. We have to ride into the Jabahl Bahra.'

'Hashashin territory,' said Ahmed quietly. 'This is not a good thing.'

'All I know is this. Ruthin's son is in possession of a great knowledge. Something so important it can cause peace or war in the Holy-land. He is intent on finding it for the sake of his brother and will travel there with my help or without it. If he goes alone, he will be dead within days.'

'As will you I fear,' said Ahmed. 'The lands of the Hashashin are no place for seasoned young men let alone those who gather the years around them like folds of a blanket.'

'I can still handle myself well enough,' said Brother Martin.

'In your mind, yes but against one half your age, how would you fare?'

'This old dog still has some tricks,' laughed the Monk. 'Anyway, we divert from the conversation. Your plight weighs heavy on my heart but it is obvious your scouting days are over.' He reached beneath his cloak and retrieved two silver coins 'Here,' he said, 'take this. It will feed you and your family for a few weeks.'

Ahmed felt the coins placed in his palm.

'Your generosity falls second only to the size of your heart, my friend,' he said. 'I will accept your gift if only for the sake of my wife.'

'I have to go,' said the Monk, 'but promise I will return, God willing.'

'Wait,' said Ahmed, 'I think I can help. There is one who knows the valleys of Jabahl Bahra like they know their own hands. I will speak to this person and see if they will accompany you on your quest. Where are you staying?'

'In a house near the Constable's castle. The door is blackened by fire.'

'We will find it,' said Ahmed. 'Travel well my friend. Until the next time.'

The Monk grabbed the offered hand and gripped it tightly, hating the plight of the man who had ridden alongside him so often.

'Until the next time,' he said and left the house.

The following morning, the sun had not fully risen when Garyn was woken by someone hammering on the door.

'Open up,' shouted a voice. 'Sir John of Cambridge demands the attendance of Garyn ap Thomas.'

Garyn sat up sharply and watched as one of the many men sharing the room raised the bar on the door and allowed a foot soldier entry.

'Who is the one called Garyn ap Thomas?' he asked.

'I bear that name,' said Garyn.

'Then you are to come with me immediately,' said the man. 'Sir John would have words.'

'The hour is early,' said Garyn.

'He said it is in your interests to attend immediately,' said the messenger, 'he has news of your brother.'

151

Garyn clambered to his feet and faced the messenger.

'What news?' he asked, 'is Geraint here?'

'I know nothing of the detail,' said the man, 'but will say this. It is a brave man who keeps the Castellan waiting.'

Garyn looked across at Brother Martin who had joined him from a different room.

'What do you think?' asked Garyn.

'No harm in seeing what he wants,' said the Monk. 'After all, it is why you came here.'

Garyn nodded and turned to the messenger.

'Give me a moment,' he said.'

Ten minutes later they followed the messenger through the quiet streets toward the Castle of the King's Constable. The guards let them through the gates and they crossed the courtyard before entering the great hall. All around, men were seeing to the business of the morning. Some were cleaning their equipment, some were talking amongst themselves while others still struggled to rise from their mats, their heads aching from the previous night's revelries.

'It seems there was much celebration,' said Garyn to Brother Martin.

'It would seem so. An expected indulgence after such a journey, perhaps.'

'This way,' said the messenger and led them through into a smaller courtyard where a man stood stripped to the waist, splashing water over his browned torso. 'Sire, said the messenger, 'Garyn ap Thomas is here.'

'Squire Thomas,' said Sir John, 'welcome to Acre.'

'Thank you, Sire but alas I am no Squire.'

The man nodded before pulling on his linen jerkin.

'And this is?'

'This is Brother Martin. A fellow traveller and close comrade.'

'I have heard your name mentioned,' said the Castellan, 'I am Sir John of Cambridge, 'master of the Castle of the King's constable. Have you broken your fast?'

'No, Sire,' said Garyn, 'we came as soon as we were summoned.'

'Yes, apologies for the hour but I have business outside of the city and seek early departure. Please, sit down and share my fare.'

The three men sat at a table while servants brought a maize porridge and goat's milk. They ate in relative silence before Sir John spoke again.

'So,' he said eventually. 'Master Garyn. I have heard tell you engage on a quest to save your brother.'

'I do, Sire.'

'Save him from what, exactly.'

Garyn paused, realising there was no right answer.

'He needs to know his family have died, Sire and I am hoping he will return home to tend our lands alongside me.'

'And what makes you think he will want to go home. Did he not choose this way of life?'

'That is a risk I take, Sire but I have to try. I promised my mother as she took her last breath.'

'Even if he also wishes this, if he is contracted to a master then he may not be able to leave.'

'Again I understand this may be a problem but I hope that a deal I made with someone back in Wales may ease the process.'

'Ah yes, the Abbot of St Benedict in Brycheniog.'

'You know of him?' asked Brother Martin in surprise.

'We often have dealings,' said Sir John. 'In fact, I received a letter from him not six weeks hence telling me of your situation.'

'Then you must be the one he talked about,' said Garyn, sitting forward in his seat. 'The one who has Geraint's fate in his hands.'

'I am indeed,' said Sir John. 'He landed here many months ago as part of a relief force on behalf of Henry and has been stationed within Acre under my command.'

'Where is he?' asked Garyn. 'Can I see him?'

'Alas, no,' said Sir John. 'At least not yet. You see, the letter asked me to place your brother under armed guard until such time certain promises made by you were honoured. Now, I have no idea what those promises are but of course I had to carry out the whim of such a holy man as the Abbot.'

'You imprisoned him?'

'I have. Oh he is safe enough at the moment but I have to admit, his circumstances are somewhat uncomfortable.'

'Where is he?' shouted Garyn standing up. 'You have to let him go, he has done no wrong.'

'Well, that isn't exactly true,' said Sir John. 'You see, he has been accused of aiding the enemy and awaits execution for being a traitor.'

'That's absurd,' shouted Garyn. 'Why would my brother aid the infidel?'

'Garyn sit down,' said Brother Martin, seeing the coldness in the Knight's eyes. 'Hear the man out.'

'Very sensible,' said Sir John as Garyn regained his seat. 'Your brother's quarters were searched and we found a purse of Muslim gold beneath his mattress. Of course he denied all knowledge but the evidence was damning. He has been sent to gaol until I decide his fate.'

'Is there to be no trial?' asked Garyn. 'What about the King's law?'

'Out here I am the law,' said Sir John and you would do well to remember it. So, down to business. I need to know what it is you seek and how you intend to get it to me.'

Garyn stayed silent and stared at the Castellan.

'Garyn, let's dispense with the games of children,' sighed Sir John. 'I do not have the patience of your Abbott or indeed the inclination to enter into futile debate. I am a wealthy man and have estates throughout England. Before the year is out, I will once more gallop amongst those hills with the sweet rain on my face so it matters not if you tell me or not.

One of two things will happen here today. One, you will tell me what I want to know and your brother lives or two, you keep silent and your brother is hanged within the hour. Should the second option come to pass then before this sun sets, you, young man will be found to be in possession of a similar purse of Muslim gold and will also be put to death as a traitor, but only after weeks of unbearable torture. The choice is simple and it will be made now.'

Garyn stared at the Castellan with hatred, not understanding the speed with how things were unfolding.

'Then why are you doing this?' he asked. 'If you have so much, why kill someone who has never done anything wrong?'

'Because I can,' said Sir John, 'and because you have stirred my curiosity. Money I have, station I have but depending on this artefact, I could have a place in history. So, this is the last time of asking. What is it you seek?'

'Tell him,' said Brother Martin quietly.

'I can't,' said Garyn

'Tell him,' said the Monk even louder.

'You don't understand,' said Garyn, 'I can't for I do not know myself.'

The Castellan stood.

'Then our business is done,' he said, 'and your brother will die within the hour.'

'Wait,' shouted Garyn, 'I can't tell you for I truly do not know. The man who told me was a Muslim prisoner and said he was a poet amongst his people. He would not tell me where or what the actual relic was in case I had a loose tongue but said if ever I was to see the Holy-land, most men of note would understand his words.'

'What words?' asked Sir John.

'He told me a poem,' said Garyn, 'and made me memorise every word. He said that within the poem was everything I needed to know about a relic so powerful, it could start or end wars.'

'Tell me the poem,' said Sir John.

'If I do, how do I know you will keep your word and release my brother?'

'You have the word of a Knight given before a man of God,' said Sir John.

Garyn looked toward Brother Martin who nodded silently.

The boy took a deep breath and closed his eyes as he remembered the words.

> 'Oh blinded men who will not see,
> the truth is not where it should be.
> When Sah-la-Dhin came close to death
> from steely blade with Sinan's breath,
> the price he paid for lengthened life
> protection from assassin's knife,
> was not of slaves or swathes of gold
> but bounty from a battle old.
> Where Christian wood, the cause of tears,
> a remnant of a thousand years
> was hidden from the Sultan's gaze
> and cost the bloodiest of days.
> Where murder was the story made,
> three thousand slain by Christian blade,
> the price of life was nought but tree,

155

a simple gift that couldn't be
for Sah-la-Dhin no longer knew
the resting place of aged yew,
the bounty of those glory days
won hard beneath the Horned one's gaze.
So seek the trophy not within
the treasuries or Sultan's whim
but in the place where all men sleep
and place their trust and bones to keep.
Where mountain men with feared name
ensure it's not seen again.
The yew that Christians so desire
was not destroyed in Muslim fire
but hides away in trees afar,
the Castle of Jabahl Bahra.'

When he had finished, Garyn opened his eyes and saw both men staring at him with open mouths.

'Do you know what it means?' he asked.

'Oh yes, Garyn,' said Sir John standing up again. 'I know very well what it is.'

'I don't believe it,' said Brother Martin. 'It has been lost for a hundred years but if these words are true, then the holiest of relics lies within our reach.'

'What is it?' asked Garyn. 'Will someone tell me?'

Brother Martin turned to him.

'It is the holiest of holies, Garyn. Your poem reveals the resting place of a sacred artefact stained by the life blood our Lord Christ himself, the remnants of the true cross of Cavalry.'

Sir John paced back and forth across the small courtyard deep in thought. He had dismissed the Monk and the boy and instructed them to be ready for an expedition to Jabahl Bahra within two days. However, Sir John knew that although Jabahl Bahra was less than ten day's ride away, it may as well have been ten thousand for between Acre and the Bahra mountains, Baibaar's forces dominated the countryside in a grip of steel. Any unprepared column setting out would be cut down within days and to raise a force strong enough to fight through would need detailed explanation. That was something he did not want to do. If Longshanks found out about this, he would

156

surely retrieve the relic and claim the glory himself. No, he had to be clever and make a plan alone. There was plenty of time and although Baibaars was indeed an obstacle, ironically the arrival of Longshanks meant the situation could change at any time. Sir John knew that all he had to do was wait and make sure nobody else knew the whereabouts of the relic.

Across the city Brother Martin was busy packing his meagre belongings into a leather sack. Garyn stood behind him with a perplexed look on his face.

'But why?' he asked. 'I don't understand.'

'Garyn,' said the Monk. 'I have seen men such as he before and the greed was written across his face as if it had been inscribed. You have to trust me in this. It is too dangerous to stay here for if I am correct, we will either be framed for treason very soon or feel an assassin's blade across our throats. We have to leave and do it now.'

'But if I run, I will be condemning my brother to death.'

'I don't think so,' said the Monk. 'If we run and are successful in retrieving the relic the only lever he has against you is your brother. He would be a stupid man to lose that advantage and believe me, stupidity was not an evident trait. I think he will keep him alive at least until this situation runs its course. Besides, if I am wrong there is nothing you can do to save your brother. Even if we knew where he is being held, which we don't, there is no way we can get him out without a fortune in compensation. The die are cast, we have to get out of here.'

Garyn paused but finally turned to his own equipment. A few minutes later a knock came at the door and one of the other young men answered before turning to shout across the room.

'Brother Martin,' he called, 'there is a comely young wench asking to see you. Are you allowed to lay sight on such a fine woman?'

The rest of the men started laughing as the Monk walked to the door to find the slave girl from Ahmed's house standing outside.

'Misha,' he said, recalling her name. 'Has your master sent you with a message?'

'He has, Sire,' said the girl, 'but I would seek privacy to share it.'

'Come in,' said the Monk, 'we can talk in the rear yard.'

They walked through the crowded room, ignoring the lewd shouts of the men as they passed.

'Let me know her price, Brother,' shouted one. 'I have several coins to spend.'

'After you, my friend,' shouted another.

The laughter continued as they made their way through and finally stood alone in a tiny yard covered with dried goat droppings.

'Is the boy here?' asked the girl.

'He is,' said the Monk.

'Then summon him for these words are for his ears also.'

Brother Martin called Garyn and they stood together as the girl relayed the message.

'Sire,' said the girl. 'My master promised word of a guide who knows the way to Jabahl Bahra and the ways of the people there.'

'He did,' said the Monk. 'Do you know of such a man?'

'I do,' said the girl, 'though it is no man. I am the person with such skills.'

Both men looked at the slight girl in confusion. Her black hair fell to her waist and matched the almond brown of her eyes. She was draped in a long white cape that covered her small frame and an ornate chain of simple steel lay around her throat. Her wrists were heavy with dozens of bracelets.'

'I don't understand,' said the Monk. 'You are but a girl.'

'My name is Misha ain Alsabar,' she answered, 'and my people are descended from a line of esteemed servants to the Sultans. My mother served the descendants of Rashid ad-Din Sinan himself, and I grew up in the forests of Jabahl Bahra.

'But why are you willing to help us, Misha?'

'My master has promised me freedom if your quest is successful,' said Misha 'and I yearn to see my family again. He said you are an honourable man and once you have obtained that which you seek, you will let me go with my master's blessing.'

'What is to stop you running away as soon as we leave Acre?' asked Garyn.

'I have been brought up in the ways of the Hashashin and my word is worth more than life itself.'

'And you think you can take us there?'

'I can though the journey is dangerous.'

Garyn looked at the Monk.

'What do you think?' he asked.

'I think we have no choice,' said Brother Martin. 'We have to get out of here and this meeting is opportune.' He turned to the girl. 'Misha, we will accept your master's offer. How soon can you be ready to travel?'

'I have already prepared,' said Misha, 'and have a horse waiting outside the city walls.'

'You have a horse?' asked Garyn in surprise.

'My master used some of the coins left by your friend,' said Misha. 'He has also organised supplies enough for ten days. After that, we are on our own.'

'Then I guess there is no reason to wait,' said the Monk. 'Tell us where and when.'

'Meet me within the hour outside Saint Anthony's gate,' she said. 'Be prepared to ride hard and be guided by all I say.'

The Monk nodded.

'We will be there.'

The girl turned to leave and was escorted back through the quarters to more cat calling from the young men. Finally they were outside but before she left she turned to the Monk once more.

'Be careful,' she said, 'for the Castellan has eyes everywhere. You need to move quickly but I suggest you do one more thing before you leave.'

'Which is?'

'Make peace with your God, Christian for there is a possibility none of us will return alive.' With that she walked back up the whitewashed street and disappeared into the busy city.

Chapter Seventeen

The Castle of the King's Constable

'*Gone*,' shouted Sir John. 'What do you mean gone?'

'They left this morning, Sire,' said the messenger, 'and were seen leaving the city via the Gate of St Anthony.'

'Were they alone?'

'It would seem so.'

They are fools if they think they can travel without escort,' said Sir John. 'The old man hasn't been here for many years and the boy is yet wet behind the ears. Gather some men and a local guide. They will have travelled northward. Find them and ensure their journey is cut short in brutal manner.'

'Yes, Sire,' said the messenger.

'Sir John,' called a voice and another Knight ran into the room carrying a rolled parchment.

'Sir Bennet,' said the Castellan looking up at the intrusion.

'Sire I have news,' said the Knight, 'about the Lady Jennifer of Orange.'

'What of her?'

'Sire, she is alive and well and held as hostage by the Mamluks.'

Sir John stood up in shock as did many of the men around the room.

'What?' he gasped. 'This cannot be. She was killed by the infidels less than a year ago.'

'Apparently not, Sire. This is a ransom demand from Baibaars himself. In it he lists over a hundred prisoners in his hands. Amongst them is your wife. She is alive, Sire. Your wife is alive.'

The room burst into activity as men raised their voices in support. The Lady had been a great favourite and was greatly missed but despite his outward appearance of gratitude, inside Sir John was seething. The supposed death of his wife had meant he could marry again into another rich family and he had already sent word to England for his trusted friends to make representations on his behalf. Now, with her potential reappearance it meant that not only would his plans be curtailed but he would have to devise a new way of ridding himself of her. His mind snapped back to matters in hand.

160

'Great news indeed,' he said, 'for surely God himself looks down on this house this day. Show me the parchment.'

For a few moments he read the document, calculating the total cost of the ransom. It included commoners, men at arms and Knights alongside several women and one Lord. Though the price was high he knew it was available within his treasury and could easily be recouped by higher taxation but what was more interesting was the arrangements for payment. At the bottom of the parchment was the instruction to make the exchange at a Wadi in the north, a lush place of green hills and waterfalls but more importantly, within ten miles of Al Kahf Castle. His mind worked furiously as he realised fate had presented him with an ideal excuse to ride north with an armed column. He looked up at the cheering men and finally held up his hand.

'Loyal Knights,' he said, as the noise subsided. 'We should calm ourselves for though the opportunity is indeed ripe for the taking, we have to consider the morals of those who demand the ransom. These may be empty words designed to trick us into the open without sign of the prisoners for it wouldn't be the first time the heathen have turned to the tricks of Satan. The names on this list deserve repatriation no matter what the cost and I recognise many of those we have fought alongside and long thought dead. Yes, the Lady's name is amongst them but so are Knights of this very hall. I swear we will do everything to raise this ransom and if this message rings true, then we will bring them back here to the safety of Acre. However, we will not walk into a trap, we will not be tricked into handing over unwarranted wealth and we will not be intimidated by those not fit to hold your shields. No, we will ride out under the banner of the Lord with sharpened blades and steely hearts and show this Baibaars we are not to be meddled with. I hear Longshanks himself already makes inroads into the Sultan's Halqas and they fear the touch of English steel like no other.'

He looked around the room.

'Ordinarily I would not think twice in commanding you to ride alongside me but as my wife is amongst those held, I will not risk men's lives for the healing of my own heart. To this end I seek men to ride with me to retrieve our fellows, the support of a hundred who, of their own free will and if called by Almighty God, will fall to gift their brothers their rightful freedom. So, fellow Knights, I say this. Who amongst you has the heart for the fight? How many are willing to run the bloodied course of true men and die so that others may live?'

The cheering was deafening as every man raised their clenched fist in support. Over and over again their voices rang around the room and Sir John's trusted servant turned toward him, struggling to make himself heard.

'Sire, the support is total. Surely such fervour will ensure the Lady Jennifer will soon be safe within these walls.'

'I'm sure she will,' answered Sir John, but inside his heart he was already planning the retrieval of a bounty far greater than anything the servant could imagine and if that meant all the prisoners and all the men present in the hall would die in the process, then so be it.

The darkness fell as if the God had thrown a blanket over the land. Garyn saw to the horses while Misha and Brother Martin scurried around searching for firewood before it got too dark to see.

'We should have stopped earlier,' said the Monk.

'A cold night is a small price to pay for the security of cover,' answered the girl.

Brother Martin looked around at the dense thicket that was their home for the night. The tangled brush provided a thorned barrier and meant that anyone approaching would be heard long before they came upon the travellers. They had ridden hard along dried stream beds and hidden valleys before turning back east toward the coast and the Monk was glad to have reached the refuge to ease the aches of the ride. Finally they sat around a small fire eating dried strips of goat meat and sipping water from the skins Misha had loaded onto a pack horse.

'So,' said Brother Martin, 'this is it, Garyn, the Holy-land. Sitting around a tiny fire, eating meat as tough as leather and hoping we are not killed in the next few minutes. Is this how you envisaged your Crusade?'

'I don't know what to think,' said Garyn, 'I worry only for my brother.'

'He will be fine,' said the Monk. 'All we need to do is return with the relic. If we can do that, I'm sure we can buy his freedom.'

'If we can find it,' said Garyn. 'It seems to me our fate changes by the minute and I'm not even sure where we are going.'

'I have been told only take you to Jabahl Bahra,' said Misha, 'and know nothing of what you seek.'

'Then perhaps now is the time to explain,' said Brother Martin. 'Garyn was told a tale by a poet who once stayed at Al Kahf and the

162

words relate to the resting place of one of Christendom's most sacred relic, the remains of the true cross.'

'And what is that exactly?' said Garyn.

'It is said that when Christ was taken down from the cross his disciples took away the timbers and hid them from the Romans. In time, when the region embraced Christianity, it reappeared and became the object of pilgrimage for many years. They were troubled times and the continued fighting saw it taken from Jerusalem to Constantinople before being returned to Jerusalem hundreds of years later. By now it had been carved up and only a small piece remained, set into a bejewelled crucifix of solid gold.'

'Which explains the interest I suppose,' said Garyn.

'On the contrary, compared with the treasures of Kings and Sultans, the gold and jewels are paltry. No the value is in the sliver of wood embedded in the gold itself for it represents the cross upon which our lord died. Any man in possession of this relic could demand his own price or cause wars to be waged in its name.'

'So how do you know where it is?'

'The cross was taken from the church of the Holy Sepulchre in Jerusalem during the first crusade but was captured by Sah-la-Dhin at the battle of Hattin. Many tried to buy it from the Sultan but it was never seen again, not even when Lionheart demanded it in return for the lives of three thousand prisoners. Sah-la-Dhin promised its return but when he didn't keep his word, Richard had the prisoners executed.'

'Three thousand slain by Christian blade...' said Garyn quoting from the poem.

'Exactly,' said the Monk. 'The horned gaze refers to the twin Volcanoes that overlooked the battle of Hattin but that much was already known. What wasn't known was the fate of the cross and the thought was that Sah-la-Dhin sacrificed those prisoners out of stubbornness. If your poem is to be believed, it seems he did not have it for it was in the hands of one of his other enemies, the Ismailis.'

'Who are they?'

'A secretive people who dominate the Jabahl Bahra mountains,' said the Monk, 'led by someone called Rashid ad-Din Sinan. Twice they fought back the armies of Sah-la-Dhin and it is said he withdrew only after he had come close to death by the hands of the Hashashin, a sect of the Ismailis who perfect the art of silent murder.'

'Sah-la-Din was almost murdered?' asked Garyn in surprise.

'He was, the story is that he woke to find a message from the Hashashin left in his sleeping tent as a sign of how easy it was to get to him. Sah-la-Dhin swore it was left by Rashid ad-Din Sinan himself and ordered his councillors to make immediate peace with the Ismailis. The story is a strange one for the Hashashin are not known for their mercy and the death of Sah-la-Dhin would have been a great victory for them but for some reason they let him live despite the opportunity. Some wonder if Sah-la-Dhin actually bought his life that night but no mention has ever been made of any price paid.'

'And you think he may have handed over the cross?'

'It's what your poet believed,' said the Monk, 'and it makes sense. The cross was invaluable and easily worth a Sultan's life. The relic disappeared from history and no mention of it was ever made again. This makes sense for a man as great as Sah-la-Dhin would never have admitted to such an act and despite their lethal reputation, the Hashashin are men of their word. Neither side would have mentioned the transaction.'

'But surely all this is guesswork.'

'It is said,' the Monk, 'but why would a man pass on this information with his dying breath? It also ties in with why Sah-la-Dhin could not produce the cross at Acre, when Lionheart slaughtered the prisoners.'

'So you think it is somewhere in the castle of Jabahl Bahra.'

'I do,' said the Monk, 'in a castle called Al Kahf, the castle of the cave. It was Rashid ad-Din Sinan's stronghold and has never been taken by any enemy. The poem refers to a mountain man and Sinan was also known as the old man of the mountain. I believe he is the final link to the location of the cross.'

'But surely he died almost a hundred years ago.'

'He did,' said the Monk, 'but your poem makes the location clear. Where do all men eventually sleep and entrust their bones?'

Garyn's eyes widened in understanding as the poem finally made sense.

'Sinan is buried in the castle,' he said quietly

'He is,' said the Monk, 'and that's where I expect to find the cross. In the grave of the mountain man, Rashid ad-Din Sinan.'

'But that doesn't make sense,' said Garyn. 'Why would a Muslim King be buried with a crucifix? To take a cross to his grave

164

goes against everything they believe. I heard they worship the devil himself.'

'Oh no, Garyn,' said the Monk. 'Nothing could be further from the truth. The God of the Muslims is the same one worshipped by Christians in the scriptures of the church and though they acknowledge Jesus was born of the Virgin Mary and carried the word of God, they maintain he was but an apostle and not his son.'

'Why not?'

'We believe that God is all holy and neither begets nor is begotten,' said Misha.

'So who was Muhammad?'

'A prophet who came after Jesus.'

'So you accept Jesus died on the cross?'

'No. We believe that he ascended into heaven whilst still alive and that another man died in his place. '

'So I ask again,' said Garyn, 'why would there be a cross in the grave of a Muslim?'

'It certainly wouldn't be for religious purposes,' said the Monk. 'Perhaps it was put there as a gift, or a sign of dominance over the Christian invaders. It may even have been put there after he died by someone else. Think about it, what better place to hide something so important to Christians. It would be the last place they would expect to find it. We may never know but the point is, if the poem is correct then the cross lies there.'

'So what happens next?' asked Garyn.

The Monk turned to face Misha.

'Well, that's in the hands of this young lady. You should ask her.'

Misha looked up from the fire.

'I can get you into the Castle,' she said, 'but will not desecrate the grave of any man.'

'Understandable,' said the Monk. 'How long will it take to get there?'

'If we travelled the road, ten days but we will take a different route. An extra three days.'

'Why?'

'So I can keep you alive,' she said. 'The countryside is thick with Mamluks and even if we get past them, the Jabahl Bahra will be filled with the eyes of Hashashin. This way, if we are lucky, the journey will be uneventful and the danger will lie only in the approach to the castle.'

Brother Martin nodded in agreement.

'It makes sense,' he said. 'What route will we take?'

'Along the coast,' said the girl, 'and then head inland. After tomorrow, we will travel by night only and lay up during the day.'

The conversation gradually waned alongside the receding flames and the group finally rolled themselves in their sleeping blankets against the chill of the night air, unaware that back in Acre, a powerful unit of men were already being armed and provisioned for a similar journey, led by someone who also had his heart set on retrieving the cross.

Brother Khoury sat amongst the rest of the prisoners. His head was down and his heart was heavy. His once bald head was now a tangled mess of hair which intertwined with the greying beard about his filthy face. Sores festered from the continued beatings he had suffered at the hands of his captors but it was not the wounds that caused him the greatest pain, but the fact he had been imprisoned in the dungeons of his own castle for almost a year. Silently he had endured everything his captors had thrown at him, praying each evening for forgiveness until finally they had forgotten about him and his jailers kept him alive only for the ransom value. Eventually the deal had been made and over twenty prisoners were dragged from their cells and blindfolded before being loaded onto carts to be traded for a ransom from the Castellan of Acre.

For several days they had travelled north until finally their blindfolds had been removed and they were herded into a disused building along with other Christian prisoners from across the Holy-land. At first he kept his own council and tried to sleep in the crowded room, the combined body heat the only blessing in the mass of stinking prisoners. He was awake long before dawn and watched as the light crept through the slats of the wooden shutters to fall on the faces of his fellow prisoners. He had been locked alone in a dungeon for almost a year and these people were the first he had seen apart from his jailers. Slowly he looked around the room. Suddenly his eyes opened in surprise and confusion as he recognised the bedraggled woman curled into a corner, Her hair was a mess but the colour was unmistakable. Khoury got to his feet and walked across the room before falling to his knees before her.

'Lady Jennifer,' he said quietly, 'Jennifer of Orange, is it truly you?'

The woman opened her eyes and stared at the unkempt man before her.

'Do I know you?' she asked weakly.

'We met once,' said Khoury, 'in Acre. I was asking your husband for aid and I knocked you over.'

The woman smiled as she recalled the meeting.

'I remember,' she whispered lifting her hand to touch his face. 'You are the Hospitaller Knight.'

'I was,' said Khoury. 'Now I am destitution itself, hoping for forgiveness from God.'

'Why, what have you done?'

'I know not but am sure he has a plan for me. How are you here?'

'I was sent to Tripoli by my loving husband,' she sneered. 'But the Mamluks had other ideas.'

'Are you alright?'

'I have been better,' she said.

Khoury moved closer and lifted a strand of hair from across her face.

'Did they hurt you?'

'You don't want to know what they did to me,' she said, her voice breaking.

Khoury pulled her in to his embrace and she sobbed against his chest.

'Be strong, Lady,' he said. 'Something is happening and I believe we are to be ransomed.'

She looked up at him and used the heel of her hand to wipe away the tears.

'Do you think so?' she asked.

'I do,' he said, 'but there is still danger. There is much distrust between the two sides and often these things go wrong, You must be strong and hold out until the deal is done.'

'I have no more strength to give,' she said. 'They have taken everything.'

'Then I will be your strength,' he said. 'From now you must stay by my side. I will protect you the best I can and though ultimately your fate is in the hands of the Lord, until that day comes I will do everything to protect you.'

'You are very kind,' she said, wiping at the tears once more.

'On the contrary,' he said, 'all Knights need a Crusade, your safety will become mine. It is you who are saving me.'

The door swung open and a Mamluk guard threw in two skins of water. Fighting broke out amongst the men as they scrambled to reach the skins but Khoury strode amongst them and used his giant frame to pull them apart.

'Behave like the soldiers you once were,' he shouted, 'rather than the wretches you have become. There are women amongst us who thirst as much as we. They will drink first and the rest will be shared equally.'

He walked over to the three women and handed them one skin of water.

'Drink deep,' he said, 'for who knows when we will next have the opportunity?'

168

Chapter Eighteen

The Lands North of Acre

For the next twelve days, Misha led Garyn and Brother Martin through deserted valleys and hidden Wadis, keeping to the lesser trails known only to the local herdsmen of the area. Though the nights were cold, they made good time as the clear skies ensured good visibility. Slowly the terrain became greener as they neared the mountains and soon they were within the thick forests that covered the Jabahl Bahra region. Finally Misha reined in her horse and dismounted, indicating the others to do the same.

'The Castle is less than an hour's ride that way,' she said, 'but from here we will walk. Do you have any coins.'

'I do,' said Brother Martin, 'why?'

'There is a village down near the river and I know a family there. Their son is a goatherd and for a price he will watch our horses while we are away.'

'Won't they be Ismailis?'

'They are but like all such peoples, the poor are kept so by the rich. They have nothing and hold no such allegiance to the Hashashin.'

The Monk nodded and retrieved a purse from beneath his robe.

'Two coins,' said Misha, 'one for each day we are away. If we are not back by then, we never will be.' She took the silver and disappeared down the hill.

'Do you think she will return?' asked Garyn.

'I do,' said the Monk. 'Come, we should hide within the thickets.'

Hours passed and Garyn fell asleep against the trunk of a tree before eventually being woken by a gentle kick against his leg. He jumped up instantly, surprised to see Misha back along with a boy about half her age.

'Misha,' he said, 'I never heard you coming.'

'No,' she said simply, 'you wouldn't. This is the boy I spoke of.'

'What's his name?' asked the Monk.

'His name is no concern of yours,' said Misha. 'Just know that he will wait here until dawn the day after tomorrow. That gives us the remains of this night as well as tomorrow to retrieve what you seek. Eat what you can now and travel lightly. We will have to walk through the day to be there by nightfall tomorrow but there are paths I know that will keep us hidden. In case we are seen, you will wear these.' She threw them each a white thawb, the dress of the desert Arabs.

'What use are these?' asked the Monk. 'If we are challenged our skin alone will betray our race.'

'They are intended to deceive distant eyes only,' she said. 'If we are challenged then all will be lost anyway. We will walk quickly and keep to the lesser paths. Hopefully any who see us will be of a similar mind of this boy's village and pay us no heed.'

'And if we are seen by one of the Hashashin?' asked Garyn.

'Then we are already dead,' said Misha. 'Now, strip away your heavy western clothing and leave your swords behind.'

'Won't we need weapons?'

'You will not get an opportunity to use a sword, she said, 'Knives will be adequate. Now hurry, we need to leave soon if we are to reach Al Kahf by nightfall tomorrow.'

Ten minutes later they left the horses behind them and started up the steep slopes leading toward the higher mountains.

Twenty miles away, a force of a hundred Knights and two hundred men at arms also camped within the trees though relied on force rather than subterfuge to protect them from any enemies. Sir John had brought his column from Acre and they now waited patiently near to Wadi al Ayun for the exchange of prisoners to take place. Representatives of both sides had made contact and the arrangements had been made for dawn a few hours later in a nearby clearing.

As the sun rose Sir John of Cambridge sat shivering on his horse, waiting for the sun's warmth to penetrate the trees above. The clearing before him was empty but as the darkness fell away he could see a line of kneeling prisoners along the forest edge, each with a Mamluk swordsman directly behind them. From amongst the trees two riders emerged and rode to the centre of the clearing.

Sir John looked along the line of bedraggled prisoners and soon made out the red hair of his wife hanging down to the floor before her bowed head. For a second his heart seemed to miss a beat as memories of better times came flooding back, but he soon put aside his thoughts and reminded himself of his true goal and the risky actions that were about to unfold before him.

'Is everything ready?' he asked the Knight at his side.

'Exactly as you ordered, Sire,' said Sir Bennet.

'Good,' said Sir John, 'now let's get this done.' He spurred his horse gently and both men rode forward to meet the Mamluk riders waiting in the centre of the clearing.

'Salaam,' said one of the Mamluks when they finally faced each other.

'Well met,' said the Knight, 'I am Sir John of Cambridge, Castellan of Acre. I come in peace under God to retrieve our people from your custody.'

'You have brought the asking price?' asked the Mamluk.

'We have,' said Sir John and nodded to Sir Bennet. The Knight lifted a hessian sack from his saddle and passed it to the second Mamluk. The warrior opened the bag and ran his hand through the pile of golden coins inside.

'Do you wish to count it?' asked Sir John.

'That won't be necessary,' said the first warrior. 'I will take your word as a Christian Knight.'

'Then let the exchange take place,' said Sir John. 'Release our people.'

The Mamluk turned to give the signal but before he could speak, an arrow flew from the trees behind the prisoners and, thudded into the side of Sir John's horse. The animal whinnied in pain and reared up, throwing the unsuspecting Knight to the floor before galloping away with blood spurting from its pierced lung.

'Treachery,' screamed Sir Bennet drawing his sword, 'your words are those of the devil himself.'

'Wait,' shouted the Mamluk, raising his arm but before he could say anything else the Knight lunged forward and smashed his blade down into the warrior's neck, carving deep into the man's chest.

With a scream of 'Allah Akbar' the second Mamluk threw himself onto the back of Sir Bennett with a drawn knife but the Knight's chain mail saved him from the killing blow. Both men fell to the floor and Sir John stamped on the Mamluk's head, crushing his skull beneath his heel. He turned to his men who were milling around at the edge of the clearing, unsure what to do.

'Archer's,' he screamed, 'take out the executioners. Men at arms, advance. Rescue the prisoners.'

Immediately the air was thick with arrows as Sir John's men ran beneath the volley toward the enemy. Mamluk warriors ran from the trees to meet them head on and some of the executioners wielded their weapons to kill the hostages. All along the line, bodies fell forward with cleaved skulls or opened throats but many escaped the slaughter as their would-be killers fell to the volley of arrows from Sir John's hidden archers.

'Sire are you all right?' shouted Sir Bennett above the sound of battle.

'Nothing hurt but my pride,' answered Sir John. 'To the fray, brother, the hostage's lives are in our hands.' The two Knights joined the assault and both sides fought a bloody battle beneath the rising morning sun.

Across the clearing, Khoury leaned forward as his executioner fell across his body with an arrow lodged in his throat. For a moment he lay confused but his instincts kicked in as he realised what was happening. He looked across to Lady Jennifer and saw her executioner had also fallen but they were still at risk from the surrounding Mamluks engaged in the heat of battle. He reached out with his bound hands and picked up the dead warrior's knife.

'My Lady,' he shouted, 'take this and cut my bonds. Quickly.'
'But...'
'Do it,' screamed Khoury.

Lady Jennifer took the knife and sawed across the thin rope binding his wrists. The knife was razor sharp and the bonds fell away easily. Khoury took the knife and cut the ropes around his feet. Almost immediately a warrior saw the threat and ran at him with a curved blade but Khoury was a seasoned warrior himself and threw his body at the Mamluk's feet, causing him to fall to the ground. Immediately he grabbed the man's head and forced it past breaking point until he heard a satisfying snap. He grabbed the knife again and cut Jennifer's bonds, knowing full well they had to get out of there. A second wave of Mamluks ran from the trees, cutting down the remaining prisoners as they came.

'This way,' shouted Khoury and dragged Jennifer into the nearby trees. Together they ran on, leaving the battle behind them and crashing through the undergrowth without purpose, just desperate to get away.

Behind them the battle raged on as each side poured their fury on the other and for a while it looked like the Mamluks would triumph until a trumpet heralded the arrival of Sir John's Knights thundering from the trees. Within moments the battle turned and any remaining Mamluks either fell or fled, leaving their wounded behind them. The foot soldiers raced after them but soon returned and after despatching the enemy wounded with their blades, gathered on the battlefield around their leader.

Sir John's heart was racing but more than that, he knew this was the moment he had been waiting for. He had to act immediately and grasp the opportunity before him.

'Brothers in arms,' he shouted, 'this day you have witnessed what we long feared, that a Mamluk's word is worth nought but scorn.' He paused as the men roared their agreement. 'We trusted them,' he continued,' believed their promise that there would be fair and equitable exchange, emptied our treasuries to pay the price of our brothers' lives yet the greed of the devil filled their eyes and treachery filled their hearts. Never was there intention to use force of arms but you saw with your own eyes as they cut my horse from beneath me before executing the prisoners.'

The men shouted in anger as he continued.

'Almost a hundred innocents lie on the field, their throats opened by Mamluk blades. Those few not killed have been dragged away to heaven knows what fate, including the Lady whom I thought returned. We have been wronged and I would ask this. Do we sit back and allow them their victory or do we do unto them what they tried to do unto us?'

'Retribution,' screamed the men, being carried away with the passion of the moment. 'Pursue them,' shouted some, 'kill every last one,' shouted others.

Sir John let the frenzy build before once more holding up his hand.

'I share your anger brothers and agree they should feel our wrath. Not a day's ride from here is one of their strongholds, a place never conquered and filled with gold. They do not expect assault and with stealth I feel we could take the gate by surprise and wreak God's vengeance inside. What say you?' Cry over our dead and return to Acre as beaten children or show the heathen why Christians will never fall to the devil?'

Again the men roared their approval until Sir John lifted his hand for the last time.

'Then the choice is made. Today we bury our dead and pay tribute to the fallen but tonight we travel through darkness and fall upon the gates of Al-Kahf with the dawn. Girder your hearts, fellow brothers for tomorrow we strike with the Lord's wrath.'

The men started cheering again before being dispersed by the sergeants. Sir John walked over to his mortally wounded horse and knelt beside him. He talked gently to the steed as he smoothed its neck.

'I am sorry, old friend,' he said, 'but this is where our journey ends.' Quietly he slit the animal's throat and held its head as the life blood drained away. When the deed was done he stood and walked over to Sir Bennett. At the forest edge an archer stood alone, watching the two men.

'Has he been paid?' asked Sir John.

'A purse of silver, as you ordered.'

'Can he be trusted to keep his silence?'

'He is a good archer,' said Sir Bennet, 'but a commoner nonetheless. Who can say?'

'Then you must ensure that the secret remains between us two only,' said Sir John. 'If the men find out that the first arrow was our own, then it is over.'

'Leave it to me,' said Sir Bennet, 'he has seen his last sunrise.'

Sir John nodded and walked away. The subterfuge had worked and apart from Sir Bennet, his trusted friend since boyhood, nobody would ever know the arrow that killed his horse was released from a Christian bow.

Twenty miles away, Garyn, Misha and Brother Martin lay at the edge of the cliff overlooking Al-Kahf Castle. The heavily wooded slopes stretched down to the valley floor before rising sharply again to form a large spur at the centre of the valley, a rocky escarpment joining seamlessly with the base of the castle walls above. The cliffs on all sides were sheer and un-scalable and from their position, Garyn could see no way up to the smooth walls of the castle.

'Where is the entrance?' he asked.

'There is a path that winds its way around the escarpment,' answered Misha. 'The only access is through a cave at the base of the mountain and it is well defended. The path is wide enough only for two horses at a time and all the way up, guards are posted in defended positions, even at night. The Castle has never been taken and is considered impregnable.'

'Then how are we to gain access?'

'Our route does not lie that way, but via a direction that no man has ever taken before.'

'And where is this route?'

Misha pointed toward the river at the base of the escarpment. A line of people took turns to fill buckets of water from a pool in the river before disappearing into the nearby undergrowth.

'The garrison maintains full water chambers at all times,' she said 'filled by a train of slaves on a daily basis. Should they come under siege they have adequate water to sustain a long defence. The entrance to the cave lies hidden beyond those trees and a pool has been dug to enable the slaves to fill the buckets easily. You can see the water is calm and clear.'

'Are you suggesting we try to pass ourselves off as one of the water bearers?'

'No, you will be spotted immediately.' She pointed further along the river. 'Look downstream and tell me what you see where the river bends.'

'I see nothing except water,' said Brother Martin.

'Look again,' said Misha.

'The water is grey where it has eaten into the bank at the river bend,' said Garyn.

'It is,' said Misha. 'That is because it is fed from a small rivulet of filth that seeps down a fissure in the rock face. It pools at the bottom before being washed away by the river.'

'Human waste?' asked Garyn.

'The product of the Castle latrines,' she said. 'Nobody defends the fissure for it is covered with the slime of body waste and is considered impossible to climb.'

'Wait,' said Garyn. 'Are you saying you expect us to climb through Muslim shit to access this Castle?'

'It is the only way,' said Misha, 'there is no other access.'

'I will not do it,' said Garyn.

'It is either this way or we return to Acre,' said Misha.

'But we don't even know if it is possible,' said Brother Martin, 'you said that no man has ever taken this route before.'

'And as far as I know it is true. However, I know of one who descended from the castle this way.'

'Did he live?' asked Garyn.

Misha stared at him without answering. Finally Garyn realised the implications and his eyes widened in understanding.

'You,' he said. 'It was you who climbed down the fissure.'

Misha nodded.

'I was one of the water slaves for a year,' she said, 'imprisoned by the Hashashin for a falsehood spread by an enemy of my family. I was determined to escape or die trying. I managed to climb down but was still on foot as I ran through the night. I know now they would have caught me eventually but Ahmed Mubarak found me and hid me from my pursuers. I owe him my life.'

'And that is why you serve him?'

'It is.'

'From one form of slavery to another.'

'I am no slave, I am a servant.'

'Is there a difference?'

'As wide as the Hom's gap,' said Misha.

'So,' interrupted Brother Martin. 'How do we go about this?'

'At nightfall, anyone outside the walls retreats up the hill and the gates are barred within the cave as well as the castle walls. Once they are gone, it will be easy to approach the fissure unseen. The crack has many handholds and ledges but is very slippery. You must leave your robe behind and climb as light as possible.'

'What about tools for digging?' asked Garyn.

'You will need no tools,' said Misha, 'the castle is built on solid rock. The Mountain man is buried in a surface tomb and covered with a simple slab. Remove the slab and the body will be exposed.'

Brother Martin looked at Garyn.

'What do you think,' he asked.

'Is there no other way?'

Misha shook her head.

'Filth can be washed away,' she said, 'the responsibility for your brother's death would remain on your soul forever.'

Garyn stared at her as her words sunk in.

'You are right,' he said finally, 'and I am ashamed of my hesitation. The two of you have risked your lives for me for no return, yet I am the one to doubt my resolve. You have my gratitude, Misha and I will undertake this task with the support of God and strength of my family behind me.'

'Then take the opportunity to rest,' said Misha. 'There is an hour until darkness and then you must climb quickly. If you are caught you will die but if you descend unseen we will need as much of the night as possible to get back to the horses.'

A cough from behind them made them fall to the floor in fear and crawl into the nearby bushes.

'Have we been discovered?' hissed Garyn.

'Shhh,' said Misha and crawled forward alongside Brother Martin.

Within a few moments two people stumbled through the trees toward them, a large bearded man, supporting a red haired woman. Both were bedraggled and were obviously on the point of collapse through exhaustion.

'A rest,' said the woman weakly to her helper, 'please, I beseech thee.'

'A moment only,' gasped the man. 'We have to keep going.'

Brother Martin grabbed the arm of Misha in their hiding place.

'In the name of the Lord,' he whispered, 'they are Christian souls. We have to help them.'

'Wait,' hissed Misha, 'your goal is the cross of the Christ. If you are distracted now, you will fall short.'

Brother Martin paused before answering.

'No,' he said, 'you are wrong. You too were once desperate for help and were delivered by God. If Ahmed Mubarak had turned his back on your plight you would be within those very walls with only servitude your future. We will do what we can.'

Before she could answer, he stood up and walked out of the thicket. Misha paused before joining him, as did Garyn. Immediately the bedraggled man turned and crouched into a defensive stance, an obvious sign of training. Brother Martin held up his hand to placate him.

'Be calm, Brother,' said the Monk, 'I am a friend and offer only aid.'

'Who are you?' hissed the man?

'My name is Brother Martin,' said the Monk, 'Who are you and what are you doing here deep in an enemy's stronghold.'

The man looked between the three as the woman stepped behind him.

'My name is Sir Abdul Khoury,' he said, 'Knight Hospitaller. This is the Lady Jennifer of Orange, wife of Sir John of Cambridge, Castellan of Acre. We escaped from Mamluk captivity and are lost amongst these hills.'

The Monk's eyes widened in surprise at the revelation but stepped forward as the Lady Jennifer collapsed to the floor with exhaustion. Within moments they had her in the safety of the thicket and made them both as comfortable as possible. When she recovered, they shared what little water and food they had and both ex-prisoners ate hungrily until finally they had strength enough to tell their tale.

'I don't understand,' said Brother Martin when they were done, 'are you saying that Sir John is nearby?'

'He is,' said Khoury. 'It would seem he arranged an exchange for the hostages but was fooled by treachery.'

'But why did you not join him when you had the chance?' asked Garyn.

'At the time we just needed to escape. In the heat of the moment we lost our way and got separated from the battle. Since then we have wandered lost amongst this forest.'

'There is another reason,' said Jennifer.

All heads turned toward her.

'My husband is not what he seems to be,' she said, 'and holds no honour as a Knight. Even though I fear for my very life, I will never stand alongside him as his wife again. I believe he was responsible for my capture and the sight of me alive frustrates his ambition to marry into the court of England.'

'You don't know that to be true,' said Khoury.

'I do,' said Jennifer. 'You do not know what depths he is capable of.'

'There is another concern,' said Brother Martin. 'He knows of our quest and the fact he is here with a force of many men is surely no coincidence. I saw cunning in his eyes and wouldn't put it past him to try his own assault upon Al-Kahf.'

'What is so important within Al Kahf?' asked Khoury.

'Something I cannot share, Sir Knight,' said Brother Martin, 'but suffice to say many have died in its name. We hope to retrieve it in the name of God.'

Khoury nodded.

'I respect your privacy, Sire and will not ask again.'

'The thing is,' continued Brother Martin, 'we need to know what to do with you. Ordinarily we could have taken you to safety before continuing our quest but I fear if Sir John is so close we cannot put it off any longer.' He looked around the group before coming to a conclusion. 'What I propose is this. Misha, you will take our friends here back to the horses. Take them to the coast path and set them on the road to Acre. Once done your debt to us is paid and you are free to join your family.'

'No,' said Khoury, 'whatever it is you plan, I will offer my aid.'

'You are too weak,' answered the Monk, 'and besides, the journey back is still fraught with danger. Your skills may yet be needed to protect the Lady before you reach Acre.'

The Hospitaller Knight paused before nodding. It made sense.

'And what about you?' he asked.

'Garyn and I will finish what it is we came to do. If it is God's will that we fall, then so be it but we will not see you enslaved when so close to freedom.' He looked toward Garyn. 'Is this agreeable to you?'

Garyn nodded.

'It is the best course,' he said, 'and if we fail, then at least it will not be in vain. Pursue freedom, Sir Knight and if we never see you again, say a prayer in our name.'

'I will do that,' said Sir Khoury and got to his feet.

Misha also stood and helped Jennifer up.

'A few hours more,' she said, 'and we will reach the horses. One more effort and you will be on the road to safety.'

'May God go with you, my friends,' said Khoury and followed the women into the darkened forest.

Garyn watched them go before looking toward Brother Martin.

'Be calm, Garyn,' said the Monk, 'God is with us.'

The sky was already dark when they approached the bend of the river but they knew they were near due to the overwhelming stench. As their eyes got used to the darkness they followed the rivulet of filth up to the rock face and peered upward.

'I can see no further than the height of three men,' said Garyn.

'Put your trust in God, Garyn,' he said, 'the girl climbed down so it is possible.' Garyn started to take off his thawb.

'What are you doing?' asked the Monk.

'If I am going to do this, at least this way I won't be weighed down by shit laden clothes. Besides, when I return I will be immersing myself in that river and will need dry garb.'

'Good idea,' said the Monk, and started to disrobe.

'No,' said Garyn, grabbing his arm. 'You are not coming with me.'

'Don't be stupid,' said Brother Martin. 'The two of us will climb.'

'No,' said Garyn again, 'the task is mine and mine alone. You have already done more than could be expected of any man. This last stage holds the most risk of failure and I have no right to ask you to fall in my name.'

'Garyn, everything I have done so far has been of my own free will. I will not stand back now and cast you adrift. Besides, the chances are you will not be able to open that tomb alone.'

'That is a chance I have to take,' said Garyn. 'If it is too heavy to move then the chances are that two men would not be enough anyway. I have to do this, Brother Martin. I have travelled across the world in a quest to save my brother, relying on the goodwill of others. Now the time has come to prove my mettle and I will not risk your life any further. I will climb alone and would have no more argument. You stay down here and ensure we are not compromised. If I cannot move the slab, I will return immediately but in any event before the dawn. If I am not back by the time the sun rises, you must leave this place as fast as you can for I will have been captured and I do not know long I could withstand torture.'

'Garyn,' said the Monk eventually. 'When we set out I joined a young man on a fool's errand. Before me stands a man on his own righteous Crusade. Your father would be proud of you.'

Garyn nodded and threw the thawb over to the Monk. He tied the rope belt around his waist along with the pouch containing his knife and started the climb dressed only in his Braccae, the knee length undergarment made from fine wool.

The first touch of the slimy walls made him cringe and the smell was putrid but slowly, his hands sought out the next hand hold and he made his way up the cleft. Over and over again he gagged at the stench but his resolve was firm and within minutes he was out of sight of the Monk.

For the next hour he climbed, resting regularly and found the climb easier than he had expected. The higher he went the worse the smell became and he found himself scooping fresher waste from the ledges to obtain hand holds. On two occasions someone above emptied buckets down the fissure and he clamped his eyes and mouth shut as the contents splashed over the back of his head but each time he thought of his brother and continued the climb. Finally the darkness seemed to ease and he realised the moon's light was seeping down from above as he neared the top.

The sound of people talking made him stay inside the cleft for a long time, crouching on a ledge as he waited for the people to pass. Eventually the noises eased and he climbed up to peer over the wooden fence placed to stop people falling down the cleft.

Before him was a courtyard, enclosed on four sides by steep stone walls. Wooden buildings nestled against all four sides and Garyn could see candlelight through the slats. Misha had explained that the poorer classes lived here, and the Hashashin themselves lived within the inner stone keep. She had also told him that the tomb of Sinan lay in the next courtyard against the far wall but the huts in that area were occupied by the common soldiers of the Ismailis.

Slowly he made his way through the shadows and under the archway to the next yard. He paused as he took in the detail. Similar huts lined the walls and an open stable contained several horses covered in their blankets. Sounds of talking filtered through the shutters but he crept onward slowly, taking care not to scare the animals. The lack of guards was surprising but he guessed that they were so secure in the safety of the castle, they never saw the need for guards within the walls itself.

Finally the tomb lay before him and his heart sank as he saw the size of the task. The hardness of the bedrock meant that those responsible for the internment of Rashid ad-Din Sinan had built the tomb upward rather than dig down. The simple base had been constructed with tightly fitted stone blocks to waist height and a single ornately carved slab formed the lid. Though the tomb itself was simple, either side was guarded by life sized stone sculptures of prancing horses.

He ran forward and tried to slide the slab aside but it failed to budge and his heart sank as he realised he would not be able to move it alone. Over and over again he strained against the rock without success and finally sat back amidst the shadows as he considered his options. Even if he climbed back down and brought up the Monk, he doubted even two men could move the slab but there was no way he could give up now. He stared at the tomb in frustration. For a moment the clouds parted and the tomb was lit by the moonlight, giving the stone horses an eerie life of their own and suddenly Garyn had the answer.

As soon as the courtyard fell dark again, he hurried back to the stables and finding a coil of rope, and a harness, led the horse back across the yard. He secured the rope around the lid and tied it to the horse's harness before holding its head and encouraging the beast forward.

'Come on,' he whispered gently, 'this way.'

The horse shuffled forward and took the strain but again without any success.

'Come on,' said Garyn again and encouraged the horse forward. Over and over again they strained together and finally Garyn's heart leapt as the sound of sliding stone on stone reached his ears.

'That's it,' he whispered, 'again.'

Suddenly the horse lurched and the stone slab slid forward to teeter on the edge of the base. Garyn eased the horse back before running to the tomb. Deep inside he could see a shrouded body and though his heart raced, he knew he had little time. He reached in and searched the tomb, running his hands alongside the corpse but found nothing. For a few seconds he was devastated. Surely Masun hadn't been lying all those months ago? Slowly realisation dawned. If this important man had indeed been buried with the cross, it wouldn't have just been thrown in the tomb without thought, it would have been laid within the shroud as a burial gift.

He took a deep breath and drew his knife before leaning in and cutting through the remains of the long dried fabric. The shroud fell open and Garyn ripped the cloth apart revealing the naked body of the long dead Sultan. The man's skin was shrivelled and blackened and the skin had rotted back on his skull, revealing the exposed death grin typical of all long dead corpses. For a second, Garyn thought his heart would stop in fear but then his eyes fell to the man's chest and he saw the prize he so desperately craved.

He picked up the relic and lifted the thick golden chain over the corpse's skull. He wiped away the dust and for a moment stared as the gold surface shone in the moonlight. The sheen was mesmerising but more than this, the image of a sliver of timber embedded into the vertical bar of the golden crucifix made him almost forget to breathe. If it was authentic then this small piece of wood had been touched by the body of Christ himself.

Garyn wanted nothing more than to fall to his knees there and then and pray to the Lord above but he knew he had to get out of there. So far he had been lucky and it was only a matter of time before he was discovered.

Leaving the tomb open, he left the horse behind and made his way quickly back to the first courtyard. Silently he climbed over the fence and back down the cleft. Climbing up was hard but climbing down was even harder and several times he almost fell. Finally he reached the floor and stood gasping for breath as Brother Martin approached.

'Garyn,' he said with excitement, 'thank the Lord. You have been gone hours, are you alright?'

'I am,' said Garyn.

'Did you find it?'

Garyn reached into the waistband of his Braccae and retrieved the cross.

'I did,' he said, 'and it is even more beautiful than we expected.' He handed over the cross before brushing past the Monk and walking quickly away.

'Where are you going?' hissed Brother Martin.

'Where do you think?' asked Garyn, 'the river.'

'Be quick,' said the Monk, 'for we have to be gone as soon as we can.'

'I will be as quick as I am able,' said Garyn, 'but I have to rid myself of this filth. I would rather face a Hashashin blade than bear this stench a moment longer.'

The Monk nodded and as Garyn disappeared, he did what Garyn had wanted to do in the castle. Holding the cross to his chest, he fell to his knees and prayed.

Chapter Nineteen

The Forests of Jabahl Bahra

Since the battle with the Mamluks at Wadi al Ayun, Sir John's force had made good ground through the forests toward Al Kahf. His guides were the best available and they knew the routes well. The men were motivated and up for the fight but despite this he knew they were not equipped for a siege and success depended on surprise and good fortune. Those who knew the castle told him it was impossible to breach its walls but a surprise attack at the cave gates could catch the defenders unawares and leave the way open to the castle above. Sir John had his doubts but knew he had to see it for himself.

The dawn approached, though the darkness within the trees still made the column nervous as they made their way through enemy territory and took up offensive positions. Two scouts approached and reined in their horses alongside Sir John.

'Sire, our men overlook the castle,' said one. 'The gates are still locked but will be opened with the dawn. If we can be in place by then, the time will be opportune.'

'How far away is it?' asked the Knight.

'An hour's march.'

'Then delay no more,' said the Knight, 'and lead us there with all haste.' He turned to Sir Bennett. 'Order the men to leave their packs. From now we travel lightly bearing arms only. If we are routed, our rendezvous will be here.'

Sir Bennett carried out his orders and within minutes, the column was a frenzy of activity as they made ready for war. Soon they were formed up again, each man carrying his weapon of choice. The archers ran forward with the scouts to deploy at advantageous positions above the castle, while the mounted Knights took a circuitous route to approach the gateway unseen. The foot soldiers waited patiently, knowing their skills would only be required should the horsemen be successful. Once the gate was taken however, their violence would know no bounds and already bloodied steel would once more shine with the glaze of Mamluk blood.

Brother Martin and Garyn ran through the woods back toward the village, where they had left the horses. They knew the animals would be gone, for Misha would have given them to the Hospitaller Knight and the Lady but the Monk still had his purse and they hoped they could buy a horse from the village. They stopped for a rest and after they caught their breath, Garyn asked to see the cross once more. The Monk handed it over and watched as the boy examined the artefact in detail.

'It is truly beautiful,' he said.

'Which part, Garyn,' asked the Monk.

Garyn looked up, confused.

'All of it,' he said. 'Why do you ask?'

'No reason,' said the Monk, 'but I have seen great men fall to avarice when faced with such treasure. The gold and jewels are indeed wonders to behold but are courtiers only to the true treasure.'

Garyn looked again at the cross. The solid gold crucifix was heavy in his hands and the jewels sparkled like the night stars yet always his eyes were drawn by the dull brown of the wooden sliver at its centre.

'Fear not Brother Martin,' said Garyn. 'To my eyes the golden glow is but mud compared to the sunlight that emits from the heart of the piece.' He handed it back to the Monk before continuing. 'Now you must tell me something.'

'Go on,' said the Monk.

'You are a man of God,' said Garyn, 'and you hold in your hands one of the holiest relics in Christendom. Your heart must be bursting with fervour yet deep inside you must know I intend to trade this bauble for the life of my brother. Does this not cause you angst?'

The Monk stared at the boy before answering.

'You are growing into an astute young man, Garyn,' he said, 'and yes, you are correct. This relic belongs in a place of God and the Pope himself would send armies to reclaim it should he know of its location. The Pious man within me demands I take it immediately to Rome and place it before the Pontiff. Christ's glory demands this shard, this beauteous splinter soaked with his very blood is revered at the very centre of the Christian world. Until I found out what we were seeking I held no such doubts but now we have it within our hands, my heart is torn in two. I am nothing if not an honest man, Garyn and I will admit to doubt. On the one hand, my pledge demands I see out my debt to you and your family but does my honour outweigh my debt to Christ? Is honour no more than pride, which in itself is a mortal sin?'

'Your words concern me, Brother Martin,' said Garyn. 'My brother's life hangs in the balance and you hold the only means of my ever seeing him alive again. If you feel this way, how do I know you will not change allegiance at the last and deny me the outcome I seek?'

'Truth be told, Garyn, I'm not sure how I feel at the moment but what I do know is this. I know that many would benefit from this gift and the spiritual lives of many outweigh the physical life of one. The truth of the matter is this, the cross belongs in the hands of a church, not the treasury of one Knight. The glory of Christ belongs to all men, both Knave and King.'

After a few moment's hesitation he handed the cross back to Garyn.

'Here,' he said, 'take it into your keeping. I have lived a long life, Garyn and though I finally chose the way of Christ, the early years were not ones of virtue. I have killed the innocent and fornicated with whores. In my time I have stolen, lied and cheated and though I finally turned to the cloth, I fear the darker side of my soul lies just beneath the surface. This cross is the means to riches and fame for those with lower morals and at this moment, I feel I am a mere scoundrel faced with temptation.'

Garyn took the cross in silence.

'We should be going,' said the Monk, 'dawn is upon us and the Hashashin will find the opened tomb at any moment.'

Garyn nodded and both men set out once more, setting a fierce pace to distance themselves from the castle.

Five miles away, Sir John of Cambridge lay above the valley of Al Kahf Castle. His men were deployed and his Knights were poised at the forest edge. The plan was simple, he had several men at arms hidden in the undergrowth near the cave gate as well as two dozen archers. As soon as the entrance opened, his archers would slay any horsemen that emerged while his men at arms would slay the gatekeepers. Though they were few in number, their role was only to engage the enemy as long as possible until the Knights arrived and charged through to the castle path. It was a risky strategy but with good fortune, Sir John calculated his horsemen could be at the upper gates before any alarm was raised. Once there, and with the support of the following force of foot soldiers, they would wreak havoc amongst the garrison while he sought the cross.

'Are the men ready?' asked Sir John.

'They are,' said Sir Bennett. 'The gates will open any second now.'

'Then gird your loins,' said Sir John. 'History beckons.'

For several minutes they waited but still the gates remained closed. Down below, he could see the upturned faces of his hidden soldiers looking to him in confusion. The sun was well up and yet the gates remained closed.

'What trickery is this?' asked Sir John, 'surely our presence is not known?'

'It can't be,' said Sir Bennett, 'We were silent in our approach.'

A noise behind them made them turn and they saw one of the scouts running toward them.

'What's happening?' demanded Sir John, 'you told me the gates opened at dawn.'

'And indeed they do Sire,' said the scout, gasping for breath, 'but there have been developments.'

'Explain.'

'Sire, my men have been watching the castle from the high bluff and since dawn there has been much activity within its walls. As soon as the sun rose, we saw the glint of mirror messages being sent from their towers and have seen answers from distant hills. Something is wrong and though we know not what causes their angst, the walls are being manned with defenders as we speak.'

'Then we are discovered,' said Sir Bennet.

'I don't think so,' said the scout, 'we have also seen them preparing a column of horsemen on the upper slopes. If they feared a siege they would keep their men inside their defences. It seems they are sending a patrol somewhere but fear an attack.'

'Then the gates will soon be open,' said Sir John, 'the day may still be won.'

'No Sire,' said the scout. 'Though you may take the gate, the garrison is on full alert and you will not get halfway up the slopes. Hashashin archers are the best there are and they already man the walls.'

Sir John looked across at Sir Bennett who stared back at him in silence.

'Withdraw the men,' he said eventually, 'I will not send them to their deaths with no chance of victory.'

Sir Bennett issued the orders and a messenger ran down the hill to pass on the message.

'What now?' he asked.

'Retreat to the rendezvous and prepare a defensive position,' said Sir John, 'until we know what is happening, we will take no chances. This may quieten down in a few days and we can try again.' He turned to the scout. 'You, I want to know what is going on. I don't care how, just get me some information before nightfall.'

'I will try, Sire,' said the man and disappeared into the trees once more.

Within the hour the Christian column was making its way at full speed back to the glade where they had left their equipment. Sir Bennett organised a defensive perimeter while the rest of the patrol set about building a temporary defence against attack. All day the men cut the smaller trees and lay them across any approaches to the camp. Finally they manned their makeshift defences and though it was no palisade, it would certainly stop a cavalry charge. The camp settled into silence and night approached without event.

'A rider approaches,' said one of the guards and Sir Bennett stood as he recognised the scout.

'Let him through,' he said and a few minutes later the scout stood before Sir John.

'Report,' said the Knight.

'Sire,' said the scout, 'we watched the patrol leave the castle in great strength and once they had left, the gates were secured once more. Nobody has been allowed in or out since.'

'Did you find out why?'

'Not at first so we followed the patrol.'

'And?'

'They rode into a nearby village with a great anger. Many villagers were beaten and some even killed. Their cries echoed around the forest but there was no mercy and their wrath only eased when they moved on to the next village.'

'Why would they do this?'

'One of my men crept forward and questioned a dying man. It would seem someone had entered the castle overnight and robbed the tomb of one of their ancestors. Some of the villagers had been there the previous day trading supplies and the Hashashin suspect one stayed behind to carry out the deed. It is the only possible way.'

Sir John's eyes widened at the news.

'You say a tomb has been robbed,' he said, 'did he say the name on the tomb?'

'Yes, Sire, the tomb of the mountain man.'

Sir John looked at Sir Bennett, his mind racing at the news.

'Sir Bennett, rally the men,' he said, 'we leave with the dawn.'

'But the castle,' said Sir Bennett, 'do you not want to stay and see if circumstances change?'

'They have already changed,' said Sir John, 'and possibly for the better. It wasn't Muslim hands that desecrated that tomb but Christian and if I am not mistaken, those responsible are headed for Acre even as we speak.'

Chapter Twenty

The Deserts North of Acre

Garyn and Brother Martin walked along the paths near the coast, their garb dirty from the dusty road. They had retrieved their clothes from the hiding place where they had left them but couldn't risk approaching a village to buy a horse due to the increased Mamluk patrols in the area. For ten days and nights they stumbled along the hidden paths, hiding in thickets during the day and making what headway they could at night. Weak from hunger they spent the last of each day's light scouring the shoreline for whatever they could find, often prizing out the flesh of pool shellfish to be eaten raw. Sometimes they used the dark of night to steal whatever they could from local houses or planted fields, before stumbling on again to put some miles between them and the Jabahl Bahra.

Brother Martin looked over at Garyn. Despite the boy's resolve the Monk knew he was suffering badly. His feet were covered with bleeding blisters and his skin was raw where his sweat sodden clothing rubbed remorselessly against skin un-toughened by the rigour of warmer climes. They had once more spent the night walking south and it was only an hour or so before the dawn was due to break.

'Enough for the night, Garyn,' he said eventually. 'We have made good ground and need to find somewhere to lie up.'

Garyn didn't answer but the Monk saw a hint of relief on his face.

'Come, he said, we will go down to the shore.'

'Why?' asked Garyn.

'Those sores will become infected if left untreated.'

'And I suppose you have an apothecary waiting upon the sands?' asked Garyn.

'We have no need of false potions,' said the Monk. 'Nature will provide what we need.'

'Like what?'

'Salt water,' said the Monk. 'You need to bathe your wounds.'

'Since when does sea water heal?'

'It may not heal but it should stop any infection taking hold,' answered the Monk. They turned down the slope of the hill and headed toward the shoreline, walking along the narrow strip of sand, seeking a sheltered place to rest.

'This will have to do,' said the Monk as they came across some weather blown bracken. 'There's a stream over there, you strip and bathe in the sea while I wash our clothes.'

'Why don't I just wear my clothes in the sea?'

'Because when they dry off, they will be covered with salt and that will irritate your skin even more. No, you bathe and wash your sores well. When done, come back here and get dressed. The clothes will be wet but the sun rises soon and we will dry off quick enough.'

Garyn nodded silently too exhausted to argue further. Twenty minutes later he returned, shivering in the morning air.

'Here said the Monk, I have rung them out as much as I can but they are still wet. You will be cold for a while but that will pass. As soon as you are warm, crawl into the bracken and pull the leaves down over you, they will protect you from the sun.'

'What about you?' asked Garyn.

'I will join you shortly,' said the Monk. 'I need to see to my own hygiene and I think there may be fish in the stream. I will try to catch us a meal.'

'Do you need any help?'

'It is a one man job, Garyn. You get some sleep and I will join you soon enough.'

Garyn nodded, his eyes already heavy from exhaustion.

'How much further, Brother Martin?' he asked.

'Not far now,' said the Monk, 'we are almost there.'

Garyn smiled and after getting into his wet clothes, crawled into the hiding place.

The Monk sat for an age, knowing full well they were not even half way to Acre and the boy's injuries were holding them back. He sat pondering everything they had been through and knew if it carried on like this, neither would survive the journey. Though he had a commitment to Garyn, he also had a commitment to the cross. Finally he made a decision and picking up Garyn's pack, walked away from the sleeping boy, heading inland without as much as a backward glance.

'Sire we have news,' said the Scout.

'Sir John stood up from the camp fire,' in anticipation.

'What news?' he asked.

191

'Two men in western garb were chased from a farm west of here a few nights ago. They were stealing crops but the farmer caught them in the act.'

'Where are they now?'

'I don't know Sire but it is said they were last seen heading south along the coast.'

'It must be them,' said Sir John, his excitement rising. His patrols had spent the last ten days scouring the country between Jabahl Bahra and Acre, questioning everyone they found about any strangers in the area. Ordinarily the countryside would be too dangerous for such activity but further east, Longshanks' formidable army was busy engaging the Halqas of Sultan Baibaars and the resulting tensions meant the Mamluk presence in the immediate area was minimal.

'Send your men in pursuit,' ordered Sir John and if you find them, bring me their heads as evidence but let me make one thing clear, you will bring all their possessions back with you unopened. Do this and I will make you a rich man but if I think you have cast your eyes on that forbidden to you, then I will hang you from the nearest tree along with your comrades. Is that clear?'

'Yes, Sire,' said the scout.

'Then be gone,' said the Knight and turned to Sir Bennett.

'Place guards at all approaches to Acre. Send word to the city, they are to send out foot patrols to intercept any approaching the walls. I want a ring of steel surrounding the city.'

'Yes Sire,' said Sir Bennett.

'Once the cordon is made,' continued Sir John, 'I want you to take the Knights and run them down like the thieves they are. Our fortune has changed, friend and our future just took a step upward. If they possess what I think they do, a place at the court of Henry awaits us both. This is a chance too great to miss, failure is not an option.'

'Then rest assured I will succeed or die trying.'

'The sentiment is appreciated, Sir Bennett though unnecessary. They are but a boy and an old Monk. What resistance could they possibly offer?'

'I hear the Monk once wore the spurs of Knighthood.'

'A mercenary, no more,' said Sir John, 'and his days have long passed. No, once they have been found they will be swatted like the flies they are and we can pursue our destiny unhindered. Rouse the men, Sir Bennett, the final stretch is before us.'

Garyn stood at the side of the thicket staring at the line of footprints disappearing across the sand. He had slept most of the day through and the sun was already setting in the west. At first he was confused, as it was obvious the Monk had not taken shelter at all and there was no sign of him. Thinking the worst he ran back to the thicket and searched for his pack but it had gone, along with the cross. Garyn's heart sank. The Monk's words of doubt days earlier had finally turned to reality and he must have succumbed to temptation. Brother Martin had deserted Garyn and taken the cross with him.

Garyn slumped to his knees in fatigue. After everything he had been through, it was over. His wounds meant he could hardly walk, he was in a strange country with no food and the only man able to help had deserted him when he needed him most. For an age he sat in the sand until finally he stood and started walking south. He had no idea what he was going to do, but the one thing he wouldn't do was give up.

Brother Martin walked for a day and a night, always heading south and at first his mind was set, he would travel to Rome and present the cross to the church but the further he went, the greater the doubts became until finally he sat at a forest edge above a tiny fishing village. No matter what the importance of the relic to Christianity, his heart was heavy for though he had the death of many men on his hands, the fact that he had abandoned the boy stabbed at his heart with more pain than the sharpest blade. Silently he prayed for forgiveness but no matter how hard he tried, he couldn't reconcile the boy's certain death with the safety of the Relic. In the cold light of day, the cross was gold and wood. Put against flesh and bone, surely there was no comparison. Over the years many men had died for this relic and he would not be responsible for any more. He stood up and stared down at the village. The Devil had tempted him with avarice and for a while he had succumbed but now the Lord had made the way clear. One soul was greater than all the gold in Christendom and he knew what he had to do. Without a backward glance, he strode down into the village, hoping deep in his heart that he hadn't left it too late.

Garyn ran through the trees, gasping for breath as the whip-like branches cut across his face. For three days he had wandered alone, half-starved and light-headed through exhaustion. In desperation he had stolen some bread from a passing traveller, waving his knife as a threat but no sooner had he stumbled away than the man raised the alarm and Garyn was chased into the woods by a baying crowd. He knew he could not escape them and his only hope lay in hiding amongst the trees but he was far from the thicker forests of the north and the small copse soon petered out before him. Within moments he was left facing sparse scrubland leading down to the water's edge. In panic he ran along the shore but finally stumbled and landed face down on the jagged rocks. Blood poured from his forehead as he turned to face his pursuers in desperation. He had no more strength to flee, his race was run and his fate was no longer his own. He was done.

The shouting of the villagers filled the air as they ran toward him but above their voices was something stronger, the sound of a man calling out his name.

'Garyn!'

He looked around but the shoreline was empty.

'Garyn!' came the call again, 'out here.'

He turned to face the sea and saw a small fishing boat off shore. At its helm was a man he had never seen before but in the centre stood the Monk.

'Brother Martin,' gasped the boy.

'Quickly,' shouted the Monk, 'come to me.'

Garyn got to his feet and stumbled toward the water's edge. He splashed through the waves and was soon up to his chest but the boat was still several yards away. Behind him most of the screaming mob had stopped at the water's edge though some pursued him with knives drawn.

'Swim,' shouted the Monk.

'I can't,' answered Garyn. 'I don't know how to.'

'Swim or die, Garyn,' shouted the Monk.

A knife spun past Garyn's head and he forced himself forward. Within seconds he was submerged, panicking as the water filled his mouth. His feet found the bottom and he pushed off hard, bursting from the surface to gasp for air. Again he sank and once more pushed off the sea bed but this time as he surfaced, the weight of a thrown rope fell across his face. Frantically he took hold and the Monk pulled him in.

'Get us out of here,' shouted Brother Martin as the sailor pulled hard on the tiller. The Monk pulled the boy over the edge to fall gasping into the bottom of the boat. Behind them the mob returned to the shore, shouting insults after the escapees, while Brother Martin stared landward in silence, a look of concern on his face.

Garyn stood up and joined him by the mast.

'I thought you had forsaken me,' he said.

'As did I,' said the Monk, 'but we have other worries to concern us before we address the issue.'

'We are safe,' said Garyn, 'they cannot reach us out here.'

'It is not the anger of those peasants that causes me angst, Garyn but the wrath of a man whose greed has blinded his faith.' He nodded toward the high ground behind the shore. Up on the hill, a patrol of ten armoured horsemen stood quietly in the fading light, watching the events unfold below. Eventually the Knight at the head of the patrol turned his horse and rode out of sight, closely followed by his men.

'Who is it?' asked Garyn.

'Unless I am mistaken, they are Knights of Acre.'

Garyn looked up with hope.

'Then surely we should summon their aid,' he said.

'No,' said the Monk. 'If they answer to Sir John then we would be as flies into a web. Don't forget, he covets the relic and I feel he will stop at nothing to make it his. Our only chance is to reach one of the other orders and seek sanctuary. The Hospitallers or the Templars are pious men and will protect us from his greed.'

'Then surely,' said Garyn weakly, 'all we need to do is sail down the coast to Acre and seek their aid.'

'It is indeed what I planned,' said the Monk, 'but alas that option has been denied us.'

'How?'

'Sir John has access to his own fleet. Once word of our situation reaches him, he will send ships to pluck us from the sea.'

'Then what are we to do?' asked Garyn.

'The services of this boat cost most of my coins,' said the Monk, 'but I have enough left for a horse. At least this man's village falls under the influence of Acre and we can buy a steed in safety. They will be expecting us to travel by sea so may relax any patrols seeking our whereabouts. Perhaps we can now reach the city overland and sneak in unseen.'

'I don't see why we don't allow ourselves to be captured and be done with it,' said Garyn. 'He will get the cross and I will get the release of my brother.'

'No,' said the Monk. 'He will want the details of the cross kept secret to meet his own ends. If we hand it over, what's to stop him killing us and your brother?'

'So what do you propose?'

'A public exchange before men of honour. If witnessed by fellow Knights then not even Sir John would go back on his word. He would be forced to release him into your care without threat of retribution.'

'And that is the only way?'

'It is.'

Garyn sat down and tilted his head back, exhausted. The sailor brought over a loaf and a flask of wine along with a platter of cold but cooked fish.

'Eat,' said the Monk, 'it has been a while.'

Garyn needed no second invitation and tore pieces of bread from the loaf before ripping at the fish.

'Steady, Garyn,' said the Monk, 'or the fish bones will do for you long before Sir John's henchmen.'

Garyn washed down the first mouthful with wine before staring at the Monk again.

'Where is the cross?' he asked.

'Fret not, Garyn, it is within my pack.'

'You left me to die back there'

'I did,' said the Monk, 'I felt the task we have set ourselves was an impossible one and unlikely to succeed. I couldn't bear the thought of the cross falling into the hands of the English royalty, so I sought a way out and grasped at the easy option.'

'But why now?' asked Garyn, 'what made you succumb to temptation.'

'It was not temptation for earthly riches,' said the Monk, 'but a need for spiritual salvation. I am getting old Garyn and the chill in my bones will soon demand the comforting wrap of a shroud. In my weakness I thought the return of the cross would grant absolution from my sins.'

'But you are a Monk.'

'I have done bad things in my time, Garyn and I feel that the few years I have spent in God's service fall way short of guaranteeing me a place in heaven.'

'Yet you returned.'

'I did,' said Brother Martin.

196

'Why?'

'I knew what I did was wrong, Garyn, yet I was overburdened with the responsibility for such a holy relic. I prayed to God, pleading that a burden as great as this cross is more than any man should bear.'

'And did he answer?'

'He did. I was asking for God's guidance and the answer came to me. Our Lord, Jesus Christ carried this same piece of wood on the way to Cavalry, not a mere sliver as lays in our hands but the whole cross. Yet he did not seek guidance or succour, he shouldered the burden and died so we may live. Who am I to question this spiritual burden when the Lord Christ has already led the way?'

Garyn stayed quiet for a moment, watching as the Monk stared quietly over the side of the gently rocking boat.

'So what now?' he asked eventually.

'Now we return to this man's village and buy a horse. With fortune we can be back within sight of Acre within days.'

'And after that?'

'There is no worth in planning beyond,' said the Monk. 'The options get smaller all the time. Get some sleep, Garyn, The village will take half a day to reach.'

The sailor threw Garyn a sheepskin cape and Garyn pulled it around him. Though he thought he would stay awake all night, within minutes he fell deep into an exhausted sleep.

'Garyn, wake up.'

Garyn opened his eyes and saw the Monk standing above him.

'We are at the village,' said Brother Martin. 'Our friend has gone ashore to buy a horse and we must make ready.'

An hour later both men were walking through the village to the high ground beyond. Finally they crested the ridge and the Monk turned to Garyn.

'Mount up,' he said, 'the beast must carry us both.'

'He is but skin and bones,' said Garyn.

'These animals are tougher than they seem and used to a life of toil, besides, it was all I could afford. We will ride hard but rest regularly.'

Within ten minutes they were riding across country but always heading south. For a day they made good ground but halfway through the second, it became obvious the horse wasn't up to the strain and it collapsed through exhaustion. They cut away the saddle and encouraged it to stand before leading it to a nearby stream.

'Its day is done, Garyn,' said the Monk cutting the horse free of its harness. 'From here we walk. With good fortune, tomorrow we will see the walls of Acre,'

'And not a moment too soon,' said Garyn.

The Monk looked at him, realising the boy's skin was drawn tight over his flesh. His hair was a tangled mess and his face was gaunt through hunger and exposure to the sun.

'No point in waiting further,' said the Monk, 'we should go.'

Again they started on their march, the rocky road playing havoc with their feet and soon their pace slowed as the rigours of the past few weeks caught up with them once more. They cut branches from a tree to use as sticks but the pain was almost unbearable.

'I can't go on,' gasped Garyn collapsing onto a grassy bank. 'I have nothing left to give.'

'It's not far, Garyn, just over that next hill.'

'You have said that since yesterday,' said Garyn. 'I am serious, Brother Martin, I am spent.'

'My words were meant as encouragement,' said the Monk, 'but I truly recognise the hill before us. The town is no more than a half day's march.'

'A half day that I cannot do,' said Garyn.

The Monk started to speak again but fell silent as movement caught his eye. He raised his hand to block out the sun and his face fell as he recognised the sight on the trail behind them.

'Garyn, get up,' he said.

'You are not listening to me,' started Garyn.

'Get up,' shouted the Monk and grabbed the collar of the boy's jerkin.

'What's the matter?' asked Garyn.

'Look,' said the Monk and pointed back the way they had come.

In the distance they could see a column of fully armoured Knights riding under the banner of Acre. Even as they watched, the column broke into a canter having obviously seen their quarry.

'We are seen,' shouted the Monk, 'come on we must run.'

'Where?' shouted Garyn, 'there is nowhere to go.'

'Into the scrub,' answered Brother Martin and dragged Garyn off the track. For several minutes they limped as fast as they could but finally realised there was nowhere else to go. Capture was inevitable.

The column bore down on them and the Monk's heart fell when he saw the armour. The tabards were varied with each bearing a different coat of arms and while the flag bore the emblem of Acre, there was no standard bearing the cross of England.

'Mercenaries,' said the Monk, 'no doubt in the pay of Sir John.'

'Then it is over,' said Garyn. 'It has all been in vain.'

The Monk didn't answer, just stared at the approaching column. Two of the Knights galloped forward and lowered their lances parallel to the ground. Brother Martin's heart sank as he realised there would be no quarter These men had been tasked with their deaths and meant to carry it out with ruthless efficiency.

'Make peace with God, Garyn,' he said, 'I fear our time is done.'

The horses galloped toward them but without warning, pulled up in a cloud of dust less than a hundred paces distant The men raised their lances once more, trying to control their mounts as the excited beasts strained to restart their charge.

'What's happening?' asked Garyn, 'why have they stopped?'

Before the Monk could answer, a dozen horses galloped past them from behind and spread out to face the mercenaries. A second wave came through, supporting the first and placed a fully armoured line between the Mercenaries and the two bedraggled fugitives. Both sides faced each other as Garyn and the Monk stared in disbelief.

'Who are they?' asked Garyn.

The Monk looked at the Surcoats of the newly arrived Knights and the matching flag attached to one of the lances.

'A white cross on a black field,' he said. 'They are the Knights of St John of Jerusalem, the order of Hospitallers.'

'But what are they doing?'

'Open your eyes, Garyn, they are saving us from certain death.'

One of the Hospitallers pushed his horse forward and lifting the visor on his helmet, addressed the opposing line.

'Who commands here?' he demanded.

A Knight clad in full armour and red Surcoat rode forward to face him, his visor already lifted.

'That honour is mine,' he said, 'Sir Bennett of Nottingham and I demand you clear our path Sire, this is no business of yours.'

'What master do you ride for, Sir Bennett?' asked the Hospitaller.

'We are paid men of Sir John of Cambridge, Castellan of Acre and act on his authority.'

'And is the killing of humble pilgrims now a task he embraces?'

'These are no pilgrims, Sire but common thieves and they have in their possession something that belongs to my master.'

'And how do you know this to be true?'

'It is from the word of Sir John himself.'

'If it is indeed true,' said the Hospitaller, 'since when are men summarily executed without trial. These people are innocent until proven guilty by the laws of your own King Henry. If you are worthy of the title of Knight then you know this. Surely your code demands justice, not murder.'

'I am no murderer Sire,' said Sir Bennett, 'I follow the commands of my betters. Your order has no jurisdiction here so I say again, get out of my way.'

'On the contrary,' Sir Bennett, 'our order are sworn to protect the pilgrims and in my eyes these travellers are simply that. However, I will ask you this. What man holds chivalry so low that he will kill a weary man of God, of any faith?'

A murmur spread around the mercenaries as the message hit home. Killing a holy man was always bad luck, especially a Christian one.

'Your point is well made, Sir Knight,' said Sir Bennett, 'and we will relinquish the custody of the older man to you. The boy however is a traitor and will feel our summary justice.'

'Look at him,' said the Hospitaller, 'he is already half dead yet you, a fully trained Knight intend to run him through like a deer. Where is the honour in this?'

Silence fell again as the words sunk in and another mercenary rode forward to whisper in the ear of Sir Bennett.

'There is a solution,' said Sir Bennett a moment later. 'You will keep the old man but the boy will fight for his name.'

'To face a Knight is no fair contest,' said the Hospitaller.

'I agree,' said Sir Bennett, 'so he will fight an untrained man of similar age.' He turned to face the main body of men at his back.

'Bring him forward,' he said. A few moments later a smaller horse appeared, ridden by a much younger man.

'Strip to your breeches,' ordered the Knight. 'You have an opportunity to gain honour before those you aspire to be.'

The young man dismounted and faced away as he removed his chainmail and undershirt. Finally stripped to the waist, he turned around and faced the Hospitallers. Garyn looked at him and his mouth fell open in shock. It was Squire Dafydd.

'I understand these boys travelled together from England,' said Sir Bennett. 'They trained as comrades and found equal skills. You asked where is the honour, so I say this. Fair contest between two equals is honourable and the outcome just.'

'But our man is exhausted?' shouted Brother Martin.

'That is not my problem,' roared Sir Bennett.' He chose to be a brigand and will now bear the consequences. It is a fair fight.'

Garyn stepped forward and faced his friend in silence.

'Why did you do it, Garyn?' asked Dafydd. 'Why have you turned your back on Cadwallader after all that he did for you?'

'I only ever asked for passage, Dafydd. My quest was always the release of my brother. I made no secret of that.'

'But he fed and trained you on the journey.'

'And in return he had my sword arm if it was called on. There is no debt.' He paused before continuing. 'And what of you, Dafydd, How do you ride with mercenaries instead of under Cadwallader's banner?'

'Cadwallader was summoned to support Longshanks while I had a fever so left me behind. I was left in Acre, nothing more than a Page so begged Sir John for service. When news came that two wanted men were in the area he relented and appointed me Squire to Sir Bennett. I had no idea it was you we sought.'

'And now we are to fight?' said Garyn.

'It would seem so.'

Two Knives fell in the dirt before them, thrown by one of the mercenaries. For a second they stared at the blades at their feet.

'I will not fight you, Dafydd,' said Garyn.

'You have to,' said Dafydd, 'there is no other choice.'

'I can just refuse.'

'You can, but you will then be hung as a thief. At least this way you have a chance.'

'I am weak, Dafydd. Even when strong I struggled against you. What chance do I have?'

'Perhaps none,' said Dafydd, 'but I will do it quickly. Better to die on a blade than on the end of a rope.'

Garyn paused before bending forward to pick up the knives.

'Then let it be done,' he said and handed one knife to Dafydd.

'Let there be fair contest,' shouted Sir Bennett,' a fight to the death with no quarter shown and no intervention.'

Both young men backed away, each holding their knives lightly in their hands as they had done countless times in training.

'Begin,' shouted the Knight and they both stepped forward, each staring into his opponent's eyes, hoping to see evidence of any sudden move.

Dafydd lunged forward but his arm was swatted away by Garyn before responding with a lunge of his own. Warily they circled each other until Garyn took the initiative and ran forward swinging his knife wildly. Dafydd stepped back, easily avoiding the blade without effort. Again Garyn attacked and this time Dafydd tripped him up to sprawl in the dust.

'Stand up,' said Dafydd, 'and be the man I trained with.'

Garyn struggled to his feet. The wound had reopened on his head and blood ran down his face.

Over and over again Garyn stepped into the attack, each time being easily eluded by his opponent. Dafydd's eyes narrowed in concern as he realised the depths of his friend's exhaustion and wasted little energy in avoiding Garyn's attacks.

'Get on with it,' shouted Sir Bennett, frustrated at the poor quality of the fight.

Garyn stumbled forward again but once more Dafydd stepped aside avoiding the clumsy lunge and Garyn fell once more.

'Finish him,' said Sir Bennett.

'Sire,' answered Dafydd, 'he is exhausted and proves no contest.'

'I said finish him,' ordered the Knight and threw a lance at Dafydd's feet.

The squire picked up the lance and rested the point against his friend's throat.

Garyn looked up at him.

'Do as he says, Dafydd,' he said, his voice barely audible. 'You are honour bound as a Squire to obey any Knight.'

Dafydd adjusted his grip but still hesitated.

'Squire Dafydd,' said Sir Bennett loudly. 'Your hesitation is admirable for the man is unarmed. However, you won in fair contest and he is but a brigand. Honour is served and his life is yours. Be the man you want to be and make the kill. Do this and I will petition Sir John to advance your journey to Knighthood.'

Dafydd swallowed hard as the Knight's words sunk in. One thrust and at the very least, he would be one step closer to gaining his spurs. Again he altered his grip and Garyn closed his eyes as the lance point cut into his skin.

'Do it,' shouted Sir Bennett but instead of piercing Garyn's throat, Dafydd lifted the lance and turned to face the Knight.

'No Sire,' he said, 'I will not. He is wounded and in need of aid. Yes I crave Knighthood but will not seek it out with the murder of innocents.'

'You will do as I order,' shouted the Knight, 'or spend the rest of your days in the Accursed Tower along with this boy's traitor brother.'

'I will not do it, Sire,' said Dafydd, 'and trust God to deliver whatever justice he sees fit.' He stepped forward and handed the lance back to the Knight

Sir Bennett stared in hatred at the young man and without warning, swung the lance to smash the haft across Dafydd's unprotected face, sending him sprawling in the dirt. The Hospitallers rode forward a few paces in a defensive manoeuvre but again Sir Bennett cried out.

'Remove your men, Sir Knight,' he said, 'for again I say this. You have no jurisdiction here and I will have my quarry even if it costs the blood of Christian Knights.'

'Not one step backward, Brothers,' shouted the Hospitaller to his men.

Brother Martin thought furiously, realising the seriousness of the situation. There was only one way to stop the bloodshed that was seconds away.

'Garyn,' he shouted, 'claim sanctuary.'

The boy looked at him in confusion.

'I don't understand,' he said.

'Curb your tongue, Monk,' said Bennett, 'your calling may allow such trickery but the boy is no priest and is subject to the law of the King.'

'Garyn,' said the Monk, ignoring Bennett, 'listen to me. If there is proven religious cause to claim sanctuary, every Knight is honour bound to grant the plea. He threw Garyn's leather bag over to land before him. Do what you need to do.'

Garyn looked at the bag and realisation dawned. Within the bag was the relic and the possessor would surely granted the sanctity of religious protection. For a second he hesitated for he knew once the cross became public knowledge, then the one lever he had to free his brother would be lost.

'But my brother...' he started.

'If you die then he has no chance at all,' said the Monk. 'At least this way you will live and we will all have a chance.'

'What chance?' cried Garyn, 'I am a commoner in a strange land. What voice do I have?'

'We can petition Cadwallader,' said the Monk, 'or even Longshanks himself. We will do everything we can but you have to live. If you die here in this place, then it is over and your brother will die with you. For his sake, do what you have to do.'

Garyn looked back at the bag at his feet. He was tired and in pain. All he wanted was for all this to end but he knew in similar circumstances, his brother would not give up. Slowly his hand crept under the flap of the bag and his fingers clasped the cross.

'What trickery is this?' demanded Sir Bennet, 'we have waited long enough. Men at arms, arrest this boy in the name of the King.'

Garyn withdrew the artefact and slowly held it up, gleaming in the sun.

'Sanctuary,' he gasped weakly, 'in the name of Jesus Christ our lord I seek the sanctuary of the church.'

The two opposing forces gasped in astonishment and the horses milled around as confusion reigned

'Sacrilege,' shouted Sir Bennet, 'the order stands. Arrest him.'

Immediately the Hospitallers lines stepped forward again and their lances lowered toward the Mercenaries.

'It looks like the circumstances have changed, Sir Bennett,' said the Hospitaller Knight. 'Our code demands we honour this request. These men now fall under my responsibility and we will defend them to the death.'

Sir Bennett was livid as he realised he had been outmanoeuvred.

'I will have revenge for this,' he snarled, 'you may hide your face under beaten steel, stranger but I will find out who you are and have retribution.'

'My face I will show and name is no secret,' said the Hospitaller, removing his helm, 'I am Sir Abdul Khoury, Hospitaller Knight of the order of St John of Jerusalem.'

Garyn and the Monk stared up in amazement as they recognised the man they had saved at Jabahl Bahra but before they could say anything, Khoury spoke again.

'Brother Najaar,' he said, 'get the pilgrims mounted and prepare to move out.'

'What about Dafydd?' shouted Garyn.

'Garyn, your friend is one of them,' said Brother Martin,' there is nothing we can do.'

'But he spared me,' shouted Garyn, 'we can't leave him.'

Two of the Mercenary Knights dismounted and grabbed Dafydd, dragging him back to the horses.

'Dafydd,' shouted Garyn, 'be strong. I will seek your release.'

Dafydd made to answer but was silenced as Sir Bennett struck him with the back of his chain mailed fist.

'Tie him to his horse,' snarled the Knight, 'I want his shame to be evident to all.'

Khoury spun his horse around to face his men.

'Hospitallers,' he shouted, 'withdraw to Acre. We are done here.'

Within minutes the Hospitallers were galloping back toward the city, taking the Monk and Garyn with them

'What now?' asked one of the Mercenaries.

'Follow them,' said Sir Bennett, 'for this issue is not yet concluded.'

Chapter Twenty One

The Hospitaller Castle in Acre

Garyn had no knowledge of the first few weeks in Acre as he caught the fever rampant in the city and in his weakened state, fell into unconsciousness. The Hospitaller's staff nursed him through the illness, bleeding him with leeches and administering potions from the apothecaries but the fever raged through him and Brother Martin feared the worst.

The Monk stayed in a cell alongside Garyn's but spent most nights at the boy's side, mopping his brow and feeding him sips of water. Garyn flitted in and out of consciousness but showed no sign of recovery.

A knock came on the cell door and a young woman entered with a tray holding a jug and a lidded clay pot.

'Excuse me, Sire,' said the girl with a slight courtesy, 'the apothecary is on his way. I have the leeches and some fresh water.'

Brother Martin sighed and stood up.

'Tell him not to bother,' said the Monk, 'the boy is beyond earthly remedies now and his life is in the hands of the Lord.'

The girl curtsied again and left the room The Monk stared at Garyn, at a loss what to do. Finally he reached beneath the bed and dragged out Garyn's pack Reaching inside he retrieved the cross and after pausing to stare once more at its beauty, placed it on the boy's chest before falling to his knees to pray

'Lord in heaven,' he said, 'spare this innocent I pray Grant him your mercy and take me in his place. This I beseech you in Christ's name.'

For an age he stayed on his knees, praying deeply but finally he stood and poured water onto a rag before bathing Garyn's brow once more.

'I have done everything I can, ' Garyn,' he said quietly. 'The rest is between you and God.'

The following morning, the Monk was summoned from his bed by one of the attendants. He hurried into Garyn's cell fearing the worst but was relieved to see the boy sitting up, being fed a light broth.

'Brother Martin,' said Garyn. 'How are you?'

'How am I?' asked the Monk in shock, 'worried sick, that's how I am. For an age we thought you were lost.'

'Really? How long have I been sick?'

'Ten days,' said the Monk, 'which in itself is a miracle. You should have died days ago.'

'Where am I?' asked Garyn.

'In a Knight's cell in the Hospitaller headquarters in Acre. It is only an arrow's flight from The Castle of the King's constable but we are safe here. Sanctuary is sacrosanct and will not be breached by any man.'

'My brother,' said Garyn, 'is there any news?'

'No,' said the Monk. 'Sir John refuses to share any information unless we hand over the cross, but enough talk, the fever may have lifted but you still need the healing that rest brings. I will leave now and make arrangements for audience with the Castellan. In a few days we can make the transfer and you can go home.'

Garyn laid back on his pillow as the Monk left, knowing Brother Martin was right. Even if he could get out of bed, he doubted he could walk.

Five days later, all signs of the fever were gone and though he was still weak, Garyn took part in regular walks around the courtyard of the Hospitaller headquarters. He asked about his brother daily but as Sir John was away, there was no chance of furthering his quest. Slowly he regained his strength, exercising in the courtyard before eating the hearty broth supplied by the Hospitallers and resting in his cell. Each night he took the cross from his pack and prayed at the foot of his bed, holding the crucifix before him. There was no doubt the cross was holy but he was under no illusions and knew he had to hand it over if his brother was to live.

On the morning of the twelfth day since he regained consciousness, Brother Martin knocked on his cell door.

'Garyn, get dressed. You are summoned to the great hall.'

Garyn donned the clothes he had been supplied and rushed out to meet the Monk.

What news?' he asked, 'is Sir John back?'

'I know not,' said the Monk, 'but Sir Khoury requests we join him.'

Together they crossed the courtyard to the hall and entered to find Brother Khoury sitting at a great table along with several other Knights.

'Brother Martin, Garyn, please be seated,' said Khoury.

The two men did as they were bid. It was the first time they had seen the Hospitaller leader since their rescue and stared at him in wonder. The man they had rescued almost two months earlier was no longer evident. In his place was the strong leader who was once Castellan of the greatest castle in the Holy-land. His head was freshly shaved and his beard was carefully tended, an image common to most Knights on Crusade.

'Garyn,' said Khoury, 'you are well I hear'

'Getting better by the day, Sir Knight,' answered Garyn.

'Good. As you are aware we have business to conclude and I have news to that end but first there is something I will say. A year ago, I allowed myself to be tricked into surrendering Krak des Chevalier. I was taken prisoner and suffered at the Infidel's hands. Though I was shamed, I saw it as part of God's plan and believed he would lead me from captivity. I admit there were times my faith wavered but he kept me alive for further purpose.' He paused and stared at Garyn. 'I now know that you were that purpose, Garyn. God allowed my judgement to falter so that our paths would cross and ultimately be there for you in your hour of need, as you were there in mine.'

'I don't understand,' said Garyn. 'How was I the purpose.'

'For you were the vessel by which the relic was returned to us. Everything that has happened led you here bearing the glory of Christ and for that I will be eternally grateful. God led the Lady Jennifer and I from that killing field in Wadi-al-Ayun and ensured our paths crossed with yours near Al Kahf.'

'Where is the Lady?' asked Brother Martin.

'She is safe,' said Khoury, 'though her mind is greatly troubled. At first she was treated well by the Mamluks but then she was taken away from the protectorate of Baibaars and placed in the custody of a lesser man. Let's just say she suffered more than any woman should.'

'I hope she finds peace,' said Brother Martin.

'Misha Ain Alsabar is with her,' said Khoury, 'and eases her days.'

'The slave girl? I thought she had sought her freedom.'

'The choice was hers but during the journey back, she grew close to the Lady Jennifer and decided to continue with us. She now serves as a free woman. Truth be told, if it wasn't for her, we wouldn't have made it back and furthermore, she told us of your arrival in the fishing village. Her network of contacts is impressive.'

'As you would expect of an Ismailis, I suspect.'

'There is talk of Hashashin blood flowing through her veins but I will not question her on her heritage. We owe her our lives, it is as simple as that.'

'So what happens now?' asked Garyn.

'First I have something that belongs to you,' said Khoury and led them outside. In the courtyard a Squire held the reins of Silverlight, Garyn's horse while another held his father's sword.

Garyn walked over and stroked the horse's neck

'I thought I would never see him again,' he said. 'Thank you.'

'No, thank you,' said Khoury. 'It was your steed that conveyed us to safety.'

'Do we have audience with Sir John?' asked Brother Martin.

'No, we don't,' said Khoury. 'The emergence of the true cross has sent awareness across Palestine greater than a desert storm. This is no longer a matter for one crooked Knight but a power much greater. The reason it has taken so long to get audience is that you will present your case at the highest level. Prince Edward has returned and will adjudicate on behalf of all parties. Garyn will have his day of justice but it will be before Longshanks himself.'

Chapter Twenty Two

The Castle of the King's Constable

Garyn sat nervously in the Hall of Sir John. At last it was coming together and soon his brother would be freed but the last thing he had expected was to have audience with the future King of England. Since the meeting with Sir Khoury two days earlier, he had locked himself away in his cell with only the crucifix for comfort, refusing to open the door to anyone including the Monk but finally he had emerged and was ready for the meeting.

'He looks much calmer,' whispered Khoury.

'I think he has found peace,' answered Brother Martin.

For almost an hour they waited for the Prince to arrive, talking quietly amongst themselves. The hall was filled with Knights, some sat around the many tables while others lined the walls.

'Is he coming or not,' whispered Garyn

'Longshanks will not be rushed, Garyn,' said Khoury. 'He will be here when he arrives and no sooner.'

'How will we know it is him?' asked Garyn.

'You will know,' said Khoury simply.

Another half hour passed before a Squire ran in and whispered to the herald at the far door.

'All stand for Prince Edward,' shouted the Herald and as one, two hundred men got to their feet.

The doors opened and a dozen men marched through the hall, each clad in full armour and tabards emblazoned with three Lions, the coat of arms of Edward.

Garyn bowed as they passed but though the procession of nobles was impressive, his gaze was drawn by the person of Edward. He was half a head taller than all the other Knights and his stride bore a confidence that could only be described as majestic. They reached the top table and took their seats with Longshanks at the centre.

'Be seated,' ordered the prince. 'Fellow Knights and honoured guests, you have been summoned here today to see justice served in the name of the King and of Christ himself. Let the one who brought petition stand forward.'

Sir Khoury stood up and introduced himself.

'My Lord, I brought the petition on behalf of several parties.'

'And you are?'

'I am Sir Abdul Khoury, Knight Hospitaller of the Order of St John of Jerusalem.'

'Khoury,' mumbled Longshanks, 'there was one of that name who was Castellan of Krak des Chevalier. Was he kin of yours?'

'I am that man,' said Khoury, ignoring the angry murmurs around the room.

'Really?' said Longshanks. 'It is said that you handed over the Homs Gap to Baibaars without struggle. I am surprised that Hugh De Revel has not had you punished for your incompetence.'

'Incompetence is subjective, My Lord,' answered Khoury, 'and if there is punishment to be suffered then it will be handed down by God.'

Longshanks stared at the Hospitaller Knight with distaste but pursued the matter no further.

'To business,' he said, 'I am informed that there is one here who claims to be in possession of the true cross. Is this correct?'

'It is, My Lord,' said Khoury, 'the Boy's name is Garyn ap Thomas and he hails from a place called Brycheniog in Wales.'

'I know of Brycheniog,' said Longshanks. 'Let the boy make himself known.'

'Stand up,' whispered Brother Martin.

Garyn stood and felt every pair of eyes in the room staring at him.

'Who speaks for you?' asked Longshanks, 'is it the Hospitaller?'

'No, Sire,' interrupted Sir Khoury, 'I will speak on behalf of my own order who also lay claim to the cross.'

'I will speak for the boy,' said Brother Martin, standing up.

'And on behalf of the house of Cambridge?'

'I will speak for myself,' said Sir John, also taking his feet, 'and will prove this peasant is no more than a common thief.'

'All in good time, Sir John,' said Longshanks. 'First we will establish the facts from the boy's own mouth.'

'Sire there is another complainant,' said a voice and all eyes turned to see the man at the end of the hall.

'And you are?'

'My name is Father Williams, said the man, and I am the Abbot of the order of St Benedict based in the Abbey of Brycheniog.

'I have no knowledge of your presence in Acre.'

'No, Sire. I am freshly arrived from England this very morn.'

Garyn's eyes opened wide in astonishment as did those of Brother Martin.

'And your stance?' asked Longshanks.

'I claim the relic in the name of the church and God himself,' said Father Williams.

A murmur echoed around the room until Longshanks lifted his hand for silence.

'Are there any others with petition to bring?'

The room fell silent again.

'Good. Then we will begin. Garyn ap Thomas, take the floor and tell us your tale, the Christian world is waiting.'

For the best part of an hour, Garyn retold the story of how he had come about the poem and the subsequent quest to Jabahl Bahra. Sometimes he stumbled over his words and he often had to go back over the story to recount something he had only just recalled. Occasionally there were murmurs of admiration, especially when he recalled the tale of how he breached the walls of Al Kahf but there were also whispers of disapproval. Overall it was an adequate presentation and when he was done, an awkward silence filled the room.

'Do you have this relic with you?' asked Longshanks.

'I do, Sire,' said Garyn.

'Then let us see what it is that causes such angst.'

Garyn picked his pack from the floor and approached the Prince but before he reached the table, two guards lowered their pikes, barring his way. A Squire stepped forward and checked the bag to make sure there were no scorpions or the like before retrieving the hessian wrapped object. Carefully he unwrapped it and his eyes widened as the golden crucifix glistened before him. Many men in the room stood for a better view and voices were raised in wonder.

'Silence,' ordered Longshanks and the Knights returned to their seats.

The Squire turned to the Prince and handed it over. Longshanks stared at the Crucifix in awe, turning it over slowly in his hands before gently drawing his finger down the embedded sliver of wood. He nodded to a nearby priest who came over and took the cross from him before disappearing through a side door.

Garyn's brow knitted with doubt.

'Where's he taking it?' he asked.

'Silence,' demanded a Knight, 'how dare you question the Prince.'

Longshanks raised his hand.

'It is a fair question,' he said. 'Fret not, young man, it has only been taken for examination by the priests. You have to understand, there are many such claims of holiness across the known world and each needs to be checked by men of God. However, while we wait we will hear the petitions. Sir Khoury, take the floor.'

The Hospitaller Knight walked to the centre and addressed the room.

'My Lord, fellow Knights, honoured guests. First I will say this. We do not doubt the authenticity of the relic. On the contrary, we fully believe it is a fragment of the true cross and should be revered as such. In addition, we also acknowledge the bravery and fortitude of Garyn ap Thomas as well as the Benedictine Monk. Indeed we commend them both for their service in God's name. However, they set out to retrieve the artefact for one reason only and that was to free the boy's brother from service.' He paused and looked around the room. 'The quest was noble and the outcome something to be lauded. Indeed they should be rewarded not only with the release of the boy's brother but with sufficient funds for safe passage home and adequate reward for their endeavours. However, make no mistake, blood has been spilt in the pursuit of this relic, men have died and people have suffered, none more so than my comrades.' He looked around once more before continuing. 'Over fifty Hospitaller Knights fell in the protection of the Muslim poet prior to his transfer to England, fifty brothers who paid the ultimate price to make available that which has been hidden all these years. For this reason we claim the cross. Let it be handed over in their honour and let Hugh de Revel present it to his holiness in Rome. This way all men can bask in its majesty and the Cross displayed to the glory of Christ and in honour of the men who fell.' He turned to face the prince once more. 'Sire, therein lays our claim.'

The room broke out into conversation as the merits were discussed between all present. Sir Khoury sat back down amongst his comrades and watched as Sir John walked to the floor to present his case.

'Pray silence for Sir John of Cambridge,' ordered the herald and the noise died down to allow the Castellan the chance to speak.

'My Lord,' he said, 'fellow Knights. The testimony from the order of the Hospitallers is indeed a heartfelt plea and yes, I acknowledge fifty men fell that day, a fact to be mourned by all present here. But put that number against those who fell at Jaffa or Jerusalem. Compare them against those who died in battles across the Holy-land from Hattin to Antioch and the uncountable skirmishes between. Yes the Hospitallers died in the service of Christ but let it not diminish those who fell before and those yet to give the ultimate sacrifice. The Hospitaller dead are acknowledged but in the case of the true cross, their numbers are irrelevant. Acre is the one true stronghold left in the Holy-land and is the beating heart of the Christian presence here. Since Lionheart ousted Sah-la-din we have been the gateway to Jerusalem for pilgrim or warrior alike and it has fallen to this city to provide safe passage to all who crusade. Within these city walls we harbour Knights of all orders, Hospitaller, Templar and Teutonic, both Christian and Secular. We house dozens of nationalities from German to African and look after the welfare of pilgrims across the world. Outside of these walls, countless villages rely on our fist to protect them from the ravages of the infidel and we serve them selflessly, often falling in their name.'

'State your case, Sir John,' shouted a voice, 'you bore us with your boasting.'

'The truth is this,' continued Sir John, scowling at the man, 'our sources had already identified the resting place of the cross at Al Kahf and we were but a day away from not only securing the relic but inflicting a devastating blow on the Hashashin, seizing a castle into the bargain. Our men were in place, primed for the assault when this boy,' he pointed dramatically at Garyn, 'climbed in and stole the cross like a common thief, craving the gold for himself and his traitorous brother. So I say this, the cross belongs to Acre and the Castellan therein. Any glory or financial gain from the discovery belongs to me and my men. As for the boy, far from being rewarded he should be hung as a common criminal.'

Again the room broke into argument before Longshanks called for silence.

'Strong words, Sir John, now regain your seat for the last of the submissions. Father Williams, the floor is yours.'

The Abbott walked forward and the room fell silent.

'Gentlemen,' he said, 'my plea is simple and made under the auspices of the Law of England. The order of St Benedict is an

214

honourable one and our Abbey falls under the jurisdiction of King Henry himself. Your words about the bravery of your men are indeed impressive but the simple fact is this. The boy made a deal back in Brycheniog and under the law of the land, is duty bound to honour that agreement. He came here to gain possession of a relic, not in the hands of any Christian but hidden away by the infidel. He has stolen nothing in the eyes of the law or indeed God and I say this. Trumpet not the tales of Knights who failed to find it over a hundred years but laud the achievement of a simple boy and a Benedictine Monk who succeeded where others have failed. The cross was obtained legally, on behalf of the Benedictine order, from infidels outside of God's grace. It is the object of an agreement lawfully made under the auspices of King Henry and as such, the payment should be made forthwith. My case is so made.'

Again the gathering broke into loud discussion before Longshanks turned to Garyn.

'Boy, do you or your spokesman have anything to add before I make judgement?'

Garyn stayed seated but Brother Martin stepped forward.

'My Lord,' he said as the noise died down, 'we have listened to all petitions and our answer remains the same. We seek not honour or glory and have no opinion as to where the final resting place of the cross may lay. Indeed we seek no payment in handing it over, all we ask is that which was promised at the beginning, the release of Garyn's brother. He is but one man and languishes within the dungeons of Sir John under false accusation. We are law abiding citizens, my Lord and the decisions regarding the artefact are above the likes of simple men. We leave this in your royal hands but we ask, nay, beg one thing of your royal mercy. Grant us the life of Geraint ap Thomas and allow him home to till his lands alongside his only surviving family. Our petition is thus made.'

Longshanks and his advisors stood and the noise died down for the last time.

'Fellow Knights,' said Longshanks loudly, 'this audience is suspended until dawn. I will make my considerations overnight and deliver the judgement on the morrow. Until then, we are adjourned.'

The Prince and his Knights marched out leaving the gathering deep in argument. Brother Martin grabbed Garyn and pulled him from the room, followed by Sir Khoury and his comrades.

'Another night to wait,' said Garyn as they eventually entered the Hospitaller headquarters, 'will this never end?'

'A few hours only, Garyn,' said Brother Martin, 'and then it is done, one way or the other.'

The following morning Garyn and Brother Martin once more made their way to the hall in The Castle of the King's constable. The room was busy with many of the same Knights but access had also been granted to the less important people who made the castle their home. Squires and soldiers jostled for position while Pages found what room they could alongside the several ladies who had also turned up to see Longshanks deliver the King's justice. Finally the Herald called the room to order and the noise settled before Longshanks once more entered accompanied by his advisors. This time, the Prince did not sit down but stood at the centre of the hall.

'Good people,' he said, addressing the crowd, 'The hour is early and there are tasks that we must be attending. Therefore I will be brief. I have given the matter much thought and have come to a decision that hopefully will satisfy most, if not all. The priests have examined the relic closely but cannot agree on authenticity. However, the feeling is that it is indeed a fragment of the true cross.'

A gasp echoed around the room.

'In the circumstances and if proved true then it has the potential to become one of the most important relics in Christendom and must be treated with the respect it deserves. My judgement is thus. It seems that two parties want the cross to be placed in the hands of the church, albeit in different locations. The true cross belongs in one place only and that is in Rome under the protection of his Holiness the Pope. In an effort to acknowledge all parties, I charge Father Williams to convey the cross at all speed to Rome under the protection of the Knights Hospitaller. Those chosen will be held personally responsible for its safe passage. Sir Khoury, do you accept this charge?'

The Knight stepped forward and bowed his head.

'We do, Sire.'

'Father Williams, do you accept?'

For a few seconds the Abbott paused and though he had an angry look upon his face, he knew he had no option. Finally he stepped forward.

'I do, Sire.'

'Good,' said the Prince and turned to Garyn.

'Garyn ap Thomas, your part in this whole affair gives me concern. You kept secrets from the church and deliberately avoided the involvement of those better than you. Your secrecy and stubbornness put many lives at risk and bearing in mind the enormity of the potential gains, you would have been better served involving the crown. However, your role cannot be ignored and without your stubbornness, the cross would still be in the hands of the infidels. You are accused of treachery by Sir John and ordinarily that alone would warrant redress but in recognition of your part in this, you will be released immediately without charge though banished from the Holy-land with immediate effect. Safe passage will be provided as far as Venice, from where you and the Monk will make your own way to England.'

'What about my brother?' asked Garyn but the Monk dragged him back into the crowd.

'Shut up,' hissed Brother Martin, 'he has not finished.'

Longshanks turned to Sir John.

'Sir Knight,' he said, 'your continued policing of the Holy-land does indeed deserve merit and you are commended for your relentless pursuit of the relic. As a reward you will be presented to the King on your return to England and suitable position found for your service. However, I find your accusations against the brother of Garyn ap Thomas unfounded and demand his immediate release from your gaol. In addition, in way of compensation and in recognition of their part in this, you will gift him and the Monk each a purse of silver from your own treasury equivalent to the weight of the cross. These monies to be repaid by the crown on your return to England.'

Silence fell as Sir John faced the Prince, his face seething in anger. Despite the acknowledgement of his work and the promise of a place in court, everyone in the room knew he had just suffered a very public rebuke.

'Sire,' he said quietly,' I pray permission to humbly protest and appeal the gift of silver. This boy and his brother are guilty of subversion and treachery. The only thing they both deserve is a noose around their necks.'

'You forget yourself, Sir Knight,' said Longshanks, 'but in the circumstances I will overlook your impertinence.' He turned to two of the armed men at the door. Guards, go to the Accursed tower and find the one called Geraint ap Thomas. Bring him here immediately.' The two men ran from the room and Longshanks turned to face Sir John. You may stand down, Sir John.'

'No, I will not,' answered Sir John to a gasp from the room. 'With respect, Sire, I am Castellan of Acre and have ruled in Henry's name for three years. I am the senior King's man in Palestine and as such demand respect. The chivalric code demands I have fair audience without redress and I challenge your decisions in the name of the King. I demand the cross remains here until we return to England and we can both stand before your father while I appeal my case.'

Before Longshanks could answer a woman's voice rung out across the room.

'And what chivalric code is this, dear husband?'

All eyes turned to see the dishevelled figure of Lady Jennifer of Orange walking across the hall floor. Her hair was a mess and tears ran down her face.

'Lady Jennifer,' gasped a voice, 'we thought you were dead.'

'I may as well have been,' she said, looking to one side. 'In the eyes of my husband I have been long dead and buried, much to his pleasure and dare I say, amusement. But I have returned and have charges of my own to press.' She turned to face the Castellan again. 'So I ask again,' she said, 'this chivalric code you preach. Is it the one that allows you to beat your wife until she bled as if wounded, or the one that tells you to steal a portion of all taxes collected for your own treasury? Is it the one that allows you to hang innocents, charged under falsified evidence so you can seize their holdings or the one that allows you to send stolen money home to buy lands in England to better your standing. Which code is it, dear husband for I am sure we all await your explanation.'

'This is nonsense,' shouted Sir John. 'The Lady Jennifer is obviously suffering from illness of the mind and needs help. She has been in the hands of the Infidel this past year and has suffered greatly. Someone escort her back to her room.'

Two of the ladies stepped forward but Jennifer pulled a knife from beneath her wrap.

'Stay away from me,' she shouted and turned to the Castellan again. 'Yes I have been held captive,' she said, 'and suffered unspeakable horrors but who is responsible, Husband? Who sent me through Muslim lands with just a handful of mercenaries as protection? You knew we would be captured and I wager you thought I would die, but I didn't.' She stepped closer with the knife raised.

'Death would have been a welcome relief from the hell they put me through but I resisted cutting my own wrists and do you know why? For a moment such as this. To see you shamed before your peers and bleed upon my blade.'

Again she stepped forward but Sir John drew his sword and held it against her stomach.

'Your mind is possessed, woman,' he said, 'and your words the product of witchcraft. Put down your knife or I will run you through right here.'

'No,' shouted a voice and another woman ran forward into the hall.

'It's Misha,' gasped Garyn, 'the slave girl.'

'Hold your sword, Sire,' shouted Misha, 'I beseech thee. She is with child.'

The crowd gasped again as the full implications sank in.

'With child?' sneered Sir John eventually, 'so you are both a witch and an adulteress. Your fate is sealed, Harlot, the noose awaits.'

'I am no adulteress,' growled Jennifer.

'Then who is the father,' asked Sir John loudly, 'for I have not set eye on your sour face for a year hence. Name the Sire of your bastard before these noble men, say his name so we can all know how low you will stoop.'

Jennifer sneered.

'You demand a name,' she said, 'but I cannot answer for I know not.'

'So you have slept with more than one?' asked Sir John triumphantly.

'If you mean lay down with a man voluntarily then no, there has been none. If however you want the name of one who took me against my will then choose one from many for I lost count.'

'You were ravished?' demanded Longshanks loudly. 'Name the knaves and they will pay the price this very day.'

'They are not of Acre, Sire,' said Jennifer, 'for they ride their horses amongst the Halqas of Baibaars.'

The crowd broke into angry shouting as realisation dawned.

'Silence,' shouted Longshanks and turned to the two people still staring at each other on either end of a sword.

'Are you saying you carry a Mamluk child?'

'I do,' said Jennifer, 'an innocent fathered by an infidel in a union of hatred.'

219

'Then there is no hope for you,' snarled Sir John, 'and no place in this world for you or your heathen spawn.' Without warning he stepped forward and run his sword through her stomach, driving the thrust until the hilt rested against her body. Cries of no, and murder echoed around the room as Jennifer fell against Sir John, still impaled on his blade. Her eyes closed in pain and blood trickled from her mouth.

'I hope you rot in hell,' he snarled into her ear.

'I probably will, dear husband,' she said weakly, 'but we are wed and I belong at your side.' With the last of her strength she lifted her own blade and thrust it up through his stomach into his heart. 'We will go there together.'

Within seconds both fell to the ground in a pool of blood and the hall erupted into a frenzy.

'Clear the hall,' shouted Longshanks, 'summon the apothecaries.'

The soldiers ushered the commoners out but as soon as they were clear, the two guards sent to bring Garyn's brother from the dungeon ran back into the hall.

'Sire,' shouted one. 'The boy is not there.'

'He has to be,' said Longshanks, 'all prisoners are kept in the Accursed tower. Search again.'

'Sire, we were told by the guards he was taken many weeks ago and nobody knows where.'

Silence fell as the words sunk in. Garyn pulled himself from the Monk's grip and ran forward to where the priests were administering the last rites to the Castellan and his wife. He pushed one of the priest's out of the way and grabbed the Knight by the shoulders.

'Where is he?' he shouted, 'what have you done with him?'

The Knight' eyelids lifted weakly and looked at the boy.

'Tell him,' said Brother Martin, 'let your last act be one of mercy and you may yet enter the Kingdom of the Lord.'

'He is beyond even you, boy,' whispered the Castellan, 'he is with the devil himself.'

The man died before Garyn's eyes and the boy's head sunk to his chest in defeat as he realised he would never see his brother again.

Half an hour later the hall had been cleared and the blood soaked up with sand before being swept away. Brother Martin sat

alongside Garyn at a table while Longshanks talked quietly at the far
end of the hall, discussing the day's extraordinary events. Garyn's
head was down and he cradled a tankard of warmed mead provided by
the dead Castellan's kitchens. Finally Garyn stood up and started to
walk toward the Prince. Brother Martin grabbed his hand and pulled
him back.

'What do you think you are doing?' he asked.

'I want audience with Longshanks,' said Garyn simply.

'Garyn, you do not just walk up to the future King of England.
We are only allowed to stay in here out of sympathy and will be
thrown out soon enough.'

'I know,' said Garyn, 'but I would have word.' He pulled
himself from the Monk's grip and stepped forward again. Immediately
two guards blocked his way.

'Withdraw, boy,' said one. 'The day is done.'

'I seek audience,' said Garyn.

'Not today,' said the Guard.

'Sire,' shouted Garyn toward the Prince. 'I seek audience.
Please spare me a moment.'

One of the guards grabbed him and dragged him toward the
door but stopped as Longshanks' voice echoed around the empty
room.

'Let him through.'

The guard released his grip and Garyn approached the table.

'That's near enough, boy,' said a Knight quietly. 'State your
case.'

'Sire,' said Garyn. 'You granted me the life of my brother in
your judgement. It would seem he is now dead so I seek a different
favour in his stead.'

'There is no bargaining to be done here, boy,' said
Longshanks. 'The judgement was made fairly. The fact that your
brother is dead is no fault of mine.'

'I know, Sire but I don't plead for gold or lands, all I ask is the
life of another who still lays in the Accursed tower.'

'And who would this man be?'

'A comrade who also suffered the injustice of Sir John's rule.'

'Be careful what you say, Boy,' said Longshanks, 'for though
the manner of his demise was unfortunate, the accusations made by the
Castellan's wife were never proven nor ever will be. As far as we are
concerned, he died a valued comrade and true Knight of Henry.'

'I understand, Sire,' said Garyn, 'but nevertheless, my friend rots in the dungeons of the Accursed tower and I beg his release in place of my brother.'

Longshanks sat back and stared at Garyn.

'You are a strange boy, Garyn ap Thomas and display the impudence of youth. I should have you whipped but I will not for I recognise that trait within myself. I will grant you your request but then you must leave Acre for I fear you are nothing but trouble. Take one of my guards and have the prisoner released in my name, now, be gone and don't let my eyes fall upon you again.'

'Yes, Sire,' said Garyn and turned to leave the room, passing Brother Martin on the way.

'Where are we going?' asked the Monk trotting to keep up with him.

'First we are going to get Dafydd,' said Garyn, 'then we are going home.'

Chapter 23

The Port of Acre

Dafydd stood at the stern of the ship watching the city come to life as the sun rose. He was wrapped in a horsehair blanket and his hair was tied back, revealing the bruises still evident around his face. Since he had been released from the dungeon he had spent several days regaining his strength in the Hospitaller headquarters while recovering from the injuries inflicted by the dungeon guards. Finally Brother Martin had secured Passage to Venice and they had boarded the vessel hours earlier in preparation, as the crew finished loading the stores. The two young men had found a dry corner in the hold to make their sleeping spaces and store the meagre possessions supplied by the Hospitallers, while Brother Martin made his way back ashore.

'Where's he gone?' asked Dafydd quietly as Garyn appeared beside him.

'I don't know,' said Garyn. 'He said he had to do something.'

'Well I hope he hurries up,' said Dafydd,' I want to get out of this accursed place.'

'Aren't you disappointed the path of Knighthood is closed to you?'

'A title and armour does not a Knight make, Garyn. That much I have learned.'

He fell silent once more and they watched the activity together as they waited for the boat to leave.

Across the city, Brother Martin knocked on the door of his old friend, Ahmed Mubarak. The same woman answered as she did many weeks earlier though this time with a look of recognition.

'You must be Maysam,' said the Monk, 'Ahmed's wife.'

'I am,' she said, 'what do you want?'

'I have come to say goodbye,' he said. 'I am leaving Acre and fear our paths will never cross again. Can I see him?'

'He is very weak,' said Maysam, 'and coughed throughout the night. He finally sleeps but I know he would want to see you. Come in, I will wake him.' They made their way to the back room where Brother Martin saw his friend fast asleep on a bed of reeds covered with a sheepskin.

'I will wake him,' said Maysam.

'No,' said the Monk grabbing her arm, 'let him sleep. I will just sit with him.'

Maysam nodded and left the room. For an hour Brother Martin sat quietly alongside his friend, remembering the adventures they had shared together. He thought of waking him but decided against it. Parting was always so hard and obviously this would be the last time they would see each other in this world. Finally he stood and touching his friend on the shoulder, said goodbye for the last time.

'Until the next life, Friend,' he said and left the room. Maysam was sitting at a table and stood to open the door.

'Do you want me to give him a message?' she asked.

'Just say this, he was more of a Knight than I ever was.'

The woman nodded and watched him go before closing the door. An hour later the voice of her husband came weakly from the back room and she got up with a sigh. He was probably hungry, as was she but she hadn't dared to go out begging while he was asleep in case he woke and needed her. She walked through to his room.

'I am here, Ahmed,' she said.

'Maysam,' he said, turning his head toward her, his sewn eyes a blank red space in the candlelight. 'Someone has been here in the room. Who was it? tell me quickly.'

'It was your friend, the man from England. He came to say goodbye.'

'Is he still here, where is he?'

'He has gone, Ahmed,' she said, 'but left his eternal thanks and respect.' She paused. 'How do you know there was someone here?'

'Because respect is not the only thing he left, Maysam,' he said, 'he also left this.' He lifted his hand from the bed and held up a leather pouch before pouring the contents out onto the bed.

'What are they, Maysam?' he asked, 'for they feel like copper coins.'

'They are not copper, Ahmed,' said the woman in wonder,' they are silver and shine like the midnight stars.'

'There he is,' said Garyn as the Monk made his way across the dock.

'You cut it fine, Holy man,' shouted the Captain. 'We are about to sail.'

'I am here now,' said the Monk, 'you can cast off.'

'Where have you been?' asked Garyn.

'Saying goodbye to a friend,' he said and turned to Dafydd.

'How are you this Morn, Squire Dafydd?'

'I am Squire no more, Brother Martin as well you know. Henceforth use my name only.'

'So be it,' said the Monk as he walked away to talk to the Captain.

The two boys watched as the ship pulled away from the dock and turned gracefully under the power of the oarsmen below deck. Soon they were easing slowly across the harbour toward the raised chain that provided it with protection.

'What was it like, Dafydd?' asked Garyn quietly.

'What was what like?'

'Your time in the dungeon.'

There was a pause before Dafydd answered.

'It was awful, Garyn,' he said. 'I have never imagined the depravity men are able to inflict on each other. There were men down there praying for death, begging others to strangle them to release them from their hell. It wasn't so bad for me, for I had not yet been found guilty so I was only beaten but the rest...' He left the sentence unfinished before looking at Garyn. 'I am sorry,' he said, 'I know it's not what you wanted to hear but no man should cover up the truth of what goes on down there. I asked about your brother but nobody knew anything. Those who are sentenced to the pit are not around long enough to form friendships.'

'So all men die down there?'

'Most,' said Dafydd. 'Some are lucky like me and are pardoned but not many. Most are either tortured to death or left to starve but even they have cause for gratitude for there is a fate worse than that, saved especially for those who have caused the greatest ire to the Castellan.'

'What fate is possibly worse than torture or death?' asked Garyn.

'Nobody knows for nobody has ever returned. All I know is that it involves eternal pain and strong men weep like babes when they hear they are being sent into his embrace.'

'Who's embrace?'

'Ba'al-zebub, Garyn. The devil himself.'

Garyn fell quiet and tried not to think of his brother suffering eternal torment. The Castellan's last words were that Geraint was in the arms of the devil himself and that could only mean he had been sent to Ba'al-zebub.'

His head fell forward as he struggled to control his emotion.

'I'm sorry, Garyn,' said Dafydd, grabbing his shoulder. 'You had to know.' Without another word he left Garyn alone with his thoughts and walked across to Brother Martin and the Captain.

'What's the delay, Captain?' asked Brother Martin. 'We are dead in the water.'

'The barrier is still up,' said the Captain pointing at the chain stretched across the harbour entrance. 'Until it is lowered we cannot leave.'

'How long will that take?' asked the Monk.

'Who knows?' said the Captain. 'The wheel is situated in that tower on shore but they will not lower the chain until they receive the signal from the Tower of flies.'

'Tower of flies,' said Dafydd, looking at the lone structure in the water, 'I remember wondering about its name when we arrived. A strange title for a defensive tower such as this.'

'But a name well earned,' said the Captain. 'In warmer weather it is said the air around the tower swarms with flies and the stink is unbearable.'

'Why?'

'The Lord God only knows,' said the Captain.

Brother Martin turned to Dafydd.

'How is Garyn?'

'His heart is heavy,' said Dafydd.

'I will speak to him,' said the Monk and walked away to join Garyn.

'So how long do we wait?' asked Dafydd eventually.

'Until the Lord of the tower wakes and gives the signal,' said the Captain,' and that depends on how much ale he drunk last night.'

'Why do you call him a Lord?' asked Dafydd. 'Surely no man with such a title is responsible for such a lowly task.'

'Of course not,' said the Captain, 'he is named so in jest by all who pass due to the nature of the role. No one knows his true name, so he has been named after the tower and the Devil himself. Men call him Beelzebub, Lord of the flies.'

Dafydd ran across the deck and interrupted the conversation between Garyn and the Monk. The Captain followed close behind and listened to the conversation.

'Garyn,' gasped Dafydd, 'all is not lost, your brother may yet live.'

'What do you mean?' asked Garyn grabbing Dafydd's shoulder, 'explain.'

Dafydd retold them the words of the Captain.

'Don't you see?' he said, 'the Castellan was not referring to the fires of hell but a real place and a real man. Didn't he say Geraint was in the arms of the Devil himself?'

'He did,' said Garyn, 'but...'

'Then he may have been referring to this place,' said Dafydd. 'The Devil is known by many names, Garyn, one of which is Ba'al-zebub, Lord of the flies. The man who dwells in this tower is also known by that name and may be holding your brother.'

'You are right,' said Garyn looking toward the tower, 'I have to go over there.'

'Not so fast, Garyn,' said the Monk. 'You have no way to get there and the Captain may not allow his ship to draw close.' All eyes turned to the Captain.

'I have heard tales of prisoners kept in that unholy place,' he said, 'but the Monk is right. I cannot risk the ship so close to the rocks.' He stared at Garyn's desperate face before continuing. 'However, I too once lost a brother to injustice and I would be dishonouring his name to refuse aid. While the harbour chain is up, I cannot sail so you have an opportunity. Take the row boat and keep seaward of the ship. The hour is still early so there may not be too many eyes on the shore but I will say this, as soon as the chain drops, I will leave with or without you. I cannot risk the ire of Longshanks and to aid the release of prisoners is treason.'

'But if the boy is there and we are successful,' said Brother Martin, 'surely the story will eventually come out and your part in this will be revealed?'

'Then I will claim one of you held a knife to my throat,' said the Captain.

'Fair enough,' said the Monk. 'Where is the row boat?'

Fifteen minutes later, they pulled the rowing boat up onto the rocks at the base of the tower and sought a way in.

227

'The door is barred from the inside,' said Dafydd, 'and the walls are too high.'

'Over here,' said Garyn and pointed at the place where the huge rusty chain entered the tower through a small hole in the wall.

'I think I can squeeze through,' he said and started to undress.

'It's too small,' said the Monk, 'you will never fit.'

'Watch me,' said Garyn and bent to look through into the tower. He placed one arm forward first and then forced his head and shoulders into the hole. For a few seconds he was stuck and he wriggled fruitlessly as he tried to free himself.

'Pull him out,' said Dafydd.

'No,' hissed Garyn from within, 'push me in.'

The Monk pushed Garyn's body further in and the few inches gained meant the boy found a handhold and tugged as hard as he could. Slowly his body scraped inward until suddenly the pressure eased and he fell to the floor in a darkened room though not before a layer of skin had been scraped from his body by the rusty chain.

'Are you alright?' asked Brother Martin's voice from outside.

'I think so,' said Garyn standing up.

'Find a doorway,' said the Monk, 'and unbar the entrance.'

Garyn walked through the darkness and felt along the wall until he found a small door. At first he thought it was locked but he soon realised it was only jammed and he leaned against it to force it open. As soon as it opened he gagged at the stench that assaulted his senses. Clouds of flies filled the air and his hand flew to his mouth to mask the stench. He paused a few seconds before seeing the main door at the far end of the short corridor and breathing as shallowly as he could, walked quickly to unbolt the door.

'By all that is holy,' gasped Brother Martin as they stepped in, 'what is that smell?'

'Death,' said Dafydd.

'Where do we start?' asked Garyn.

'Look for locked doors or a stair to a dungeon,' said Brother Martin.

'Do you think there will be a dungeon here?'

'Has to be,' said the Monk. 'These places always do.'

'And you think my brother will be there?'

'It is a possibility, but you have to be prepared for the worst. He may be already dead.'

'Perhaps,' said Garyn, 'but you once assured me the Castellan would see merit in keeping him alive until he had the cross. We know that Sir John died before that happened and he may not have had the chance to send the execution order. This Beelzebub may not know of the Castellan's demise and has kept my brother alive.'

'It is a possibility,' said Dafydd. 'Come on, we don't have much time.'

Together they walked over to the entrance to the spiral stairway disappearing up the tower. Garyn looked up but Dafydd tapped him on the shoulder and pointed to the floor. Sunk into the stone floor was a trap door with a metal ring sunk into the wood. Through the ring was an iron bar which slotted into a hole in the wall, preventing the trap door from being pushed up from below.

'Why bar a door unless you want to keep someone in?' he said.

Garyn nodded and bent to withdraw the bolt before lifting the trap door. The stink from the corridor was nothing to the stench that escaped the hatch and they all caught their breath before Garyn peered forward into the hole.

'Quiet,' he hissed, 'listen.' For a few seconds there was silence before they heard a groan from below. 'Someone's alive down there,' he said, 'lower me down.'

'You don't know how far it is,' said Dafydd, 'you could break your neck.'

'I've come too far to turn back,' said Garyn, 'lower me down.'

The two men lowered Garyn through the hatch until they could reach no further.

'Let me go,' said Garyn and he fell to the floor a few feet down. His fall was broken by the softness of dead bodies and he scrambled to his feet before pressing his back against the wall in a panic. For what seemed an age he stayed there, frozen in fear before Dafydd's voice came from above.

'Garyn,' he whispered, 'take this, I found it on the stairway.' Garyn looked up and saw the boy holding a lit candle stuck onto the spike of a holder.

'Watch you don't drop it,' said Dafydd,' there are no others.'

Garyn caught the candle and after a few seconds where he thought it would go out, the flame re-gathered its strength and he held it up to examine the room by its flickering light.

What he saw was beyond his worst nightmares.

Chapter Twenty Four

The Tower of Flies

Garyn stared at the horrors of the dungeon. The floor was a carpet of bodies in various stages of decomposition, laying in a sea of dried excrement. Flies filled the air and the corpses were alive with the movement of countless maggots. A movement caught his eye and he saw the largest rat he had ever seen leave the opened stomach cavity of a recently deceased man, dragging entrails behind it. The more he looked the more depravity he saw. Metal baskets hung from the ceilings containing the cadavers of prisoners long dead, as well as those who had suffered more recent atrocities. Stocks usually used in village squares were fixed high on walls with remains of long dead men still held in their grip, their remains only held together by rotting clothing and toughened sinews.

A large wheel sat between two wooden frames and a man lay stretched backward over the curve, the look on his face still testament to the pain he suffered as his spine had been stretched past dislocation before being pulled apart by the horrific device.

Garyn was frozen with fear and disgust and wanted nothing more than to get out of this hellish place but he knew he had to go further, if only to confirm his brother was dead. Slowly he stepped forward, careful not to lose his footing in the unholy filth. A naked man lay tied to a table against a wall and at first Garyn could see no injury but then he saw a small domed cage over his groin and the dark ragged hole where the caged rats had eaten themselves up through his body. Even as he stared, the skin over his stomach writhed disgustingly as the creatures moved within the cavity. With this Garyn leaned over and emptied the contents of his stomach onto the filth ridden floor. For what seemed an age he retched until there was nothing left until finally he straightened up and stared around the room. It was pointless, even if his brother had been here, there was no way he would still be alive. He turned to leave but stopped dead in his tracks when he heard a whisper.

'Help me,'

His heart stopped and he stared around the dungeon again.

'Hello,' he said, 'is there anyone here?'

'Help me,' came the whisper again.

Garyn took a step forward and held up the candle.

'Where are you?' he asked.

'In God's name help me,' came the weak voice again.

Garyn looked toward the far wall and saw a man suspended from the rafters by his hands. His shoulders had long since dislocated and his arms had stretched above him in a deformed parody of a human shape. His feet had once reached the floor but the attentions of the rats meant his toes had been eaten away and his lower legs were blackened with infection.

Garyn walked over and stared hopelessly at the condemned soul, knowing he was beyond help. His eyes had been gouged out and his teeth broken with a blunt instrument.

'I cannot help you, Sir,' whispered Garyn gently. 'your tormentor has put paid to any hope. I am so sorry.'

'Then kill me,' whispered the man.

Garyn nodded silently and drew his knife, knowing it was the merciful thing to do. He held the point above the man's heart and rested the point against his skin.

'Do it,' whispered the man.

'I can't,' stuttered Garyn.

'In the name of merciful Jesus, I beg you to end my torment,' cried the man.

Again Garyn hesitated but the man used all his remaining strength to cry out once more.

'Do it,' he called, his voice breaking. 'I beseech you, release me from this hell.'

Garyn closed his eyes and with a cry of his own, drove the blade through the wretch's heart.

The man let out a gasp and a few second later his head fell forward onto his chest.

Garyn still held the blade and watched as the man's thick blood ran down the hilt and onto his own arm.

In disgust he staggered back and fell amongst the filth. Panicking he jumped up and stumbled across the dungeon toward the hatch but as he passed a row of corpses piled against the wall, a hand reached out and touched his ankle.

Garyn screamed in fear and he fell again, but this time pushed himself backward until he leaned against the opposite wall.

'Sweet Jesus in heaven,' he gasped as he righted the fallen candle, 'what purgatory is this?'

The body he thought was dead pushed itself up onto all fours and crawled slowly toward him, each movement a painful effort to get closer. Garyn pushed further away and looked up at the beckoning hatch above. He was about to call out when the prisoner gasped weakly.

'Help me, stranger,' it whispered and lifted his hand toward Garyn. 'In God's name I beg you.'

The candlelight cast its yellow glow on the pathetic figure as he lifted his head toward Garyn and as the hood fell from the creatures face, Garyn covered his mouth with his hand in an effort to stifle the cry rising from his very soul. Finally he lowered his hand and crawled closer to the prisoner.

'Merciful God,' he gasped, 'can it be true?' He leaned forward and held the candle closer before touching the side of the prisoner's face as gently as if a child. Tears burst forth and his body shook with emotion as he recognised the gaunt features of Geraint.

'I have come for you brother,' he sobbed in the darkness, 'I am here to take you home.'

Fifteen minutes later both boys had been hauled from the dungeon and Brother Martin gave Garyn his cloak to wrap the emaciated body of his brother.

'We have to go,' said Dafydd, 'or it will be too late.'

'What about the chain?' asked Garyn

'We heard it lowered a few minutes ago.'

'Is he strong enough?' asked the Monk, looking at Garyn's brother.

'He will make it,' said Garyn.

'Someone comes,' hissed Dafydd and they looked toward the stone stairway stretching up into the tower.

'Who's there?' shouted a voice from above.

'Quickly,' said Dafydd, 'to the door.'

'Too late,' said Brother Martin and beckoned Dafydd to hide around the corner

The sound of a wheezing man filtered down from above as the steps grew louder.

'Whoever you are,' snarled the voice, 'I will have my rats eat your heart while you still live.'

The end of a spear appeared from the stairwell and Brother Martin stepped out to grab the shaft and pull it toward him. The unexpected action pulled the man from his feet and he fell down the last few steps to smash his face on the opposite wall before falling to the floor.

Brother Martin placed his heel onto the man's neck and Dafydd stepped forward to stare at the fattest man he had ever seen, sprawled naked on the cold stone slabs.

'Kill him,' snarled Garyn from behind them.

The Monk turned to stare at the boy.

'Kill him,' repeated Garyn.

'Is murder now your trait, Garyn?'

'You didn't see what I saw,' said Garyn, 'he does not deserve to live.'

'I will not kill a man in cold blood, Garyn. I left those days behind me many years ago.'

'Then give me the blade,' said Garyn and walked over to stand above the terrified man. He snatched the blade from the Monk's hand and dropped to straddle the man's chest, placing the knife against the man's throat. The fat man's eyes widened as he felt the pressure.

'Do it scum,' he spat. 'Send me to hell.'

Garyn paused. A quick death was too good for this man. He looked at the Monk.

'Stand him up,' he said.

They dragged the fat man to his feet as Dafydd held the spear against his back. With a quick swipe of the blade Garyn sliced the tendons behind one knee and as the prisoner fell again, he repeated the action on the other knee. The man screamed but Garyn knelt on the side of his face as he sliced his knife through the tendons inside his elbows. The effect of the wounds meant the man could no longer use his hands or feet and as blood poured from the wounds, Garyn dragged him up into a sitting position.

'Never let it be said I am a murderer,' said Garyn quietly, 'for as God is my witness, the last time I saw you, you still lived. You asked for hell, stranger so it is hell you shall have.' Without another word he kicked the man in the chest and watched him fall through the trap door and into the dungeon below. Garyn closed the trap door and turned to see the Monk and Dafydd staring at him.

'His people will release him soon enough,' said Dafydd.

'He has open wounds and useless limbs,' said Garyn. 'By the time they realise something is wrong, I suspect the rats will have meted out justice on my behalf. He will know how those who share his hell felt. Now, we need to get out of here.'

'I'll help you with your brother,' said Brother Martin.

'No,' snapped Garyn. 'I will carry him. I owe it to him and to myself.' He picked up his brother and cradled him in his arms. 'Come on Geraint,' he said. 'Let's go home.'

'About time,' snapped the Captain when they finally climbed aboard, 'if I was to have waited a moment longer they would have been suspicious and raised the chain.'

'We are here now,' said the Monk. 'Get us out of here.'

'There is one thing more before we leave,' said the Captain, 'we found this amongst the cargo.' He nodded to a sailor who dragged a small figure along the deck.

'Misha,' said Brother Martin in surprise.

'You know her?' asked the Captain.

'I do,' said the Monk. 'Misha, why are you here?'

'I need to get away,' she said. 'When I went back to my village I found they had killed my family and my name is known for helping you rob the mountain man's tomb. If I stay here I am a dead woman and have no place to flee.'

'But surely you can find a place in Acre?'

'Acre will fall soon,' said Misha, 'today, tomorrow, who knows but fall it will and when it does my fate will be sealed.'

'But why have you hidden away on here?' asked the Monk. 'Surely you don't intend coming back with us?'

'Why not?' she asked. 'You are kind and will see I am not mistreated.'

'Misha, you are Muslim, England is a Christian country.'

'And that is why I will go with you,' said Misha. 'You say that the Christian God is merciful so I will be safe. One day, when my land is once more at peace then perhaps I can return.'

'I don't know, Misha,' said the Monk.

She ran forward and threw herself at his feet.

'Don't send me back, Holy man,' she said. 'I am begging you. If I return, my life will be forfeit.'

'What do you want me to do with her, Monk?' asked the Captain. 'Shall I throw her overboard?'

Brother Martin looked at Garyn and Dafydd before looking back at the Captain.

'No,' he said, 'she will come with us.'

'And who will pay her passage?' asked the Captain.

'I will,' said Garyn. 'I still have the money from the Castellan's compensation'

'Then get her below,' said the Captain, 'and keep her from my men.'

'Thank you,' said Misha and kissed the Monk's hand.' I will be no trouble and can help look after the sick one.'

Brother Martin nodded and watched her follow Garyn as they descended the steps to the hold.

'She is very pretty,' said Dafydd eventually.

'She is,' said the Monk, 'and something tells me that she is going to be the cause of much trouble before this thing is over.'

'A worry for another day, Brother Martin,' said Dafydd looking up at the unfurling sails. 'For now, let's just thank God and hope for favourable winds.'

The Monk looked back at Acre as they left the city behind them, wondering how many more men would die before the Holy-land once more was at peace.

'I agree, Dafydd,' he sighed, 'but for now, I would settle for a night's rest and the silence that sleep brings.'

'Then let us find a bed space for you,' said Dafydd, 'we have a long journey ahead.'

Chapter Twenty Five

England

The trip home had been long and arduous but despite the rigours, they had finally landed on England's shores and paid for passage back to Wales in the wagon of a trader from France. Geraint had slowly regained his strength though refused to talk about his time in the dungeons and Misha spent most of her time caring for him.

Dafydd and Garyn walked behind the wagon while the Monk rode the one horse they had managed to buy with the remainder of their money.

'The Monk looks ill,' said Dafydd as they walked.

'He does,' said Garyn, 'I fear the journey has been too much.'

'He is an old man,' said Dafydd, 'and I fear he may not make it back to Brycheniog.'

'I agree,' said Garyn, 'perhaps we should rest a while. Give him chance to regain his strength.'

Dafydd nodded and they carried on walking in silence. Finally they stopped for the night and prepared to make camp. Garyn and Dafydd set about cooking a hare they had caught en route and were in quiet discussion when Misha came running from the cart.

'Garyn, come quickly.'

'What's wrong?' he asked,' is it my brother?'

'No, it's the Monk, he is ill.'

They ran to the cart where Brother Martin had made his bed. He leant against the side panels, his body covered with his blanket. His face was soaked with sweat though his body shivered with cold

'Garyn,' he said weakly, 'I think I have the fever.'

'You are no apothecary, Monk,' said Garyn with a smile, 'but I suspect you are correct in your diagnosis. I will send to the nearest village for aid.'

The Monk smiled.

'No, Garyn,' he said, 'there is no need. My body is tired and my soul exhausted. Let this illness take its course and if I fail to recover, then so be it. I don't fear death and if truth be told the thought of eternal sleep is inviting.'

'You are not going to die, Monk,' said Garyn. 'I won't let you.'

Again the Monk smiled.

'We will see,' he said, 'but listen, there is something you should know. Something I have kept from you.'

'More secrets?' asked Garyn gently.

'Just one more,' said the Monk. 'Garyn, you head for your home but you must know this. I know the man who killed your family.'

Garyn's smile fell away.

'You do? How?

'I learned his identity before we left England two years ago.'

'And you did not tell me?'

'I couldn't, it would have put you at great risk and stopped you in your quest.'

'Who was it?' asked Garyn coldly.

'I don't know the man's name,' said the Monk, 'but I know the man who paid him to do it.'

'Who?'

'Father Williams.'

'The Abbott?'

'Yes. He found out your family knew about the Muslim prisoner's secret and arranged to have them silenced. He offered a thief freedom if he killed your family.'

'Are you sure?' asked Garyn.

'I am,' said the Monk. 'I was going to take the truth to my grave but once the Abbott returns from Rome I fear he may seek retribution for your part in this. You have turned into a good man, Garyn and deserve a long life. Do not seek vengeance but be wary of the man, he is a wolf in sheep's clothing.'

Garyn tucked the blanket around the Monk's neck.

'Thank you friend,' he said. 'I will give it serious thought. Do you need anything?'

'I am cold,' said the Monk. 'Is there another blanket?'

'I will bring you mine,' said Garyn.

The two boys made the Monk as comfortable as possible before returning to sit at the fire.

'He is dying,' said Dafydd.

'I know,' said Garyn. 'I don't think he will last the night.'

'He was a good man, Garyn You owe him a lot.'

'I owe him my life,' said Garyn, 'and that of my brother.'

An hour later they were summoned again by Misha.

'You should come,' she said quietly.

237

The two boys ran over and knelt at the Monk's side.

'It is my time, Garyn,' whispered Brother Martin. 'Do not fret, for it comes to us all.'

'I may not be able to save your life,' said Garyn, 'but I may be able to save your soul.'

'My soul is beyond redemption, Garyn and I fear the gates of heaven will remain barred to me.'

'No,' said Garyn, 'they are not. For I have the key, my friend. I have the means to give you access to glory everlasting.'

'Just bury me deep, Garyn. The rest is beyond mortal man.'

'No,' said Garyn, opening the Monk's hand. 'Not if you have this.' He placed something in the Monks palm and closed his fingers around it.

'What is it?' asked the Monk and opened his hand to see a sliver of wood. He looked up at Garyn in confusion. 'I don't understand.'

'It's the remnant of the true cross,' said Garyn. 'I cut it from the crucifix when I locked myself away in the cells of the Hospitallers. I don't know why but now I know God guided my actions for exactly this moment.'

'But the cross was intact when you handed it over,' said Brother Martin.

'It was,' said Garyn, 'but the wood therein was no more than a piece carved from chair in the cell. You hold the real relic in your hands, my friend and when we bury you, it will be with a piece of the cross that once bore our saviour on his final journey.'

'Garyn, I don't know what to say,' said the Monk.

'Then say nothing,' said Garyn, 'but promise me this. When you enter the gates of heaven, seek out my mother and tell her I kept my promise to her, tell her I brought my brother home.'

The Monk gave his last smile before answering.

'I would, Garyn,' he said, 'but there is no need. She already knows.'

Slowly his eyes closed and Brother Martin finally slipped into the eternal sleep he had craved for so long, clutching a tiny part of a greater tale, a fragment of the one true cross of blood.

Epilogue

Brycheniog

Three weeks later, Elspeth Fletcher sat at the table helping her father make flights for the Manor's archers. Several candles burned around the room and she sat alongside her mother in the dim light. Finally they put aside the shafts and bagged the goose feathers.

'Time to get some sleep,' said her father.

'I think I will get some air first,' said Elspeth. 'The dust from the feathers irritates my nose.'

'Don't be long,' said her mother, 'and do not wander.'

'I won't,' she said and stepped outside to sit on a log in front of the house. She looked up at the stars and wondered if Garyn was looking at the same ones in some far off land. She sighed and pulled out the folded piece of parchment Garyn had given her over two years ago. Carefully she unfolded it as she had done a hundred times before and though the moon was bright, she didn't need to read the oft repeated words she knew so well. Quietly she said them to herself.

> *'Elspeth Fletcher, fair of face.*
> *Easer of nightmares, creator of laughter,*
> *Hair of softest down with sparkling streams captured in your eyes.'*

Before she could finish, a man's voice came from the darkness and she jumped as Garyn walked up the path toward her, finishing off the poem.

> *'Patient be for soon the wind changes and happiness beckons.*
> *Already you hold my heart and soon yours will be mine…'*

Garyn left the last line unsaid as he walked slowly toward her. Elspeth stood up and walked to meet him, hardly daring to believe he was home. He held out his hands and she took them gently in hers.

'For evermore?' she whispered as she gazed up at him through her tears.

'For evermore,' he confirmed through tears of his own and pulled her into his arms.

The End

Author's notes

Obviously the main storyline is fictional but the locations and historical events have been based on real happenings in the past. On occasions the timelines have been tweaked to make the storyline fit but some of the more interesting facts, as far as can be ascertained with current research are listed below.

The True cross.

It is said the true cross was kept in Jerusalem for hundreds of years after the death of Christ. The age was a turbulent one and after many conflicts, it seems it disappeared for a while before being re-discovered in Jerusalem by Arnulf Malecorne of Rhodes during the first crusade around 1100ad. It is reported that a fragment of the cross was embedded in a golden crucifix and became the most holy relic of the time. In 1187, the king of Jerusalem, Guy of Lusignan, along with Raynald of Châtillon, Gerard of Ridefortand and Raymond III of Tripoli, fielded an enormous army to defeat Saladin at the battle of Hattin in modern day Israel. However, Saladin was victorious and inflicted a crushing defeat on the Christians as well as capturing the cross.

The Ismailis

The Ismaili's were enemies of Saladin and he eventually campaigned against them in the Jabahl Bahra mountains. However, a sub sect called the Hashashin (the predecessor of our word, assassin) were experts in the art of assassination and history records that during the campaign Saladin woke to find a dagger stuck in a table in his tent. Attached was a note demanding Saladin withdrew his army and pointing out how easy it would have been to kill him. Saladin swore the intruder was no less than the Ismail leader himself, Rashid ad-Din Sinan and he was so shaken up, sued for peace with the Ismaili people.

Al Kahf Castle

The castle still exists and is based on a spur of rock rising from a valley floor. It can only be approached via an entrance through a cave and is said to have been impregnable. It was built by the Ismailis and the body of Rashid ad-Din Sinan is said to have been buried there.

The Slaughter of the Innocents

When Richard the Lionheart freed Acre from Saladin's forces in 1191 he took almost three thousand prisoners, men women and children. He demanded a ransom including the return of the true cross but Saladin stalled and when he failed to produce the ransom, Richard had his men march the prisoners out onto the plains before Acre and killed every one. It was terrible act and one that has reverberated down the ages as an indictment of Crusader brutality.

The City of Acre

Acre was probably known as Akko or something similar in the thirteenth century and the name has changed through the ages. The towers listed were real as was the castle of the King's constabulary along with the Templar and Hospitaller headquarters. In 1291 Baibaars finally took the city, the last major stronghold of the Crusaders.

The Tower of flies

The tower was real and was a major strategic defensive structure at the harbour mouth in Acre. There was indeed a chain stretching between the tower and the mainland which was used as a barrier to ships. The name is reputed to have been given to the tower by the soldiers of the first crusade, thinking they had arrived at the city of Ekrom. Ekrom was a city whose deities included Ba'al-zebub which translates to 'lord of the flies'

Torture Methods

The methods of torture in the book are based on real methods at the time. Torture was seen as a punishment for most crimes and those listed herein are just a tiny selection of those that may have been employed at the time.

Krak des Chevalier

Krak des Chevalier was known as 'Crac de l'Ospital' at the time and is one of the most magnificent castles in the world. It was rebuilt by the Hospitallers in the twelfth century and sits on the remains of a previous castle built by the Kurds. In 1271, Sultan Baibaars laid siege to the castle and after causing severe damage by mining the outer walls, managed to get the defending Hospitaller Knights to surrender while the castle was still intact. It is said that the defending Castellan received a note from the order's grand master, Hugh de Revel, authorising the surrender but current thinking believes the note was a forgery arranged by Baibaars himself.

More Books by K. M. Ashman

The India Sommers Mysteries
The Dead Virgins
The Treasures of Suleiman
The Mummies of the Reich

The Roman Trilogy
Roman I – The Fall of Britannia
Roman II – The Rise of Caratacus
Roman III – The Wrath of Boudicca

Novels
Savage Eden
The Last Citadel
Vampire

The Medieval Trilogy
Medieval I – Blood of the Cross

Follow Kevin's blog at:
WWW.Silverbackbooks.co.uk

or contact him direct at:
KMAshman@Silverbackbooks.co.uk

CPSIA information can be obtained at www.ICGtesting.com
Printed in the USA
LVOW13s1212110314

376933LV00002B/439/P

9 781784 070526